JAVIER MARÍAS was born in Madrid in 1951 and published his first novel at the age of nineteen. In addition to several novels (which have won him the Ciudad de Barcelona Prize, the Spanish Critics' Award, and the Dublin International IMPAC Award, and some of which have been translated into several languages) he has written volumes of short stories and collections of essays. He is also a highly practised translator into Spanish of English authors, including Conrad, Stevenson, Hardy and Laurence Sterne. He has held academic posts in Spain, the United States (where he was a visiting professor at Wellesley College) and in Britain, as a lecturer in Spanish Literature at Oxford University.

MARGARET JULL COSTA is the translator of many Spanish-language writers including Bernardo Atxaga, Carmen Martín Gaite and Juan José Saer. Portuguese writers she has translated include Eça de Queiroz, Mário de Sá-Carneiro and Fernando Pessoa, for the translation of whose masterpiece, *The Book of Disquiet*, she was joint winner of the 1992 Portuguese translation prize.

Also by Javier Marías in English translation

Fiction
A HEART SO WHITE
TOMORROW IN THE BATTLE THINK ON ME

Short stories
WHEN I WAS MORTAL

Javier Marías

ALL SOULS

Translated from the Spanish by
Margaret Jull Costa

THE HARVILL PRESS
LONDON

The translator would like to thank Javier Marías, Guido Waldman, Christopher MacLehose, Annella McDermott and Faye Carney for all their help and advice.

M.J.C.

First published in Spain with the title *Todas las Almas* by
Editorial Anagrama, Barcelona, 1989

First published in Great Britain by Harvill, an imprint of HarperCollins*Publishers*, 1992

This paperback edition first published in 1999 by
The Harvill Press, 2 Aztec Row, Berners Road, London N1 0PW

3 5 7 9 8 6 4 2

www.harvill.com

A CIP catalogue record for this book is available from the British Library

This novel has been translated with the financial assistance of the
Spanish Dirección General del Libro y Bibliotecas, Ministerio de Cultura

ISBN 1 86046 435 1

Designed and typeset in Linotron Galliard by
Rowlands Phototypesetting Ltd, Bury St Edmunds, Suffolk

Printed and bound in Great Britain by Mackays of Chatham

Half title: photograph of Oxford gargoyles by Chris Donaghue

CONDITIONS OF SALE

For Eric Southworth,
for Vicente and Félix, my predecessors,
and for Elide

AUTHOR'S NOTE

Given that both the author and narrator of this novel spent two years in the same post at the University of Oxford, some statement may be in order on the part of the former, before he finally yields the floor to the latter, to the effect that any resemblance between any character in the novel (including the narrator, but excluding "John Gawsworth") and any other person living or dead (including the author, but excluding Terence Ian Fytton Armstrong) is purely coincidental as is any resemblance between any event in the story and any historical event past or present.

J.M.

ALL SOULS

OF THE THREE, two have died since I left Oxford and the superstitious thought occurs to me that they were perhaps just waiting for me to arrive and live out my time there in order to give me the chance to know them and, now, to speak about them. In other words – and this is equally superstitious – I may be under an obligation to speak about them. They did not die until after I had ceased to have anything to do with them. Had I continued to figure in their lives (to figure in their daily lives there) and stayed on in Oxford perhaps they would not be dead. This thought is not only superstitious, it is also vain. But in order to speak of them, I must speak of myself and of my time in the city of Oxford, even though the person speaking is not the same person who was there. He seems to be, but he is not. If I call myself "I", or use a name which has accompanied me since birth and by which some will remember me, if I detail facts that coincide with facts others would attribute to my life, or if I use the term "my house" for the house inhabited by others before and after me but where I lived for two years, it is simply because I prefer to speak in the first person and not because I believe that the faculty of memory alone is any guarantee that a person remains the same in different times and different places. The person recounting here and now what he saw and what happened to him then is not the same person who saw those things and to whom those things happened; neither is he a prolongation of that person, his shadow, his heir or his usurper.

My house was a sort of three-storey pyramid and, since my

3

duties in the city of Oxford were practically nil, even non-existent, I spent a great deal of time there. Oxford is, without a doubt, one of the cities in the world where least work gets done, where simply being is much more important than doing or even acting. In Oxford just being requires such concentration and patience, such energy to battle against the natural lethargy of the spirit, that it would be too much to expect its inhabitants actually to stir themselves, especially in public, although in the breaks between classes some of my colleagues did make a point of rushing from one place to another just to create the impression of being in a state of the most constant and extreme haste and bustle. Their classes, however, would have been or would be conducted in the most absolute calm and tranquillity, since classes were part of being, not doing or acting. Both Cromer-Blake and the Inquisitor were like that (the Inquisitor was Alec Dewar, also known as the Butcher or the Ripper).

But the person who most clearly gave the lie to all these feigned attempts at activity, and who truly embodied the stasis or stability of the place, was Will, the ancient porter of the building (called, with due Latin pomp, the Institutio Tayloriana) where, with the requisite calm and tranquillity, I used to work. Never have I seen a more limpid gaze (certainly not in my native city of Madrid where the limpid gaze simply doesn't exist) than that of Will at nearly ninety, small and neat, dressed always in some kind of blue overall, who on many mornings would be allowed to remain in the glass-paned porter's lodge to greet the lecturers as they came in. Will literally did not know what day it was and spent each morning in a different year, travelling backwards and forwards in time according to his desires or, more likely, quite independently of any conscious desire on his part. No one could predict which date he would choose, far less why he chose it. It was not just that on certain days he believed it was 1947, for him it really was 1947 or 1914 or 1935 or 1960 or 1926 or any other year of his

4

extremely long life. Sometimes you could tell if Will was living through a bad year by the slight look of dread on his face, though this was never enough to darken his cheerful, trusting gaze (he was too pure a soul to be capable of containing any anxiety, for he completely lacked the sense of futurity inseparable from that feeling). One could surmise that a morning in 1940 was dominated by his fear of the bombings of the previous night or the night to come, or that a morning in 1916 found him somewhat downcast by bad news of the Somme offensive, or that on a morning in 1930 he rose without a penny to his name and with the calculating, timid look in his eyes of a man who is going to have to ask someone for a loan but has not yet decided who. On other days, the touch of sadness that dimmed his huge smile and the brilliance of his ever friendly gaze was utterly indecipherable – beyond speculation even – because it was probably due to griefs and sorrows in his private life which had doubtless held not the slightest interest for students or lecturers. All that endless journeying through the length and breadth of his existence was almost impenetrable to other people (like portraits from past centuries or a photograph taken the day before yesterday). How were we to know in which painful day of his life Will was living when we noticed that he greeted us with only a half-smile instead of the enthusiastic wave he gave on cheerful or even neutral days? How were we to know what melancholy stretch of his unending journey he had reached when his "Good morning" to us was not accompanied by that childish wave? That hand raised aloft made you feel that in the inhospitable city of Oxford there was at least one person who was really pleased to see you, even if that person did not actually know who you were, or rather saw you each morning as someone quite different from the person you were yesterday. Only once, thanks to Cromer-Blake, did I find out exactly in which moment of his eventless life (much of which had been spent behind the glass panes of his lodge) Will found himself.

Cromer-Blake was waiting at the door of the building for me to arrive:

"Do say something to Will. You know, a few words of comfort or something. Apparently today he's in 1962, on the day his wife died, and he'll be awfully hurt if no one says anything to him on the way in. He can still manage a smile, mind you, not that he isn't genuinely sad, he's just too naturally good-humoured not to get some kind of enjoyment out of being in the limelight for a day. In an odd sort of way, he's in his element." Then, looking away and stroking his prematurely grey hair, Cromer-Blake added: "Let's just hope he doesn't decide to stick on this date; if he did, it would mean having to convey our deepest sympathies every single morning we crossed the threshold."

Will was wearing a black tie and a white shirt beneath his blue overalls and his clear, clear eyes seemed even more transparent and limpid than usual, perhaps the effects of a night spent in tears and in the presence of death. I approached the door of the lodge, which was open, and put a hand on his shoulder. I could feel his bones. I didn't quite know what to say.

"I'd wish you good morning, Will, only I know there's little good about it for you. I only just heard the news. I can't tell you how sorry I am."

Will smiled gently and once more his pink face, so pink it looked as if it had been polished, lit up. He placed a hand on mine and patted it lightly, as if I were the one in need of consolation. Cromer-Blake stood observing us, his gown over his shoulder (Cromer-Blake always carried his gown over his shoulder and spent his life observing others).

"Thank you, Mr Trevor. You're quite right, it couldn't be a worse day for me really. She died last night, you know, in the small hours. She'd been a bit off-colour for some time, but nothing serious. Then I woke up in the early hours and she was

6

dying. She died sudden like, with no warning, just like that, probably didn't want to wake me. I told her to wait, but she couldn't. She didn't even give me time to get up." Will stopped a moment and asked: "How do I look in a tie, Mr Trevor? I don't usually wear one, you see." Then he smiled and added: "But she had a good life, I reckon, and a long one too. 'Cause she was five years older than me, you know. Five years older, it doesn't matter if people know that now. Perhaps I'll get to be older than her. I'll go on clocking up the years and maybe I'll end up older than she ever was." He tugged hesitantly at his tie. "Anyway, however bad a day it is for me, there's no reason I can't wish you a good morning, Mr Trevor."

His hand may not have left my own – which still rested on his shoulder – as lightly as on other occasions but he raised it all the same to give his customary vertical salute.

That particular morning it was 1962 and so he addressed me as Mr Trevor. Had Will found himself in the 1930s that morning, I would have been Dr Nott and, had he chosen the 1950s, he would have seen me as Mr Renner. During the First World War I would become Dr Ashmore-Jones, in the 1920s Mr Brome, in the 1940s Dr Myer and in the 1970s and 1980s Dr Magill, and that was the only indication one had of which decade Will the time-traveller inclined towards each morning. Each day I was a different faculty member from the past, although always the same faculty member from any one particular period, chosen by his spirit as its habitation for that day. And he never got it wrong. In me, and in his pure, atemporal eyes, Dr Magill, Dr Myer, Mr Brome, Dr Ashmore-Jones, Mr Renner, Dr Nott and Mr Trevor all returned to live out again their own routine past; some were long dead, others retired, others had simply moved on or disappeared leaving behind them only their names, or had perhaps been expelled from the university for some serious misdemeanour of which Will, in his eternal porter's lodge, would never have had the slightest notion.

And, oddly enough, on some mornings I was a certain Mr Branshaw, about whom no one remembered or knew anything, and each morning that I heard his greeting – "Good morning, Mr Branshaw" – it made me wonder whether Will's ability to travel in time might not also encompass the future (perhaps only the near future, the future that would cover the little that remained of his life) and whether, installed in the 1990s, he might not be greeting someone who had not yet arrived at Oxford and who, perhaps, wherever he might be now, was as yet unaware that he would one day live in that inhospitable city, a city preserved in syrup as one of my predecessors once described it. Someone whom Will's dreaming, diaphanous eyes would also fail to recognise and to whom, on greeting him with his customary festive wave at the entrance to the Taylorian, he would perhaps give my name, the name he had never pronounced in my presence.

AS I MENTIONED BEFORE, my duties in the city of Oxford were minimal, a fact that often made me feel I was playing a purely decorative role there. On realising, however, that my mere physical presence was insufficient in itself to decorate anything, I occasionally felt I ought to put on my black gown (obligatory now on only very few occasions) with the primary aim of satisfying the many tourists whom I would pass en route from my pyramid house to the Taylorian and with the secondary aim of feeling both disguised and slightly more justified in my role as ornament. I would therefore sometimes arrive in this guise at the room where I gave my few classes or lectures to various groups of students, all of whom treated me with an excessive degree of respect and an even greater degree of indifference. In age I was closer to them than I was to most of the members of the congregation (as the assembly of dons and teachers of the university is called, in keeping with the strongly clerical tradition of the place) but the mere fact that I spent our few hours of eye contact perched nervously above them on a dais was enough for the gap between the students and myself to verge on that between king and subjects. I was above and they were below, I had a smart lectern in front of me and they only ordinary desks embellished with graffiti, I wore my long black gown and they did not (to widen the gap between us still further, my gown boasted the bands denoting a Cambridge rather than an Oxford degree) and that sufficed for them not only to allow any tendentious statements I made to pass undisputed but also to let me hold forth unquestioned for an hour

9

on the sombre literature of post-civil war Spain, an hour that seemed to me as interminable as the post-war period had to its writers (to those few writers opposed to the regime).

The students did, on the other hand, ask questions in the translation classes, which I taught in tandem with various of my English colleagues. The latter were responsible for the choice of texts for these classes (in order to avoid creating a purely gratuitous and, indeed, minor enigma, I would prefer for the moment not to reveal the bizarre name by which these classes were known), texts that were couched in such abstruse or obscurely vernacular language that I often had to invent spurious definitions for antiquated or unintelligible words that I had never seen or heard before and which, of course, the students would never see or hear again either. Of those pretentious, memorable words (clearly the products of sick minds) I recall with particular enthusiasm: *praseodimio*, *jarampero*, *guadameco* and *engibacaire* (and how could I forget *briaga*, a term that cropped up in a particularly elegant passage on the wine trade). At the risk of appearing a fool, now that I have translated them into English and know perfectly well what they mean, I confess that then I was totally ignorant of their existence, which, even now, surprises me. My role in those classes, that of walking Spanish grammar and dictionary, was a more hazardous one than in my lectures and caused considerable wear and tear on my reflexes. The etymological questions were the most taxing but, after a while, borne along by impatience and a desire both to please and to get myself out of trouble, I became quite unscrupulous about inventing wild etymologies on the spot, convinced that neither the students nor my teaching colleague would ever be interested enough to check the truth of my replies. (And even if they did, I was sure they would have compassion enough not to throw the blunder in my face the following day.) So, confronted by what seemed to me malicious and absurd questions such as: "What is the origin of the word *papirotazo*?", I had no compunction whatever about supplying them with answers that outdid the questions themselves in absurdity and malice.

"Ah, yes, *papirotazo*. This is a flick delivered with the thumb and forefinger and derives its name from the method used to test the toughness and thereby establish the age of papyruses found in Egypt at the beginning of the nineteenth century."

When I saw that, far from provoking any violent reaction or it occurring to any of them to point out that one *papirotazo* would have been enough to reduce any such dynastic papyrus to confetti, the students were instead diligently taking notes and my English colleague – doubtless stunned by the vulgar sonority of the word and intoxicated perhaps by this sudden evocation of a Napoleonic Egypt – was endorsing my explanation ("Did you get that? *Papirotazo* comes from the word *papiro*: pa-pi-ro, pa-pi-ro-ta-zo"), I even found the nerve to go on and compound my lie with an erudite footnote: "It is, therefore, a fairly recent word, created by analogy with the more ancient *capirotazo*, as this painful and offensive blow is also known," and I paused to illustrate the word, flicking the air with thumb and forefinger, "for it was just this kind of flicking blow that was dealt to the hooded penitents taking part in Holy Week processions, or rather, that was levelled at the tips of their hoods or *capirotes*, with the intention of humiliating them."

And my colleague again endorsed my view ("Did you get that? Ca-pi-ro-te, ca-pi-ro-ta-zo"). The delight some teachers took in pronouncing preposterous Spanish words never failed to move me, and their preference was always for words of four or more syllables. I recall that the Butcher enjoyed them so much that he would lose all composure and, raising one leg (a combination of very short socks and huge voracious shoes resulting in the exposure of one brilliant white shin), would uninhibitedly, and not without a certain grace, rest it on an empty desk and bounce it up and down in time to his own euphoric syllabification of the word in question ("Ve-ri-cue-to, ve-ri-cue-to. Mo-fle-tu-do, mo-fle-tu-do"). In fact, as I realised only later, my colleagues' applause for my invented etymologies was a consequence of both their excellent manners and a dual sense of solidarity and fun. In Oxford no one ever says anything directly (frankness would be considered the most unforgivable, not to say the most disconcerting, of sins), or at least that is how I understood Dewar the Inquisitor's parting words to me at the end of my two-year stay when, in the midst of other splendid remarks, he said:

"What I'll miss most is your extraordinary etymological knowledge. It never ceased to amaze me. I can still remember my surprise when you explained that the word *papirotazo* came from *papo*, jowl, and signified a blow delivered to another's *papada* or double chin. Really astonishing." He paused for a moment with some satisfaction to observe my embarrassment. Then he tutted and added: "Etymology is such a fascinating subject, it's just a shame that the students – poor undiscerning creatures that they are – forget ninety-five per cent of the marvels they hear, and their bedazzlement at our brilliant revelations lasts only a matter of minutes, at most for the duration of the class. But I will remember it: pa-pa-da, pa-pi-ro-ta-zo." He flexed one of his legs slightly. "Who'd have thought it? Quite fantastic."

I think I probably blushed deeply and, as soon as I could, rushed to the library to consult the dictionary and discover that, in fact, the now famous *papirotazo* did indeed come from the *papo* on which in former times the ignominious blow was received. I felt more of an impostor than ever, but at the same time my conscience felt clearer, for it seemed to me that my crazy etymologies were no more nonsensical, no less likely than the real ones. Or, rather, the true etymology of *papirotazo* struck me as being almost as outlandish as my invented one. Anyway, as the Ripper had pointed out, such ornamental knowledge, whether false, genuine or merely half-true, enjoyed only a very short life span. When true knowledge proves irrelevant, one is free to invent.

I SPENT ENDLESS HOURS walking round the city of Oxford and consequently know almost every corner of it, as well as its outlying villages with their trisyllabic names: Headington, Kidlington, Wolvercote, Littlemore (and, further off, Abingdon and Cuddesdon). I also came to know almost all the faces that peopled it three years ago and two years ago, however difficult it subsequently proved ever to find them again. Most of the time I walked with no set purpose or goal, although I well remember that I spent about ten days during my second teaching term there (Hilary Term as it is called, comprising eight weeks between January and March) walking the streets with a goal that was neither very adult nor – while it lasted – one I cared to admit to myself. It was shortly before I met Clare and Edward Bayes and in fact my interruption or abandonment (yes, abandonment is the word) of that goal came about because of that meeting with Clare Bayes and her husband and not just because, around that time, one windy afternoon in Broad Street, the goal itself was simultaneously achieved and frustrated.

Some ten days before I was introduced to Clare and Edward Bayes and began to get to know them, I was coming back from London – on a Friday – on the last train, which then left Paddington around midnight. It was the train I caught most Fridays or Saturdays on my return from the capital where I had nowhere to sleep unless I stayed in a hotel, a luxury I could only permit myself from time to time. Usually I chose to return home and, if necessary, to travel down again the following morning if something or someone required my presence there – London is less than an hour away on the fast train. The midnight train from London to Oxford, however, was not fast, but any inconvenience this caused me was compensated for by the pleasure of spending another hour in the company of my friends Guillermo and Miriam, a married couple who lived in South Kensington and whose conversation and hospitality formed the final stage of those days spent wandering the streets of London. Catching that last train involved changing at Didcot, a town of which I have never seen more than its gloomy station, and that only after dusk. The second train, which was to transport us with incomprehensible slowness from there to Oxford, would not always be standing ready at its platform for the arrival of the six or seven passengers from London making the connection (British Rail obviously believed any travellers on that train to be inveterate nightbirds who would not in the least mind getting to their beds a little later still) and then I would be forced to wait at the silent, empty station, which, so far as one could make out in the darkness, appeared to be entirely cut off from the town it served and to be surrounded on all sides by countryside, as if it were some rural halt.

In England strangers rarely talk to each other, not even on trains or during long waits, and the night silence of Didcot station is one of the deepest I've ever known. The silence seems even deeper when broken by voices or by isolated, intermittent noises, the screech of a wagon, for example, that suddenly and enigmatically moves a few yards then stops, or the unintelligible cry of a porter whom the cold wakes from a short nap (rescuing him from a bad dream), or the abrupt, distant thud of crates that invisible hands quite gratuitously decide to shift despite the complete absence of any urgency, at a time when everything seems infinitely postponable, or the metallic crunch of a beer can being crushed up then thrown into a litter bin, or the modest flight of a single errant page from a newspaper, or my own footsteps vainly pacing to the edge of the platform and back just to pass the time. A few lamps, placed some yards apart (so as not to squander electricity) timidly light those as yet unswept platforms that resemble the aftermath of some rather pathetic street party. (The women who will sweep them in the morning lie dreaming now in darkest Didcot.) In the hesitant light of each lamp, you can just make out brief stretches of platform and railway lines, just as one lamp lights both my own face framed by the turned-up collar of my navy blue coat and a woman's shoes and ankles whose owner remains engulfed in shadow. All I can see is the shape of a seated figure in a raincoat and the glow of the cigarettes that she, like me, smokes during the wait, even longer than usual that night. The shoes were lightly tapping out a rhythm on the platform, as if the person wearing them could still hear in her head the music she'd perhaps spent the whole evening dancing to; they were the shoes of an adolescent or an ingénue dancer, low-heeled with a buckle and rounded toes. They were very English shoes and kept my eyes swivelled in their direction, making the interminable hour spent in Didcot station more bearable. The butts of our respective cigarettes consorted on the ground. Whilst I flicked mine – using a genuine *papirotazo* – towards the edge of the platform over which they occasionally failed to fall, she tossed hers in the same direction with an arm movement reminiscent of someone rather feebly throwing a ball. And when she made that movement, her hand entered the beam of light allowing, for a fraction of a second, just the glimpse of a bracelet. I got up from time to time, partly to peer out at the dark rails in the distance and partly in an attempt to see something more of the woman who sat – with her legs now crossed, now uncrossed – smoking and tapping out that unknown rhythm with her illuminated feet. I took two or three steps in her direction and then returned to my place, having managed to see nothing beyond the English shoes and her ankles, made perfect by the penumbra. At last she got up and walked slowly along the platform, just a couple of minutes before the slow, sluggish appearance of the delayed train and the announcement by a slurred, amplified voice (with such a marked Indian accent that a foreigner could only guess at what was being said) of the arrival of the train in Didcot and its subsequent stops: Banbury, Leamington, Warwick, Birmingham (or was it Swindon, Chippenham, Bath, Bristol? I can't be bothered to look at the map; my memory contains both series of destinations and perhaps one has now become confused with the other). She remained standing now, swinging her small bag while she waited. I opened the carriage door for her.

I've completely forgotten her face but not her colours (yellow, blue, pink, white, red), yet I know that during the whole of my youth she was the woman who made the greatest and most immediate impact on me, although I also know that, traditionally, in both literature and real life, such a remark can only be made of women whom young men never actually meet. I can't remember now how I got talking to her, nor what we talked about during the less than half-hour journey between Didcot and Oxford. Perhaps we didn't even have a proper conversation but just exchanged three or four casual remarks. On the other hand, I do remember that, although not young enough to be a student, she was still very young and therefore not particularly elegant, and that the collar of her raincoat was open just enough for me to see the pearl necklace (cultured or real I couldn't say) which, in the fashion of a few years back, the best-groomed English girls thought the thing to wear even though the rest of their outfit was informal or apparently casual (she herself was neat rather than elegant). The other thing I remember about that woman, with her bobbed hair and forgotten features, was that she looked as if she'd just stepped out of the 1930s. Perhaps to Will the porter all women looked like that on the days he found himself in that particular decade. Anyway, whatever it was we talked about, it was not personal enough for me to ascertain any concrete facts about her. Perhaps her clear eyes finally closed with tiredness and I didn't dare do anything to prevent it. Perhaps during that thirty-minute journey my desire to look at her was stronger than my curiosity or my capacity for conjecture. Or perhaps we spoke only of Didcot, of the dark, cold station we'd left behind and to which we would both have to return. Like me she got off at Oxford but, since I was unable to do any preparatory groundwork, I couldn't even offer to share my taxi with her.

For the next ten days, I walked all over Oxford with the aim or rather with the unconscious hope of meeting her again, which was not that improbable assuming she'd not just gone there on a visit but lived in Oxford. I spent even more time in the streets than usual and with every day that passed her face became more blurred, more confused with other faces, as tends to happen with the things one struggles to remember, with all those images memory shows no respect for (that is, before which memory does not remain passive). It's no wonder, then, that today I can recall none of her features – just an unfinished portrait, an outline drawing with the colours barely blocked in, not painted – despite my having with certainty seen her a second and, I think, a third and possibly even a fourth time. But the one definite sighting I had of her – ten days after that first encounter – occurred on a terribly windy day and was over before I knew it. Coming out of Blackwell's with less than enough time to get to one of my translation classes with the punctilious Dewar, I quickened my step and walked straight ahead into the teeth of the hurricane that had blown up whilst I'd been browsing in the bookshop. About twenty paces further on, outside Trinity, I passed two female figures also in a hurry and with their heads bowed against the wind. Only when I'd taken another four or five steps (and had my back to her) did I realise who it was and turn round. What surprised me most was that she and her friend, who had also walked on four or five steps, had also stopped and turned round. At that distance of eight or nine paces we looked at each other properly. She smiled and shouted, more in order to identify herself than to indicate her recognition of me: "On the train! At Didcot!" I hesitated for a moment as to whether I should approach or not and whilst I hesitated, her friend tugged at her sleeve and urged her to continue on her way. Her skirt swirled about in the wind, as did her short hair. I remember that particularly because during the brief moment in which she stood there on Broad Street and shouted: "On the train! At Didcot!" she had one hand to her hair, holding it off her forehead, and the other to her skirt, holding it down against the elements. "Yes, on the train! At Didcot!" I repeated to indicate that I recognised her too (the hem of my blue coat beating against my legs), but then her odious, tugging friend whose face I did not see was carrying her off, not towards Dewar and the Taylorian, but in the opposite direction. I had no other firm sighting of her that year or the next, after which I left Oxford for Madrid, although not immediately to settle down there, as I now realise I have. What I regret most is that on that second occasion, I didn't manage a glance at her English shoes or her ankles which would doubtless have seemed fragile in the wind. I was too intent on observing the wary flappings of her skirt.

THE SHOES CLARE BAYES wore were never English, always Italian, and I never once saw a low heel or buckle or a rounded toe on any of them. When she came to my house (which was not that often) or when we managed to end up together at her house (even less often) or we met in a hotel in London or Reading or even Brighton (though we only went to Brighton once), the first thing she would do was to ease her shoes off at the instep and then with a kick, one for each shoe, send them ricocheting against the walls, as if she were the owner of innumerable pairs and cared nothing for their ruination. I would immediately pick them up and put them where we couldn't see them: the sight of empty shoes always makes me imagine them on the feet of the person who has worn them or might wear them, and seeing that person by my side – with their shoes off – or not seeing the person at all upsets me terribly (that's why, whenever I look at the window of some old-fashioned shoeshop with its rows and rows of shoes, I automatically see it filled by a multitude of cramped, uncomfortable figures). Clare had the habit – apparently acquired during her childhood years spent in Delhi and Cairo – of going barefoot when indoors (fortunately in England almost everywhere is carpeted) and so my most vivid memory of her legs is not the memory shared perhaps by many others, that of strong, slightly muscular calves, as seen when poised above their high heels, but rather that of two slender legs, almost boyish in their movements, as seen when barefoot. She would lie on my bed or her bed or on a hotel bed and smoke and talk for hours, always with her skirt still on, but

20

pulled up to reveal her thighs, the dark upper part of her tights or just her bare skin. She was not circumspect in her gestures and would frequently ladder her tights, often scorching them by briefly, unconsciously brushing against them with the cigarette she waved around with an abandon uncommon in England (and learned perhaps in the southern lands of her childhood), a gesture accompanied by the tinkling of the various bracelets adorning her forearms, bracelets she sometimes neglected to take off (it was little wonder that sometimes real sparks flew from them). Everything about her was expansive, excessive, excitable; she was one of those beings not made for time, for whom the very notion of time and its passing is a grievance, and one of those beings in need of a constant supply of fragments of eternity or, to put it another way, of a bottomless well of detail with which to fill time to the brim. More than once, for that very reason, because of that endless drawing out of whatever we had begun, we ran the risk of her husband, Edward Bayes, glimpsing with his own eyes the retreating back or the wake of the very thing he surely knew about and was continually trying to reject or perhaps forget. Consequently, I was always the one who had to interrupt Clare's interminable ramblings and comments, her chronic logorrhoea, her eternalising of the contents of each moment as she lay back on the bed, smoking, gesticulating, pontificating, crossing and uncrossing her legs, folding them beneath her, extolling or railing against her past and her present, jumping from one plan for her immediate future to the next, without ever actually bringing any of them to fruition. I was the one who had to set the alarm clock or keep an eye on the watch on the bedside table and decide it was time to part, or (in Oxford) keep one ear open for the city's obsessive bells chiming the hour, the half hour and the quarter hour, then inconsiderately pealing out again as evening fell; I was the one who had to hurry her along, look for the shoes I'd put away after her arrival, smooth her skirt and make sure it was on straight, remind her not to forget her umbrella or the brooch impaled in the carpet or the ring left by the washbasin or the bag containing the strange collection of purchases she always brought with her wherever we met, even if it was on a Sunday (and, if we were at her house, I was the one who had to empty the ashtray, help her change the sheets, open the window and rinse my glass). Clare always carried all manner of things with her and would spread them out wherever she arrived as if she planned to spend the rest of her life there, even on occasions when we had less than an hour to spend together between our respective classes. (I still have one pair of earrings that I never did manage to expel from my house.) Fortunately, by upbringing, she was incapable of going out into the street without her makeup on, and her hair was a mane of artificially tangled curls on which my caresses or any prolonged, intense contact with a pillow made little impact. Thus, whilst I did not have to comb her hair before we said goodbye, I did have to check that her face bore no sign of the private eternity she'd erected and maintained during the time spent in my company, that her face was not flushed, her eyes not too soft, that all signs of joy were obliterated (in Oxford the distances are so short they barely give one time to change colour). To achieve all this I had simply and briefly to rehearse with her the intellectual exercise that underpins all adultery, that is, help her in the invention of seamless stories for the benefit of Edward Bayes and to ensure she didn't contradict herself when telling them, although she herself considered the exercise unnecessary and bothersome (her expression darkened whenever we said goodbye because of my insistence on it). She was careless and frivolous and smiling and forgetful and, had I been Edward Bayes, or so I thought then, it would not have taken much scheming or effort on my part to ascertain her every thought, her every move. But I wasn't Edward Bayes and perhaps if I had been, Clare's activities and intentions would have seemed utterly impenetrable to me.

Perhaps I wouldn't have wanted to know about them, or would have been content simply to imagine them. At any rate, I was the one who, at the closing of each passionate parenthesis, had to put everything in order and almost propel her out of my pyramid house (with each floor narrower than the last), drag her from the hotel we were staying at or else free myself from her momentary, last-minute tendency to cling (grief for the ending of time) and, on the rare occasions I dared set foot in her house in Edward Bayes' absence, neutralise her rasher impulses. (Adultery is hard work.)

Clare had few scruples, but then no one who knew her would ever have expected anything else, for her charm lay in large measure precisely in her lack of consideration both for other people and for herself. She often made me laugh, the talent I most appreciate in others, but I know that my fondness for her, and hers for me, was never long-lived or solid enough to prove dangerous (for I was not Edward Bayes, nor was I ever in any danger of supplanting him). It has always seemed to me overly ingenuous to think that because someone loves us – that is, because independently of us that person has made a decision temporarily to love us and only afterwards informed us of the fact – their treatment of us will be any different from the treatment they mete out to others, as if, immediately subsequent upon that other person's independent decision and declaration, we were not certain to be relegated to join those others, as if, in fact, as well as being ourselves, we had not always been "the others". The last thing in the world I would have wanted – at least during those fragile days I lived in Oxford, with only a very uncertain sense of my own identity – would have been to have Clare treat me as she treated Edward Bayes or her father or even the ironic Cromer-Blake, who was simultaneously paternal and filial towards her, while her father was simply paternal and her husband purely marital. I suppose my relationship with her was preeminently fraternal, as has tended to be the case with women I've known well, doubtless because I had no sisters and felt the poorer for it. Although our meetings were never that frequent I did have the opportunity to observe Clare at close quarters and, without wishing to speak ill of her or – let's say – speak of things that others, on hearing them from my lips, might consider derogatory, I put myself often enough in the shoes of the others – in the shoes of her father, of Edward Bayes and even of Cromer-Blake – to know without a doubt that she showed none of them the least consideration. I put myself above all in the shoes of Edward Bayes and I remember on one fifth of November, nine months after we'd met – I remember the date because it was Guy Fawkes Day and from Clare's study window, in All Souls, in Catte Street, across from the old Bodleian Library and the Radcliffe Camera, I could see some little boys begging pennies for the guy they'd made for the occasion out of rags, string and old clothes to represent the executed plotter Guy Fawkes, who is burnt that night on bonfires throughout the land – when I put myself so successfully in his place (in the place allotted to him, but perhaps never filled) that Clare confused me with him.

The four of us, Bayes, Cromer-Blake, Clare and myself, had arranged to meet there in order to go out to lunch and I had been the first to arrive at Catte Street, deliberately getting there twenty minutes early. The previous night Clare and I had stayed on far too late at a hotel in Reading and, contrary to our custom when we visited Oxford's neighbouring town, had travelled back on the same train (when Edward Bayes was away we took Clare's car and when he wasn't we always travelled on different trains, there and back, to London or to Reading). Anyway, we'd arrived at Oxford station and walked together beneath a fickle, mellow moon, our faces to the wind, until on a corner still some distance from our respective houses, we went our separate ways. During the train journey we'd also sat next to each other since, being friends in the eyes of the world, not to have done so would have struck anyone seeing us as even odder. A member of the Russian department called Rook had certainly seen us. He was dozing, slumped in the first-class carriage we had initially got into because, from the platform, it had appeared to be empty. He saw us and we saw him when we were already advancing down the corridor, laughing in a compromising or overly frank and unEnglish manner and he, with what one presumed to be a nod of his sunken head, addressed Clare first with a "Mrs Bayes" and then – doubtless because he didn't know how to pronounce my name, or because he found it difficult to remember – bade me a simple "Good evening". We walked on to find a seat as far away as possible from him, but even there dared utter nothing but the briefest of noncommittal phrases in the lowest of voices. Afterwards, when we walked the streets of Oxford, for the first time together and alone, beneath the fickle, mellow moon, our faces to the wind, we heard his footsteps a little way behind, echoing the rhythm of our steps, or at least we thought they were his and not just the echo of our own. We neither turned round nor exchanged a word until the moment came for us to part and then we simply said "Goodbye" without even stopping or looking at each other (such is the sadness of secrecy). I heard nothing after that except, for an instant, Clare's footsteps hurrying away; I doubt she heard my own weary steps.

Rook was famous because for the past twelve years he'd been engaged on a new translation of *Anna Karenina* and because, during an academic year spent in America, he'd met and become friendly with Nabokov. His translation – though no one, not even his publisher, had as yet seen a line of it – was to be both definitive and incomparable, beginning with a fundamental innovation in the title, for, according to both Rook and Nabokov – to whom he always referred as "Vladimir Vladimirovich" to indicate his familiarity both with the man and with Russian patronymics – the correct title was *Karenin* not *Karenina*, since Anna was neither ballerina, singer or actress, the only women, however authentically Russian, whose family name it would be admissible to feminise in a text in English or in any other Western language. He and I had met on more than one occasion in the Senior Common Room in the Taylorian where, drinking cups of anaemic coffee and casting the occasional lazy, loathing glance at the scholarly contents of our respective brief-cases, we lounged around pretending to be putting the finishing touches to our lesson preparation. Rook – a man with a massive head perched on a slender body – was always only too ready to talk about Nabokov or to enlighten me about Lermontov or Gogol, but his personal life was a closed book to the other members of the Oxford congregation. For that reason one could quite happily attribute to him any habit or characteristic one liked, and the reputation he had was of being a dreadful gossip. In fact in Oxford that is of no great significance. What would be extraordinary would be for someone not to have such a reputation: anyone who's not a scandalmonger or, at the very least, malicious is doomed to live as marginal and discredited an existence as someone unfortunate enough to have graduated from a university other than Cambridge or Oxford itself, and such a person has no chance of adapting because he will never be accepted. In Oxford the only thing anyone is truly interested in is money, followed some way behind by information, which can always be useful as a means of acquiring money. The information obtained can be important or superfluous, useful or trivial, political or economic, diplomatic or epistemological, psychological or genealogical, familiar or ancillary, historical or sexual, social or professional, anthropological or methodological, phenomenological, technological or straightforwardly phallic, it doesn't matter; but anyone wishing to survive there must have (or must obtain without delay) some sort of transmissible data. Giving information about something is, moreover, the only way of not having to give out information about oneself, and thus, the more misanthropic, independent, solitary or mysterious the Oxonian in question, the more information about other people one would expect him to provide in order to excuse his own reserve and gain the right to remain silent about his own private life. The more one knows and tells about other people, the greater one's dispensation not to reveal anything about oneself. Consequently the whole of Oxford is fully and continuously engaged in concealing and suppressing itself whilst at the same time trying to winkle out as much information as possible about other people, and from there comes the tradition – true – and the myth – also true – of the high quality, great efficiency and virtuosity of the dons and teachers of Oxford and Cambridge when it comes to the dirtier work involved in spying and of their continued employment by both British and Soviet governments who vie for their services as prestigious agents – single, double and triple (Oxonians have sharper ears, Canta-brigians fewer scruples). However, the effect of this is that the aforementioned right to remain silent about one's private life is reduced literally to just that, that is, to saving oneself the humiliation and embarrassment of having to own up and make it public knowledge oneself, since, given the universal need to supply information about other people in order not to have to divulge anything about oneself, the very information that one avoids giving, others (a whole host of them) covet, spy out, pursue, track down, obtain and end up broadcasting in order, in turn, to avoid having to reveal any information about them-selves. Some weak spirits (only a few) give it up as a bad job right from the start and, with a reprehensible lack of resistance and modesty, make a full public confession of their private affairs. Though frowned upon because of the frank, easygoing and heterodox attitude it reveals towards the game, this is per-mitted because it is seen as both unconditional surrender and abject submission. On the other hand, some virtuosi in the field manage, in spite of everything, to keep secret their habits, vices, tastes and practices (perhaps by dint of renouncing *all* habits, vices, tastes and practices), which does not, of course, prevent other people from inventing and attributing to them every vice they can think of; however, the variety and resultant contradictions in such incongruous and motley reports tend to make one distrust their veracity. Occasionally, though, such virtuosi (but they have to be *real* virtuosi) do get their own way and no one really knows any hard facts about them at all. Rook was without a doubt an eminent member of that class (such a consummate master of the art, you'd think he'd been trained by the Soviets). Apart from his absolute commitment to his monumental translation and his encounter with Vladimir Vladimirovich in Britain's former colonies, nothing was known about him (his personal life was a blank) and, on the other hand, one could take it for granted that anything he knew would, the instant he knew it, rapidly pass into the realm of popular knowledge.

When I arrived twenty minutes early at her office in Catte Street, the morning after seeing Rook, crumpled and asleep, on the London train and imagining we'd heard his footsteps behind ours in the windy streets of the empty city, Clare was calmly reading the newspaper. (She opened the door to me, one finger keeping her place between the pages. She didn't kiss me.) Whilst she seemed to have slept well enough, I had barely slept a wink, so I had no option but to come straight to the point and ask her the question I'd asked myself again and again during that long, sleepless night ("Had she or had she not told Ted that she was in Reading last night?")

"Of course not; anyway, he didn't ask me."

"You're mad. That just makes it worse. If he doesn't know it already, he'll find out soon enough from Rook."

"Not directly from Rook. They scarcely know each other."

"In Oxford everyone scarcely knows everyone else, but that doesn't stop them talking to each other at all hours and leaping to the first interpretation of the facts that occurs to them. All it needs is for Rook to have met Ted this morning in a corridor or in the street. 'Oh, by the way, tell your wife I meant to offer to share my taxi with her last night. We were on the same train from Reading, but she got off so quickly I didn't have time to offer. I expect the Spanish gentleman took her home. Very polite, that Spanish chappie, we've had the odd chat before, he and I.' That's all it needs for you to be faced with a barrage of questions that I really don't know how you're going to answer."

"What questions? Ted hardly ever asks questions. He waits until I tell him things. There's no need to get so worried."

I was always the one who worried about her. I played my part and sometimes hers as well. Now I was playing all three, mine, hers and Edward Bayes', or rather the part that, according to her, Edward Bayes was not playing.

"What do you mean 'what questions'? 'What were you up to in Reading last night with our Spanish friend? Where had you been? Why did you leave the station in such a hurry? Rook saw you both. Why didn't you tell me you were going to Reading? Why didn't you tell me you'd been in Reading? Rook saw you. Rook. Reading.'"

"I'd get out of it somehow."

"Get out of it now. Tell me how you'd answer those questions. They're simple, concrete, conjugal questions."

As usual Clare was barefoot. She'd sat down behind her desk with the newspaper in her hand (her index finger still keeping the same place; I wondered what was so important about what she was reading that she didn't want to lose her place) and I was standing with my back to the window opposite her. From there I could see the tips of her toes, the dark tips (the toecaps so to speak) of her dark tights. They peeped out from beneath the desk, on the carpet. I would have liked to touch her dark feet, but Edward Bayes or Cromer-Blake could arrive at any moment. Clare was looking at me silhouetted against the light.

In her other hand, she held a cigarette. The ashtray was some way from her.

"Ted could arrive at any moment," I said, "and if he did meet Rook this morning, he might start questioning us both the minute he comes in that door. We'd better think up something first. I've spent the whole night thinking up answers. Perhaps you bumped into me in Reading. At Reading station? Why were you coming back so late? Why had you gone there? You couldn't have been shopping, there's nothing to buy in Reading."

"You're a fool," Clare said to me. "Fortunately, though, you're not my husband. You're a fool with the mind of a detective, and being married to that kind of fool would make life impossible. That's why you'll never get married. A fool with the mind of a detective is an intelligent fool, a logical fool, the worst kind, because men's logic, far from compensating for their foolishness, only duplicates it, triplicates it, makes it dangerous. Ted's brand of foolishness isn't dangerous and that's why I can live with him, why I like living with him. He just takes it for granted, you don't yet. You're such a fool that you still believe in the possibility of not being one. You still struggle. He doesn't."

"All men are fools."

"We all are, I am too."

She tapped ash off her cigarette with her forefinger but miscalculated so that it fell instead on the carpet, near her bare feet. I looked at her dark, desirable feet and looked at the ash, waiting for the moment when her feet would tread in it and become smeared with grey.

"If you were Ted you wouldn't ask me those questions because you'd know that I could simply choose to answer them or not and that in the end it would come to the same thing; when you share your daily life with someone, you look for ways of living in peace with them. If I answered your questions I could lie to you (and you would have to accept the lie as the truth) or I could tell you the truth (and you might not be sure you wanted the truth). If I didn't answer your questions, you could keep insisting and I could get angry and argue with you and reproach you and still not answer, or even look at you perplexed and remain silent for days on end and still not answer until you got fed up with my reproachful gaze and with not hearing my voice. We always condemn ourselves by what we say, not by what we do, by what we say or by what we say we do, not by what others say or by what we actually have done. You can't force someone to answer, and if you were Ted or you were married, you'd know that. The world is full of unwitting bastard children who inherit the fortune or the poverty of those who did not engender them. Family resemblances notwithstanding, no man has ever known for certain that he was the father of his children. Between married couples, neither partner answers questions they don't want to answer, and so they ask each other very few. There are plenty of couples who don't talk to each other at all."

"And what if, despite all you say, Ted chose to be like me today and he did ask those questions? What would you say if, when he came through that door, he submitted you to an interrogation? What were you doing together in Reading last night? Where had you been? Did you go to bed together? Are you lovers? Do you sleep together? Since when?"

"I'd say just what I said to you: you're a fool."

She put down the newspaper and got up, stepping on the ash she'd continued to drop without noticing on to the carpet by her feet. She came over to where I was standing and I turned round and we both stood in silence looking out of the window: it was sunny and cloudy. Her breasts brushed against my back. The boys were on the steps of the Radcliffe Camera begging for pennies for their guy. I opened the window and threw them a coin, and the clink of coin on stone made the four of them look round at us; but I'd already closed the window and they could only just make us out behind the glass. Clare stroked the back of my neck with her hand and my shoe with one of her bare feet. I imagined she would probably be thinking about her son. My shoe was smeared with grey.

THIS IS WHAT CROMER-BLAKE wrote in his diary for that fifth of November and which I transcribe today:

What surprises me most is that the disease does not for the moment stop me taking an interest in other people's lives. I've decided to behave as if nothing were wrong with me and to say nothing to anyone except to B, and to him only if my worst fears are confirmed. This doesn't prove to have been that difficult, once the decision was made. But the strange thing isn't that I'm able to behave secretly and properly, it's my own unchanging interest in the world around me that's odd. Everything matters to me, everything touches me. In fact I don't have to pretend because I still can't persuade myself that this can or will happen to me. I can't get used to the idea that with things as they are I could end up dying, and that were that to happen (I cross my fingers) I would no longer be in a position to learn about the continuing saga of other people's lives. It's as if someone were to snatch from my hands a book I'm devouring with infinite curiosity. It's inconceivable. Although if that was all it was, it wouldn't be so bad, the worst thing is that there won't be any more books, life is the one and only codex.

Life is still so medieval.

Of course, nothing more is likely to happen to me, death will have happened to me, which is quite enough. I can't get used to the idea, and that's why I don't want to go back to the doctor just yet or to see Dayanand who, with his terrible clinical eye, must already suspect something about my state of health. And that's why what will no longer matter then, matters so much now: what will become of B (I can't imagine not being a witness to his life: death doesn't just rob us of our lives, but also of everyone else's), and of Dayanand himself, of Roger, Ted and Clare and of our dear Spaniard. I saw them today, they were together, fresh from an embrace, standing by the window, looking more amused than amorous and also a little melancholy, as if they regretted not being able to love each other more. It was lucky I arrived first, and not Ted. I don't know what they want, or what Clare wants, nor why they've made me their confidant and in a way their accessory. I'd rather be in the same state of blissful ignorance as Ted. The other day Clare came to see me in my office between classes; she was even more excitable than usual and desperate to talk to me. I gave her three minutes that stretched into six (an irritated young Bottomley was waiting outside, an arrogant, critical look on his face), during which time she talked of nothing in particular, nothing coherent, she just talked about Ted, it seemed he was the only thing in the world that mattered to her. She didn't call me later to continue the conversation, silence, nothing. Today, on the other hand, to my great surprise I noticed a foot, her foot, probing my right calf under the table. Clare's foot was stroking my calf. Luckily, we were in the Halifax where they have long tablecloths. I realised at once that what she was really after was the left leg of our Spanish friend seated next to me, so, fixing her with wide, slightly reproachful eyes, I discreetly took her foot and transported it to its true and desired resting place, the foreign knee. Then, of course, I took no further interest in things subterranean, in fact I swiftly renewed my conversation with Ted, fearful lest he realise what was going on down below. I found it both extremely embarrassing and extremely amusing, and felt guilty to feel that. I worry about all three of them and wonder how it will all end. We've got months ahead of us yet, we're only halfway through Michaelmas. But I can't help seeing the funny side of things, despite my years of friendship with Ted, my general concern about Clare and about my own health. At any rate, the first thing I told B about tonight was the case of the mistaken limbs as being the most important event of the day or the one that might best distract him from his discontents. I'm just the same as ever, veering between rage and laughter, whichever life provokes in me, with no medium term; they're my two complementary ways of relating to and being in the world. I'm either furious or merry or both things at once, battling it out inside me. I don't change. This illness ought to change me, ought to make me more reflective, less excitable. The illness, however, provokes neither fury nor merriment in me. If it develops, if it's confirmed (I cross my fingers again), I'll just observe myself. I feel frightened.

MY GUIDE AND MENTOR in the city of Oxford was Cromer-Blake and, four months after my arrival there, nine months before that same fifth of November, it was he who introduced me to Clare Bayes at one of the grandiloquent Oxford suppers known as high tables. These suppers take place once a week in the vast refectories of each of the different colleges. The table at which the diners and their guests sit is raised up on a platform and thus presides over the other tables (where the students dine with suspicious haste, fleeing as soon as they have finished, gradually abandoning the elevated guests to their solitude and thus avoiding the spectacle the latter end up making of themselves) and it is for this reason rather than because of any unusually high standard of cuisine or conversation that they are designated "high tables". The suppers are formal (in the Oxonian sense) and for members of the congregation the wearing of gowns is obligatory. The suppers do begin very formally, but the sheer length of the meal allows for the appearance and subsequent development of a serious deterioration in the manners, vocabulary, diction, expositional fluency, composure, sobriety, attire, courtesy and general behaviour of the guests, of whom there are usually about twenty. At first, though, solemnity reigns and everything is regulated down to the last detail. Half the guests are members of the host college and half from other colleges (plus the occasional outsider or foreigner who happens to be passing through), who have been invited by the former in the hope of subsequently being invited by the latter to *their* respective colleges (with the result that the composition of different high tables varies very little, the guests being nearly always the same, except that sometimes they dine at one college and at other times at another, some thus dining together ten or twelve times a year, often ending up on terms of such mutual detestation that they can scarcely bear the sight of each other). The guests have to gather first in an elegant little room next door to the refectory where they enjoy a swift glass of sherry and then, once everyone has arrived, proceed to the refectory (never at the stipulated seven o'clock sharp) two by two (each member accompanied by his or her guest) and strictly in accordance with college hierarchy. Having to remember instantaneously the seniority and titles of ten or twelve worthy and extremely touchy people is no easy task, so that even before going in to eat, the odd argument or outburst of bickering takes place, and there is some shoving, jostling and elbowing on the part of ambitious or forgetful members or fellows who attempt, so to speak, to torpedo protocol and jump the queue in order to gain in prestige. The students, who wait (hungrily) seated in the dining room, rise in a hypocritical show of respect to watch the entrance of the gowned dons and their chance and often bewildered companions from the outside world, who all duly place their hands on the back of the chair assigned to them. The Warden, that is the director or administrator of the college (often a bored member of the nobility), presides over the raised table which in turn presides over the other tables, so that he thus presides twice over, and demonstrates (even before the guests sit down) the most obvious duty of this double presidency, which is to deliver the unforgiving series of gavel blows interspersed with Latin phrases that keep any poor foreigners present in a state of permanent fear and trepidation throughout the meal. For the Warden has beside him a small gavel (together with a wooden stand affixed to the table to receive the blow, just like the one judges use) with which he inaugurates the meal, decides the timing and announces the arrival of the numerous

37

changes of wines and courses, and which serves him as a dangerous plaything when (as almost always happens) he grows weary of what's going on around him. Once he has said the first prayer (in his anglified Latin), with everyone in the refectory on their feet in a silence still redolent of incense, the first abrupt gavel blow and the consequent tinkle of fine crystal gives way to the din of eager dons and even more eager students as they sit down, shout, contend for the favours of stewards, hurl themselves, spoon in hand, on the soup or consommé set before them and close ruddy fists about their glasses of red wine. It is stipulated that each (elevated) college member should speak for seven minutes with the person to his right or left (this depends on the distribution of the couples at the head of the table), and then for five minutes to the person on his other side and so on alternately for the two hours that the first stage of high table lasts. It is, on the other hand, extremely ill-advised to address the person opposite, unless both guests have simultaneously fallen victim to an error of timing on the part of their neighbours and been left momentarily with no one to talk to, a most unfortunate, not to say vexatious, situation in which to find oneself in Oxford. Oxford dons are, therefore, expert at simultaneously talking, eating, drinking and keeping track of the time, the first three activities at extraordinary speed and the fourth with great precision, for, according to a sequence ordained by the Latin phrases and gavel blows of the capricious Warden, the stewards will speedily remove the plates and wineglasses of all the guests regardless of whether the former are scraped clean, empty, half full or even untouched. I hardly ate a thing at my first high tables, preoccupied as I was with counting the minutes and keeping up a pretence at conversation in strict symmetrically duodecimal time to my right and my left. Course after course, the stewards wrested from me both my untouched plate and my wineglass, the latter in fact empty, indeed drained to the lees, since, plunged as I was into chronological and conversational despair, the only thing I did manage to do in between talking and clockwatching was to drink incontinently.

At my second high table, Clare, seated almost opposite me, observed me out of the corner of her eye, half amused at and half pitying my despair at the disappearance of yet another plate groaning with food that I hadn't even had time to look at let alone eat, despite my increasing drunkenness and growing hunger (I can picture myself now, knife and fork in hand, both implements in a state of permanently frustrated readiness, for every time I went to cut into or spear a piece of food I would remember to look at my watch or notice how the guest to my right was beginning to mutter unintelligibly, curses and swear words no doubt, or to eat more noisily than usual – I'm sure on occasions I even heard someone gargling – to warn me that his turn with his previous conversational partner was over and he was now impatiently waiting for me). During the first stage of the supper there were three, four or five main courses (according to the munificence or meanness of the college) and, as I have said, the consumption of these took about two hours, a time dictated more than anything by the long pauses between each course (during which we were left utterly alone with our glasses of wine). Thus, during these first two hours one was condemned to speak to only two people, of whom one – seated to your left – was always the colleague who had invited you whilst the other was determined by fate or, rather, by the usually malevolent intentions of the Warden who was in charge of seating arrangements. At that particular supper my host was Cromer-Blake, and he warned me that to my right I would have a promising young economist whose main defect (at least at high table) was that he had only one topic of conversation, the subject of his recent doctoral thesis.

"But what was his thesis about?" I asked while we searched and jostled for our place in the queue before going into the refectory.

As usual before answering a question, giving an opinion or telling an anecdote, Cromer-Blake stroked his greying hair and replied with a smile: "Well, let's just say it's most unusual. I'm sure you'll have more than enough time to find out."

The economist, Halliwell by name, was an obese young man with a bright red face and a small, sparse military moustache, either premature or being given an overhasty first public airing, who showed not a flicker of curiosity about my person or my country (my country being normally an excellent subject to fall back on for high-table talk) so that I had to initiate a polite interrogation which, after only four questions, led, as I had been warned, into the extraordinarily original topic of his doctoral thesis, namely: a certain and, it would seem, unique cider tax that existed in England between 1760 and 1767.

"It was just a tax on cider then?"

"Just on cider," responded the young economist Halliwell with satisfaction.

"How interesting . . . fancy that," I replied. "And why a tax on cider alone?"

"You're surprised, aren't you?" said Halliwell gleefully, and proceeded to explain in minute detail the causes and characteristics of that unusual tax about which I couldn't have cared less.

"How fascinating," I said, "do go on."

Fortunately, in a language not one's own, it's easy to make a pretence at listening and, by pure intuition, to agree or enthuse or now and again make some (obsequious) comment, which was what I did during the endless seven-minute periods with Halliwell that were my allotted span after my five minutes of conversation with Cromer-Blake. While this promising young economist spouted endlessly on about cider without even having the delicacy to ask me one single question about me, I was able to devote myself, despite my increasingly drunken state (though I'm fortunate in that nothing in my conduct or external appearance ever betrays my progressive drunkenness), to observing the other guests, with whom any direct contact was forbidden until dessert was served, and, during my designated periods of talk with Cromer-Blake, either to interrogating him about the other guests or avenging myself on the young economist Halliwell by fulminating against him (in Spanish). I should say that, just as Clare was observing me out of the corner of her eye with mingled mockery and pity, I took great pleasure in observing her and, later, as the general deterioration of manners at the table became more marked, my gaze became one of open sexual admiration. She was one of only five women at the supper, and one of only two aged under fifty. She was also the only one to reveal beneath her black gown a tasteful glimpse of décolletage but, for the moment, I'll say no more than that, since, having been the lady's lover for a certain time, it would seem boastful now to enumerate her charms. The rest of the table was occupied by gentlemen all but one of whom wore gowns, and the Warden that night was Lord Rymer, a notorious intriguer in the cities of London, Oxford, Brussels, Strasbourg and Geneva. I was separated from him by two other guests, and Clare, on the other side of the table, by only one.

As is well known, the English never look openly at anything, or they look in such a veiled, indifferent way that one can never be sure that someone is actually looking at what they appear to be looking at, such is their ability to lend an opaque glaze to the most ordinary of glances. That's why the way Continentals look at people (the way I do, for example) can cause great unease in the object of their gaze, and that applies even when the gaze in question would be classified, within the range of possible Spanish or Continental gazes, as indifferent, dispassionate, even respectful. That's why, too, it can be shocking when the veil usually covering the insular or English gaze is torn away and why it might even provoke a dispute or an argument were it not for the fact that the eyes of those likely to see that gaze stripped of its veil still wear theirs, and therefore fail to see what to unclouded eyes (to Continental eyes, for example) would be obvious and possibly even insulting. Although during my two years there I did learn – at will – to veil my gaze somewhat, I was not at first trained in self-censorship, and at those unforgettable suppers my one recourse against hunger and tedium – apart from the wine: red, rosé and white – was, as I have explained, to look about me even more intently and devote myself to observing the other guests. Anyway, if my gaze (as I myself noticed) was, after a certain point, full of sexual admiration for Clare, that of the Warden, right from the first Latin phrase and gavel blow, was one of unbridled and undisguised lust. But just as the immodesty of my gaze was cancelled out by the modesty of other people's when they looked at me (this included that of the Warden, who put on the customary insular veil whenever he managed to tear his eyes away from Clare's décolletage and face), the offensive lustfulness of his gaze was obvious to mine, which, when it detached itself from Clare's face or décolletage, was manifestly agonised (because of the hard time Halliwell was giving me) or furious (at the animal lust I saw mirrored in the Warden's eyes). The main problem, however, was that Clare's own gaze was not totally English either, perhaps because (as I learned later) of a childhood spent in Delhi and in Cairo where one looks at others neither as one does in the British Isles nor as one does on the Continent; and so she was in a position to perceive not only the bestially salacious gaze of the Warden but also my own admiringly sexual one. The second (though minor) problem was that at the other end of the table, on my side and next to the other head of table, a famous literary scholar close to retirement age of whom I was very fond and of whom I will speak later, was her husband Edward Bayes, like Cromer-Blake a member of the host college; and although his gaze was always purely insular, it's possible that the fact that the only two unveiled gazes at the table were directed at his wife might in turn have obliged him to remove the habitual veil from his own gaze in order to keep abreast of the desires, untamed or otherwise, of others. But I'm not being quite accurate, for, given his position on the same side of the table as me, while Edward Bayes could not see my gaze at all, he had an uninterrupted view of Clare's and the Warden's. He must have noticed that at times his wife was on the verge of blushing but presumably attributed this to the wine or to the drooling and unworthy attentions of the Warden, a gigantic man with strangely tight skin – I imagined him as being completely hairless – and now much the worse for drink. And if Edward Bayes noticed his wife occasionally looking in my direction, he must have thought she was looking at her friend Cromer-Blake (seated, as I have said, immediately to my left) in search of protection or at least complicity. But there was a fourth gaze too – possibly a fifth if Edward Bayes' own had in fact dispensed with its layer of English tulle – that had no reason to remain veiled, and that was the gaze of Dayanand, the doctor of Indian origin who was Cromer-Blake's friend, seated to the left of Clare and therefore immediately opposite me. Although he had lived in Oxford for decades, his eyes retained the luminous, diaphanous quality of his native land and, in the context of that supper, they seemed positively aflame. Every five or six minutes, whilst he passed calmly from his conversation with Clare to a laconic silence with the one guest not wearing a gown (a hideously ugly lecturer in mineralogy from the University of Leiden whose gaze, despite being foreign, was also veiled by the two great rectangular magnifying glasses he wore in the guise of spectacles), his black, rather liquid eyes would rest on me for a moment and look me up and down with a clinical expression, as if my way of looking openly to right and left but above all at Clare were a symptom of some well-known complaint, easily cured, but long eradicated from those lands. It was impossible to hold Dayanand's gaze and every time my eyes met his, I had no choice but to turn back to Halliwell and pretend I was still absorbed by his exhausting chatter. Dayanand's eyes flashed fire when he turned them in Clare's direction and the Warden at the head of the table thus entered his field of vision; the latter, however, experienced no difficulty in holding Dayanand's gaze, since quite probably – believing himself unassailable – he barely noticed it. The Warden, forced to talk to his immediate neighbours, who visibly irritated him (to his right sat the warden of a women's college, a real harpy; to his left, a supercilious, pontificating luminary of the social sciences called Atwater), gradually began to free himself from the bonds of protocol and to intervene in the respective conversations of Clare and Cromer-Blake, his next neighbours along on either side of the table. But seeing that neither of them felt particularly disposed to involve him in their conversations, he took to feigning an interest in the talk of the harpy or the luminary and to playing with the gavel, a frequent pastime amongst bored or drunken wardens at high table. Out of temper and angry, he failed to notice that his initially indolent beating on the stand (he kept up a lazy drumming with the gavel) was becoming a series of hammer blows that grew steadily more violent (he was brandishing the gavel with real gusto now) and were given at sufficiently long intervals to cause both surprise and horrendous confusion, since, on hearing them, some stewards proceeded to remove plates they had only just served whilst others of greater experience, aware that the blows did not form part of the ceremony, tried to retrieve the plates from their less experienced colleagues in order to return them to their intended recipients, who in some cases had barely got a sniff at them. After a couple of plates had crashed noisily to the floor as a result of these struggles, a moment arrived when all five of the stewards serving us stopped what they were doing and gathered in one corner of the refectory for a confabulation during which accusations of ineptitude were exchanged, while protests (albeit only muttered) began to arise amongst the guests, who found themselves amidst a clutter of abandoned serving dishes piled high with cold leftovers (a sight never seen at high table), equipped with only fish knives and forks to tackle a sirloin steak, or confronted by plates of food already begun or nibbled at or (most serious of all) with their glasses empty or filled with a mixture of two or more wines. The Warden was completely unaware of all this, and as each distracted blow on the stand or on the table (when he missed the stand) made the fine wood boom and splinter and set peas and mushrooms leaping and several wineglasses rolling, all I could do was calculate the possible trajectory of the gavel, according to his posture or rather his slant (for his huge body was slumping slowly on to the tabletop), were it to fly from his grasp. I leaned back slightly both in order to avoid the flying gavel and in the hope that I would thus increase the likelihood of the projectile braining the young economist Halliwell, for he, oblivious to everything, continued to douse me in sour, stale cider after every respite and breathing-space afforded by my conversational turns with Cromer-Blake, for nothing would have pleased me more than to see Halliwell rendered unconscious.

"Quite amazing this business about your cider," I was saying. "And this peculiar tax of yours, was it really only in England?"

"Yes, only in England," replied Halliwell enthusiastically.

I saw that Clare had noticed my backwards movement (so she was paying me some attention) and that she had too had leaned back, although I don't know if she did so in order that one of her neighbours might bear the brunt of the blow or in order to remove her décolletage and face from the Warden's line of sight and see if that would rouse him out of his stupefaction and bring him to his senses. Instead the intriguer followed suit, leaning his gigantic torso forward (his left elbow sweeping across the table, the front of his gown trailing over his uneaten steak and dislodging the peas from his plate), and would not countenance the eclipse of the gratifying sight he was so determined to gaze on. At one point, his gaze irredeemably lost in her décolletage, the peer was simply not there and what had been until then – as I have described – intermittent, random, arrhythmic blows with the gavel, became a continuous, mechanical hammering, to which he was wholly oblivious. The effect of this on the table was now all too apparent, for, leaping amidst the accumulated remains of the contents of several plates, were not only crumbs, peas and mushrooms (which have a natural propensity to leap) but also bits of steamed potato, the bones of several lemon sole, great gobs of thick sauces, the spectacles belonging to the ugly professor from Leiden (even uglier without them) and pools of spilled wine of various hues. (Fortunately, the gowns, as well as serving the twin functions of concealment and aesthetics, also protect the elegant clothes worn at high table from the unconscionable, seemingly infinite amounts of filth and debris generated.) The five servants, however, having reached some agreement, were now engaged in holding down the table at the other end – ruffling the hair of the literary scholar seated there – to ensure that the vibrations from the hammer blows and the weight of the Warden's monstrous body, now lying almost completely across the table, did no further damage. Gradually (although in fact it took only a matter of seconds) the refectory fell silent, or almost silent, for both the fervent Halliwell and the peevish Atwater were incapable of keeping their mouths shut for a moment and while the former continued drowning me in cider ("Even Viscount Pitt had to intervene in the affair! And Sterne mentioned the tax in one of his sermons!" he was exclaiming in rapturous tones), the latter, his thumbs tucked into his gown, continued to aim his exhortatory discourse at the Warden in the belief that the latter's fixed and bestial eyes were gazing on him, not on Clare's covered décolletage and face. Although at its wildest the hammering did not in fact last more than a minute, the situation (during that minute) became untenable. But since the only guests with unveiled eyes were not, given our lowly status in the hierarchy, in a position to take steps and the eyes of the other guests who did have that authority wore the aforementioned layer of gauze that prevented them from seeing that the peer had quite gone off the rails and that someone should either speak to him or relieve him at once of the presidency (Lord Rymer, however, as well as being Warden, was an influential politician known for holding lifelong grudges), the silence grew ever longer, broken only – apart from the gavel blows – by Halliwell's and the luminary Atwater's imperturbable murmurings and by the shrieks of the harpy to the Warden's right, who, although arrantly fawning and therefore incapable of bringing the man to his senses because of the concomitant risk of annoying him, could not help jumping at every gavel blow, so close to the battered gavel stand was her prominent and doubtless silicon-enhanced bosom.

During that one eternal minute I had the chance to observe all the other guests within my field of vision: the literary scholar at the other end of the table was slapping at the stewards who, in their eagerness to hold the table steady, threatened to overwhelm him, tousling his hair and shoving the elbows of their ten firm arms in his ears; to his right Dr Wetenhall, another of the ladies present, could have done with a helping hand in her triple attempt to cover her ears, keep two (half-empty) bottles from rolling in the direction of the Warden and to hold on to her precarious wig (possibly new) that threatened to become dislodged; her other neighbour, the head of my department (Professor Kavanagh, an easy-going Irishman, whose main interest lay in the successful horror novels he wrote under a pen name, a man considered suspect by both colleagues and subordinates alike precisely because he was easy-going, Irish and wrote novels), seemed amused and indeed was adding his own ironic contribution to the din made by the Warden, by keeping time with a teaspoon on his wineglass, the way people do to introduce an after-dinner speech; to his right, were two members of the college (Brownjohn and Willis by name, two middle-aged men of science and possessed therefore of rather slow reflexes) who dared cast only sidelong glances at the Warden and were engaged in the attempted recapture of the fugitive spectacles belonging to their Dutch guest, who, although seated and quite safe where he was, had stretched out his arms the moment he lost his glasses (thus knocking over the few objects left upright in his part of the table) as if he feared he might stumble at any moment, like a blind man who's had his stick snatched from him; Dayanand, also a member of the college and a man of strong character, was one of the few present who could have put a stop to the Warden's banging, but the fact is that, whilst he made his feelings perfectly plain, he restricted himself to throwing the Warden lethal looks and flexing his fingers menacingly ("This Indian doctor will make him pay for this even if he has to wait another ten years to do so," I thought, "he's definitely not a man to be trifled with"); the luminary Atwater and the economist Halliwell had finally ceased their verbiage and the mere fact of being quiet seemed to have a more disconcerting effect on them than the Warden's pounding, which they'd probably not even noticed until that moment of clamorous silence; I've already described the quivering harpy, and as for Cromer-Blake, his face remained an enigma: rubbing his waxen chin, he seemed simply to be waiting with just the suggestion of a smile (that of a man on the point of bursting out laughing or perhaps of one storing up his wrath) as if, all too familiar with the Warden's habits, he already knew that the minute would last just that, a minute. The other four guests, including Edward Bayes seated to the left at the opposite end of the table, were concealed from view. But, after all this time and taking considerably longer than the original sixty seconds, I notice that in making that tour of the table then and now (from this city of Madrid to which I'm now returned), I've quite deliberately omitted any further mention of Clare.

48

In fact one might say that during that one minute nobody really noticed – I mean, really looked at – the Warden: some guests threw him occasional stealthy, apprehensive glances but did not, as I've explained, actually see him; others were too concerned with maintaining some semblance of composure and with struggling to prevent the bottles, spectacles and stray wineglasses shaken by the gavel blows from rolling on to the floor; a third faction took advantage of the moment to exchange looks or, which comes to the same thing, to look directly at each other, their eyes for once unveiled. The first group included the harpy, the author of horror novels Kavanagh, the luminary of the social sciences Atwater, the cider economist Halliwell, the last two, as college members, hesitating perhaps (although only slightly) over whether to intervene and disarm the Warden or just to sit back and let someone else run the risk of being pounded to a pulp for their boldness, or more likely – later on – being avenged for it. The second group included the literary scholar or by then (almost) Professor Emeritus Toby Rylands, the scientists Brownjohn and Willis, the bewigged Dr Wetenhall and the hideous mineralogist still plunged into darkness. And amongst the third group, as far as I could ascertain during the final seconds of that minute, were Dayanand and Cromer-Blake, Clare Bayes and myself and possibly, or rather certainly, her husband. The attenuated gaze (merely distrustful or severe) that Dayanand had directed at me from time to time throughout the meal and that he now directed in its full intensity at the Warden was suddenly turned, unchanged, on his friend Cromer-Blake: that is, Dayanand, still flexing his fingers in the gesture of an exasperated man barely able to contain himself, cast Cromer-Blake one of those looks I earlier termed "lethal", and Cromer-Blake, feeling the Indian doctor's burning gaze upon him, in turn raised his eyes to meet it and, although I could not see very well, since I had a side view and could therefore see only his right eye, I noticed that what had been the beginnings of a smile hardened into a tight line I had seen before on those thin, apparently bloodless lips.

Then I looked straight into Clare's face and, though I didn't know her, I saw her as if she were someone who already belonged to my past. I mean like someone who no longer belonged to my present life, like someone we once found enormously interesting but who has ceased to interest us or has died, like someone who *was* or whom one day, long ago now, we condemned to *having been*, perhaps because that someone condemned us to the same fate long before. As is often the case with evening wear in England, the low-cut dress visible beneath her gown (the indirect cause of all that fuss) seemed to belong to another era. Even her face was somewhat old-fashioned, with its full lips and unusually high cheekbones. But that wasn't the reason. It was that she was looking at me too, and she was looking at me as if she knew me of old, almost as if she were one of those faithful but ancillary figures from our childhood who, later on, are never able to see us as the detestable adults we've become but instead, fortunately for us, will only ever see us as the children we were, their inert gaze distorted by memory. That providential handicap is more frequent in women than in men, insofar as for men children are just irritating rough drafts of adults, while for women they're perfect beings destined to become battered and coarsened, and so their retina struggles to retain the image of that transient deity condemned to lose his godliness and, when they haven't known a man as a child, they pour all the effort involved in getting to know someone into imagining the child whom they can know now only from photographs or from the traces of the child that remain in the sleeping image of the grown man, or even perhaps of the old man, or from the idly told tales the usurper will have ventured to confide to them in bed, the only place men willingly recall out loud things from the distant past. That was how Clare looked at me, as if she knew all about my childhood in Madrid and had witnessed in my own language my games with my brothers, my night-time fears and the inevitable after-school fights. And her seeing me like that made me see her in a similar way. I found out later – once I knew all about her – that in those final seconds of a minute that only truly exists now, scenes from her childhood in India had flashed upon my mind, and I saw the pensive look of the girl with little to occupy her in those southern cities, who watched the passing of a river and was watched over in turn by the dark voices of smiling servants. I didn't know I was seeing that (and perhaps I'm mistaken or lying or simply didn't see it and should not, therefore, speak of it), but I have to say that through those deep blue eyes flowed a river gleaming brightly in the blackness, the River Yamuna or Jumna that crosses Delhi, dotted with the rudimentary barges that carry on its current cereals, cotton, wood and stone, a river that is lulled from its own shores by trifling songs, its surface dimpled by the pebbles that fall from its banks as it leaves the city behind, just as perhaps my eyes were full of images of Madrid, of calle de Génova, calle de Covarrubias, calle de Miguel Ángel, streets that she had never walked or seen: perhaps the image of four children walking down those streets accompanied by an old maidservant. And there too would be the huge railway bridge that crosses the River Yamuna where it passes through the city, always there in the distance, and from which, according to tales told by her nanny when they were alone together, tales told in a voice full of mystery, many a pair of unhappy lovers had thrown themselves: the wide river of blue water broken by the long bridge of crisscrossing iron girders, deserted for the most part, in darkness, idle and shadowy, just like one of those faithful but ancillary figures from our childhood who grow dim then blaze into life again later, just for a moment, when they are called, only to be instantly plunged back into the gloom of their obscure, commutable existences, having done their brief duty or revealed the secret suddenly demanded of them. And thus they exist only in order that through them, whenever necessary, the child may once more emerge. The little English girl is looking now at the black iron bridge and waiting for a train to cross it, to see the train lit up and reflected in the water, one of those brightly coloured trains, full of light and distant noise that from time to time cross the River Yamuna, the River Jumna that she looks patiently out at from her house high above it while her nanny whispers to her and her diplomat father, in evening dress ready for dinner and with a glass in one hand, watches from behind, from the other end of the garden. It's getting close to the girl's bedtime, but before she goes one more train must pass, just one more, because the fresh image of the passing train and of the river illuminated by its windows (the men on the barges look up at it and grow dizzy) helps her to go to sleep and to come to terms with the idea of spending another day in a city to which she does not belong and which she will only perceive as hers once she has left it and when her only chance to recall it out loud will be with her son or her lover. The three of them wait, the girl, the nanny and the melancholy father, until the mail train from Moradabad that always arrives incalculably late has steamed across the iron bridge, filling its entire length with rickety multi-coloured carriages just distinguishable beneath the sliver of moon; and then, once the swaying lantern on the last carriage is out of sight and she has said goodbye to it, a goodbye that was never spoken in expectation of any response, Clare Bayes gets up, puts on her shoes, stands on tiptoe to kiss her silent father, who smells of tobacco and alcohol and mint, and then disappears at last into the house holding the hand of the nanny who will perhaps sing her to sleep with some trifling song. That was how Clare looked at me and how I looked at her as if we were each the other's vigilant, compassionate eyes, the eyes that look out at us from the past and no longer matter because they've known for a long time how they're obliged to see us: perhaps we looked at each other as if we were each the other's older brother or sister. And although I didn't know her, I knew that I would and that one day I would lie with her on a bed and tell her all the insignificant details – about calle de Génova, calle de Covarrubias and calle de Miguel Ángel – that I confided to her throughout all those months of turbulent, intermittent meetings in my pyramid house in Oxford and in her house, in those dreary hotels in London and Reading and in one hotel in Brighton.

She looked away. Suddenly, the Warden seemed to wake from his lewd reverie; he waved the gavel energetically and, finding himself the centre of an immense silence (there was not even a murmur now and all the students at the lower tables, having done what justice they could to their miserable suppers, had fled some time before, taking with them the odd knife as compensation), made a vague, scornful gesture then pointed the handle of the gavel at us:

"What's up with you lot? Haven't you got anything to say to each other or has the cat got your tongues?" And standing up, he pushed away the plate of steak (untouched and bereft of peas) with one grotesque thrust of his hips, uttered some crude Latin phrase without the least pretence now at correct pronunciation, dealt the battered gavel stand one last, furious blow and let out a euphoric cry: "Dessert!"

At high tables, this is a moment of great solemnity and (plastic) beauty, when all the guests rise and, forming up in line again (a ragged, unsteady and anarchic one this time), progress into another large room, less formal and more welcoming than the refectory, where for an hour and a half they partake in leisurely fashion of fresh fruit, tropical fruit, dried fruit, ice cream, cakes, pies, sorbets, biscuits, wafers and chocolates: plain, mint and liqueur, whilst simultaneously circulating, at great speed and in a clockwise direction, several bottles or rather carafes of various rare ports unobtainable at any ordinary vintners. During this second more auspicious phase of the supper, more medieval than eighteenth-century in flavour and known locally as "eating bananas in the moonlight", one can finally change one's conversational partners, talk to anyone for as long as one likes, and, as the port both sharpens the desire to make up for lost time and puts the finishing touches to the verbal deterioration wrought by the wines drunk during the first phase, the conversation grows generalised, unruly, violent and chaotic, even indecent at times. There is also the remote possibility that at some point the Warden (like everything else this is entirely at his discretion) will decide to toast the Queen, which is the signal that one can at last smoke. But the moment of great solemnity and (plastic) beauty I mentioned occurs when the guests leave the refectory, for as they do so each one bears in his or her hand, the napkin they've been using, however stained and crumpled, and the swaying passage of that small piece of white cloth (the moment has the slightly martial air about it inevitable when people walk in single or double file) contrasts sublimely with the slow billowing line of black gowns. As we marched in, Clare, with a nicely ironic touch, tucked her napkin into her neckline like a bib, thus covering up her décolletage. She started laughing and, I think, included me in her laughter. Afterwards, during dessert and for what remained of the evening, she sat far off from me next to Toby Rylands and near her husband and did not look at me again. After a certain moment I was free once more to smoke cigarette after cigarette, thanks to an unexpected show of tolerance or perhaps a sudden display of loyalty to the Crown on the part of the Warden.

THAT WAS THE NIGHT I knew for certain that I would remember my time in the city of Oxford as a time of unease and that whatever was begun or whatever happened there would be touched or contaminated by that one overriding feeling and would, therefore, in the context of the rest of my life, which is not on the whole troubled or uneasy, be condemned to insignificance, to dispersal and forgetting like the tales told in novels or like most of our dreams. That's why now I'm making this effort of memory and writing, because I know that otherwise it will all be obliterated, as will those who have died, those who make up one half of our lives, the half who, together with the living, complete our lives, although, in fact, it isn't always easy to tell what separates and distinguishes one from the other, I mean, what distinguishes the living from the dead whom we knew when alive. I would end up obliterating the dead of Oxford. My dead. My example.

In a way, since everyone who lives in Oxford either feels or is in some way troubled, there's nothing remarkable about the fact that my time in the city was one of unease. For the inhabitants of Oxford are not in the world and when they do sally forth into the world (to London, for example) that in itself is enough to have them gasping for air; their ears buzz, they lose their sense of balance, they stumble and have to come scurrying back to the town that makes their existence possible, that contains them, where they do not even exist in time. But I was used to existing in time and in the world (in Madrid, for example) and consequently, as I discovered that night, my unease was bound to be of a different order, perhaps contrary to the norm. Having always been in the world (having spent my life in the world) I suddenly found myself outside it, as if I'd been transplanted into another element, water perhaps, and a full realisation of the extent of my unease arose from that unexpected glimpse of my childhood in Clare's eyes, for it is during childhood that we feel most comfortable in the world, or to put it in a more precisely infantile way, when the world is most worldlike, when time has more substance and the dead are not yet one half of our lives.

After supper I went up to Cromer-Blake's rooms at the college to have a nightcap before going home to bed. Without taking his gown off, he got out two glasses and opened a bottle with assured, methodical movements. I thought: "Here in Oxford, the one really decisive factor is not just that I'm a foreigner about whom no one knows or cares, about whom the only fact of any biographical significance is that I won't be staying here for ever, it's that there's no one here who knew me as a young man or as a child. That's what really troubles me, leaving the world behind and having no previous existence in *this* world, there being no witness here to my continuity, to the fact that I haven't always swum in this water. Cromer-Blake knows a little about me, from some time back, through my predecessors from Madrid and Barcelona. But that's all, information received before I had a face and was still nothing more than a name. But that's reason enough – this friendship by proxy – to condemn him to being my strongest link with this city, the person of whom I will ask all those questions that must be asked and to whom I will come whenever some problem arises here, be it illness, infamy or a serious emotional crisis. He's the person whom I intend asking right now about the woman at supper, Clare Bayes. As soon as he's poured the drinks and sat down I'll ask him about her and her husband. Cromer-Blake, with his greying hair and pale face and the moustache which every few weeks, in a state of perpetual indecision, he grows then shaves off; Cromer-Blake with his inimitable English accent that admiring students say is exactly the way they used to speak on the BBC; Cromer-Blake with his incisive mind and his extraordinary interpretations of Valle-Inclán, with his look of a man of the cloth expelled from the bosom of the Church and with his complete absence of family feeling, is condemned to being both father and mother figure to me in this city, even though he did not know me – at all – as a child or as a young man (I'm over thirty years old now, so he can't be said to have known me in my youth). The woman at supper knew nothing about my childhood or my youth either and yet, how, I don't know, she saw my childhood and allowed me to see hers, to see her as a child. I know, however, that in this city I can't rely on her to be either the father- or even the mother-figure each of us always needs at all times and in all places, whatever our age or our status. Even the oldest and most powerful of men need such figures right to the end of their days and if they find it difficult or are unable to light upon someone to embody those two figures, that in no way denies their need for them or belies the fantasies provoked by their search or by the sense of their lack, their need, their expectation and their imagination of them.

Cromer-Blake poured me a glass of port, apologised for the inferior quality compared with the port imbibed with our high-table desserts, then sat down in an armchair. I was already seated on the sofa opposite him, also still with my gown on. We were both fairly drunk but in him that never proved a barrier to holding a conversation. We spoke sometimes in English, sometimes in Spanish and sometimes each in his own language.

"Cheers," he said and took a sip of wine. "It wasn't so bad, was it? Apart from your baptism of cider, from which, if it's any consolation, no one in college has escaped this year. There was no mischief intended in seating you next to him, you were simply the only one at table as yet unbaptised. Halliwell's new

here and that spiel of his is by way of being a very long-winded
visiting card. The worst of it is that he never gets beyond that
because no one will ever give the poor chap a second chance."

"That was hardly the worst part . . . ," I began, but Cromer-
Blake, who clearly considered that the best part of those high
tables consisted in large measure in the after-dinner post-
mortems, left me no space to tell him what I thought had been
the worst part.

"Oh, the worst part was Dayanand," he said.

I was going to mention the Warden's salacious and reckless
behaviour and take the opportunity to ask Cromer-Blake about
Clare and Edward Bayes, but that clearly held neither novelty
nor interest for him. I watched him taking tiny sips of port, his
long legs crossed, the skirts of his gown cascading about them,
his black figure crowned in white and framed by shelves full
of books in Spanish and English, as if his own attitude, his
appearance, his posture and his surroundings were nothing
more than an aesthetic disguise. But he wasn't at all a ridiculous
figure and I thought: "Women and any of the feelings they
might arouse have no importance for Cromer-Blake, even when
they might well be the mother-, father- or even daughter-figure
he needs. For, indispensable though those figures are throughout one's whole life, they're incapable of causing conflicts or
major upsets and are, therefore, unworthy of after-dinner comment. Clare Bayes might well be such a figure for Cromer-Blake
whereas for me she could be so, at best, only very incidentally
or only if she one day definitively ceased to be that other figure,
whatever conflictive, disturbing identity I decided or rather will
decide to attribute to her. One's enemies, on the other hand,
are worthy of these exhaustive, obsessive after-dinner commen-
taries. One's greatest enemies are those who are also one's greatest friends. Cromer-Blake has always introduced Dayanand, the
Indian doctor, as a great friend which, of course, equips him –
indeed is the ideal qualification – to become the most bitter of

enemies. As for the Warden, Cromer-Blake is doubtless used to him by now."

"I didn't get a chance to talk to him."

"So much the better for you. Didn't you notice the way he kept looking at us all through supper?"

"I certainly did. I was on the receiving end of one of his scorching looks; I suppose he didn't approve of my overt admiration of your friend Clare any more than he did of the Warden's."

"I don't think that's what it was about. He glowered at all three of us, at the Warden, at you and me. You don't imagine he cares what His Lordship gets up to at these suppers, do you? He's been much worse than that: once, during dessert, he insisted on decorating the bosom of the Dean of York's wife with a necklace made out of mandarin segments. It happened in plain view of everyone there, we didn't know where to put ourselves, but no one said or did anything to let on that any of us had even noticed our imaginative Warden's sudden interest in the ornamental possibilities of fruit. The Dean, it must be said, showed astonishing sang-froid, fortitude and possibly restraint, observing the scene from the other end of the table with an impartial eye, almost as if he could only see the positive side of the affair, as if they were helping him out with some future task or furnishing him with a good idea. The next day Dayanand laughed out loud every time he remembered the Dean of York's profound impassivity and the even more praiseworthy example set by his buxom lady wife, who allowed herself to be hung with jewels, offering no more than a blushing smile and a few demure words of protest. And do you imagine that Clare didn't know what she was doing when she chose to wear that particular dress? Winding up His Lordship is one of our oldest pastimes. No, Dayanand was glowering at you because you were *my* guest tonight and at the Warden because he knows that at the moment I'm doing him a few favours, or rather, we're doing each other a few favours. He and I have been working pretty much hand in glove lately. All Dayanand's glowering was aimed at me, I'm sure of it. He did it first through intermediaries, then it was my turn to be crucified with red-hot nails. How dare he?"

The last question was purely rhetorical.

"I thought you were such close friends."

"Oh, we are. And what's more he's my doctor, a splendid one I wouldn't want to lose. As soon as I feel the hint of a sore throat I'm off to his rooms for him to have me stick out my tongue and give me a few pills. I'm eternally in his debt, but not so much that I have to put up with his wild looks across the table, with twenty other people as witnesses." In other circumstances I would immediately have asked the reason for those looks that had so upset and offended Cromer-Blake and whose cause he nonetheless seemed to understand perfectly well, but I couldn't wait to find out about Clare Bayes and was waiting for a convenient opening to the conversation that would allow me to return to the subject. Not finding one, I fell silent and Cromer-Blake, as he sometimes did, adopted an air of seriousness that seemed to have nothing to do with what was going on around him nor with what his companion was saying: it was something that welled up from within him, like the false solemnity that precedes and surrounds soliloquies in the theatre. And the more he talked, the more his head sank onto his chest and the more he seemed to be talking to himself.

"I can't suit my tastes and my desires to his, I mean I can't avoid coinciding with them. If I did I'd spend my whole life feeling handcuffed and frustrated, having to ask his permission before I started up any new pastime or passion in this city; it would mean having to reject the most tempting of offers, having to put on hold my best seduction techniques in order, before carrying them through, to go to his rooms and ask him if he had any objections, if my sexual activities or even my affections in any way clashed with his past life or with his future plans, if I might in any way wound him retrospectively or in advance, if he'd noticed or was considering noticing such and such a pretty face or athletic body at that moment at my disposal in my bedroom. It would be ridiculous: 'Dayanand, do you have any objection to my going to bed with a certain naked person I happen to have in my room at this present moment? Now take a good look at him and make quite sure, just in case you change your mind later.' It would be ridiculous. But something's going to have to be done, he's taken it very badly. Who does he think he is, behaving like that? Who does he think he is, asking me direct questions about my personal life? Who does he think he is, adopting that desperate tone with me? I can't be the cause of his desperation, and I'm not. Who does he think he is, calling me to account? And right at the end of supper, it's unbelievable. Jack's the one he needs to talk to." Cromer-Blake paused, as if the name he'd just pronounced were an internal signal to end the soliloquy and grow less serious; he stroked his wispy hair, emptied his glass in one gulp and added as, with unsteady hand, he poured himself another: "The man's insanely jealous, he's a fanatic."

Drink makes me laconic, although I remain a good listener. It had no such effect on Cromer-Blake who talked resolutely on, but it did make him momentarily forget to whom he was speaking and he thus mentioned subjects which, though he made no secret of them to me (probably because I would not be staying in Oxford for ever) he would not have spoken about so frankly had he been sober. Were I a malevolent person (which I'm not), I would have made the right noises to fan his bad temper and he would have divulged to me every detail of that quarrel over sentimental or sexual rivalries. But the truth is I wasn't interested in such details that night, although I've often speculated about them since with more than mere curiosity, with a real longing to know. I'd like to have known the identity of that person (that "Jack") whom at the time both Dayanand and Cromer-Blake wanted or rather, perhaps, wanted to hang on to. I'd like to have known the identity of that vital nexus uniting them, for it seems possible that it was that person, for whom on that winter night I felt barely a glimmer of curiosity, who bound them together for life or beyond that into death, even though one of them is still in the land of the living and the other in the land of the dead. "And what about Edward Bayes? Is he a fanatic too? Or is he more like the Dean of York?"

Cromer-Blake gave a short, serene laugh and regained at a stroke the joviality he'd shown at the beginning of our conversation. "We're all capable of being like the Dean of York at one time or another. Do I take it you're seriously interested in Clare?"

"No, not really. I think my mind's still very much on a young girl I saw some days ago on the train from London and again yesterday in Broad Street. But since I don't know who she is and may never see her again I might well begin to think about your friend Clare too." – "What an idiot," I thought, "why can't I think about something more fruitful, more interesting? Relationships with those with whom we have no blood ties never are; the possible variety of paths such a relationship can take are minimal, the surprises all fakes, the different stages mere formalities, it's all so infantile: the approaches, the consummations, the estrangements; the fulfilment, the battles, the doubts; the certainties, the jealousies, the abandonment and the laughter; it wears you out even before it's begun. I feel troubled by my absence from the world and can no longer tell the difference between what I should spend my time thinking about and what is just a deplorable waste of time and thought. I feel completely off-balance and I shouldn't be thinking about either of them, the girl or Clare Bayes. The one thing I shouldn't be doing is *thinking* about them. I'm just drunk and generally confused. Here I am with all the time in the world in this static city I happen to have ended up in, and I'm turning into an idiot." I continued my thoughts out loud to Cromer-Blake: "I shouldn't be thinking about these things, I should be thinking about something more interesting. More to the point, I should be talking about something more interesting, I'm sorry."

"*Is* there anything more interesting?" Cromer-Blake had once more adopted a serious tone, though less serious than before and without losing his indulgent, good-humoured air. This was real after-dinner talk. He'd taken out a cigarette from the packet I'd placed on the table and rather ineffectively put a flame to it with my lighter. He never carried cigarettes or matches of his own. He held the cigarette as if it were a pencil. He didn't inhale. In fact he didn't really know how to smoke at all.

"I suppose not," I said and drank the last of my port while I looked for answers; Cromer-Blake refilled my glass. His hand was steady again. I relit his cigarette, properly this time.

"Thanks. I mean, take me, take Dayanand, or even the Warden; take Kavanagh, Toby or the Ripper, who, given their ages and temperaments, must surely lead chaste lives. And take Ted of course. Well, you don't know them as well as I do. Oh, yes, I know them all. Not one of us thinks of anything else all day but men and women, the whole day is just a process one goes through in order to be able to stop at a given moment and devote oneself to thinking about them, the whole point of stopping work or study is nothing more than being able to think about them; even when we're with them, we're thinking about them, or at least I am. They're not the parentheses; the classes and the research are, so are the reading and the writing, the lectures and the ceremonies, the suppers and the meetings, the finances and the politicking, everything in fact that passes here for activity. Productive activity, the thing that brings us money and security and prestige and allows us to live, what keeps a city or a country going, what organises it, is the thing that, later, allows us to think with even greater intensity about them, about men and women. It's like that here, even in this country, contrary to what we say and contrary to our reputation, contrary to what we ourselves would like to believe. Yes, it's all that other activity that's the parenthesis, not the other way round. Everything one does, everything one thinks, everything else that one thinks and plots about is a medium through which to think about them. Even wars are fought in order to be able to start thinking again, to renew our unending thinking about our men and our women, about those who were or could be ours, about those we know already and those we will never know, about those who were young and those who will be young, about those who've shared our beds and those who never will."

"That's all very nice but it's a bit of an overstatement, isn't it?"

"Maybe it is, but that's what I see in myself and all around me. I even see it in this city where you'd think study left neither time nor space for anything else. And it will always be like that. I know that when I'm old and retired and can do nothing more than receive specious honours and tend my garden, I'll still think about them and stop in the street to admire people who aren't even born yet. That's the one thing that won't change, I'm sure of it. And that's why I think about them so intensely now. I'm manufacturing and storing up future memories in order to create a little variety for myself in my old age. My old age will be a solitary one, like Toby's. You should make friends with him."

"And what about Clare? Who does she think about?"

"Oh, I don't know, I was talking about how men, the male sex, think, they're the only thoughts I know well, the only ones I can be sure of identifying correctly, with a few minor variations. I imagine Clare thinks about her husband and about her son and certainly about her father with whom she has, as far as I can make out, an intense, ambivalent relationship: a mixture

64

of resentment and unconditional love, of hope and indignation, something like that. I imagine that for her, as for me, only men count. She spent her childhood in Egypt and India surrounded by women, but on the other hand lacked the principal female figure, the mother. She never talks about her mother or at least she's never talked to me about her; I imagine her mother died when she was very young, possibly even in childbirth. I don't know, she's never spoken of it in my presence. Her father was a diplomat and she saw him only rarely. In her version of her childhood there was always a dark-skinned nanny in a long dress at her side: her eyes still soften when she sees an immigrant woman in the streets wearing the colourful clothes of the country she left behind. She's had a strange life, like that of so many English people for whom their country was only a name until they returned as adults, or visited it for the first time. There aren't that many of them left now, though, they're an endangered species. She came here as a student and ended up teaching here. That doesn't usually happen. Most of our students manage to get jobs where the real money is, in finance or management, even if the only thing they know about is Góngora and Cervantes. That's the advantage of studying here, it's assumed that after enduring our teaching methods and our continual hounding of them, which admittedly lessens with the years, they're fitted for any task, even if all they can do is scan sonnets and stammer out a few incoherent remarks about Calderón or Montaigne in an oral exam. Only the most ill-equipped for life in the world, like myself, come creeping back wearing these silly gowns."

Cromer-Blake removed his gown as he said this and I took the opportunity to take mine off too, for I never felt comfortable wearing it in private, seeing in it a suspicious and unpleasant reminder of the traditional short cloak – ridiculous but now, happily, abolished – worn in my own country. Cromer-Blake carefully hung up the black gown on the back of the door and sat down again. He was still drinking port and followed the first cigarette he'd purloined from me with a second, which he was at that point drunkenly attempting to light in the middle. He filled the air with smoke (unfiltered by his lungs), a far showier, denser pall of smoke than the (filtered) cloud I exhaled from time to time. Cromer-Blake was drunk, probably much drunker than I was, but he spoke as decisively and fluently as on the occasions when he wanted to confound some visiting colleague from another university who'd been invited to the weekly seminars that took place in the library at the Taylorian (he was particularly cruel to hagiographers of García Lorca, a writer he classified as a nincumpoop – he delighted in showing off his knowledge of dated slang – and a fraud). "Clare's case is different since she's perfectly capable of looking after herself in the real world and could easily have had a career as a diplomat like her father, who would gladly have helped her. I don't know why she's ended up here really, since she isn't exactly passionate about teaching, maybe it's just because of Ted. Despite the fact that we've been friends for years, get on magnificently well together and have a great deal in common, I don't think I know her very well. There's something odd about her, something opaque and turbid, as if her foreign past prevented you from seeing her clearly and made her ultimately incomprehensible. With most people, after a certain age you know or you can guess what they want or what their intentions are, what they're really interested in or at least how they like to spend their time. With her I don't really know, not for certain. But then, I realise, my thoughts are completely taken up by my young men, past, present and future. In fact that's all I think about, although my activities and my profession would seem to indicate that I'm also interested in Spanish literature (which doesn't interest me in the least or, at any rate, no more than that of anywhere else, in fact less than that of some other places) and promotion up the academic ladder (which only half-interests me, not out of ambition, but in order to avoid risks to myself and to be able to get on with my work more easily) and in the plots constantly being hatched in this city. The latter do interest me rather more, I must confess, but I don't dedicate myself to them body and soul, the way so many others do. When it comes down to it, the ultimate aim of all these plots is financial, it's all a question of money, but the huge sums that the colleges shift around are always institutional funds, no one can get their hands on them or profit from them. I myself have a lot of money at my disposal in the form of grants for study, research and travel, but I only have it in usufruct, as do the bursar and the Warden. There've been cases of bursars with sole responsibility for millions of pounds which, through their good management, they've been kind enough to increase, and yet, when it came to paying their funeral expenses, a collection had to be made. As soon as you retire or die the money you administer and share out, distribute and assign, the money you see and touch and nurture disappears, leaving you without the least personal gain, the least trace of its existence, and passes to another temporary keeper. The only things that count here are the institutions, and whilst you can achieve considerable power as a member or representative of one of those institutions, you can achieve nothing without them or outside them. That's why it always pays to be on good terms with the Warden, and even more so with the bursar. Everything we have, everything we enjoy, including our influential contacts in London, both political and financial, lasts only as long as our post, our activity and our life, no longer than that. One of the things Toby misses most is that now he hardly ever gets anyone in London phoning up to consult him. Destitution is possible but not inheritance. I think that's one of the reasons why there are so many bachelors here. It doesn't really encourage one to have a family knowing that, after a life of discipline and sacrifice but also of authority and wealth, one will have nothing to leave that family but the miserable pension of an obscure university lecturer. Despite all that, I still hope one day to be bursar of this college. I know it won't grieve me that much to give up the money when called upon to do so. Above all I know there'll be no ill-mannered, spoiled child to reproach me for it, I mean for the extreme poverty that would await us after the years of pomp. There's no risk of my having a family."

"Cromer-Blake doesn't want to talk to me or tell me anything about Clare," I thought. "He's quite capable of speechifying for hours on any subject in the pretence that he's talking to me about Clare, but he still hasn't told me anything it would be in my interests to know; he's capable of revealing his most intimate desires, his most deep-seated ambitions, of making all kinds of confessions I haven't asked for in order to avoid telling me anything concrete about his friend Clare. If what he wants is to distract me, to dissuade me and protect her from any attempt on my part at seduction, he's going about it the wrong way. The more he avoids and delays telling me what I want to know, the greater, more urgent, exclusive and all-embracing that interest becomes. I'm even beginning to forget about the girl on the train as being too hypothetical, too young, too autonomous, too unconscious of her own presence. Clare isn't like that. Clare is possessed of more self-knowledge, which is the kind of knowledge that makes people attractive, the kind that gives them their worth: the fact that they can shape their lives, plan and carry through their actions. The interesting thing is to act knowing that what one does or does not do has weight and meaning. There's nothing interesting about chance and the only promise innocence holds is the manner of its loss. Clare must have lovers, although Cromer-Blake doesn't want to tell me so, probably more out of friendship and respect for her husband than for reasons of discretion (according to what he's told me, Cromer-Blake needs, appreciates and indeed relies on indiscretion). What do I care about a husband I don't even know nor, if I can help it, ever will know? What do I care about the long-established marital ties of a city where I neither belong nor have any? How can anything that happened before me have any possible influence or weight? I'm free of the responsibility of having been a witness here, I've witnessed nothing. This static city was set in motion the day I arrived, only I didn't realise it until this evening of disquieting thoughts and events. And once I'm gone, what importance can whatever happens next possibly have? I'll leave no trace. This is just a stopping-off point for me but I'll be stopping long enough to make it worth my while finding what people call 'someone to love'. I can't let myself have all this time at my disposal and not have someone to think about, because if I do that, if I think only about things rather than about another person, if I fail to live out my sojourn and my life here in conflict with another being or in expectation or anticipation of that, I'll end up thinking about nothing, as bored by my surroundings as by any thoughts that might arise in me. Perhaps Cromer-Blake is right, at least in part: perhaps the most pernicious, and furthermore impossible, thing is *not* to think about women, or in his case men, about a particular woman, almost as if there were a part of our brain that could only deal with that kind of thought, thoughts that other parts of the brain flee from or perhaps despise but without which they cannot function fruitfully, properly. As if not thinking about someone (even if that someone were more than one person) could prevent you from thinking about anything. At least that's what happens to people who aren't serious. I'm not serious, I should not in fact be taken seriously, my thinking is erratic, my character weak, but few people know that and, more to the point, no one here knows that and I very much doubt anyone has given the matter much thought. So I'm going to ask Cromer-Blake directly, taking advantage of the fact that we're both drunk and that questions asked during drunken conversations always get an answer, I'm going to ask him now if Clare has or has had lovers, if she's in love with her husband, and whether he thinks I have any chance of success should I try to make her the person I'll spend my two years (already less than two years now) thinking about. Two years that will be permeated by this sense of unease. Since he's destined to be both father- and mother-figure to me, I'm going to ask Cromer-Blake for his advice and I'm going to ask if during this time I can have Clare in usufruct, with no hope of personal gain, leaving no trace once I'm gone. I'm going to ask him right now, without bothering to lead the conversation back to the subject, I'm going to ask him now point-blank, as one never asks anything in England but as one does in Madrid, even though Cromer-Blake has just repeated the word 'bursar' several times and appears to have steered the conversation right away from what I want to know. I'm going to ask him straight out and he'll have no alternative but to answer yes or no. He must know, although he could always say that he doesn't."

"Does Clare Bayes have any lovers?" I said, and the truth is that I wasn't really prepared when I asked the question, it just slipped out.

"What?" said Cromer-Blake. "Yes, I mean, no. I've no idea."

WHEN YOU'RE ALONE, when you live alone and live, more-over, in a foreign country, you take more notice than usual of the rubbish bin, because at times it may be the only thing with which you maintain a constant, no, more than that, an ongoing relationship. Each black plastic bag, new, shining and smooth, waiting to be used for the first time, evokes a sense of absolute cleanliness and infinite possibility. When you replace the plastic bag each night it signals the inauguration, the promise of a new day: everything is still to come. That bag, that bin, are some-times the only witnesses to what happens during the day of a man on his own, and it is in that bag that the remains, the traces of the man are deposited throughout the day, the half of himself that he discards, everything he has decided not to be and not to have, the negative of what he's eaten, drunk, smoked, used, produced and received. At the end of that day, bag and bin are full, the contents confused, but the man has watched them grow, become transformed, seen them shape themselves into an indis-criminate jumble of which, nonetheless, he knows the expla-nation and understands the order, for that indiscriminate jumble is itself the order and explanation of the man. The bag and the bin are proof that this day existed, has been added on to all the other days and that, whilst slightly different from the previous day and the next, it was also the same, the visible nexus between the two. They are the one record, the one proof or assurance of the passing of that man, the one task he has truly brought to completion. They act as both connecting thread and clock. Each time he goes over to the rubbish bin and throws something in, he again sees and has contact with the things he threw away before and that is what gives him a sense of continuity. His day is measured out in visits to the rubbish bin; there he sees the empty pot of fruit yoghurt he had for breakfast and the cigarette packet which, at the start of the morning, had contained only two cigarettes, the envelopes from the post he received, now empty and torn, the cans of Coca-cola and the shavings from the pencil he sharpened before starting work (even if he was going to use a pen), the screwed up sheets of paper he judged unsatisfactory or wrong, the cellophane wrapper that had contained three sandwiches, the cigarette stubs from numerous emptyings of ashtrays, the cotton wool balls soaked in the cologne with which he refreshed his brow, the discarded fat from the cold meats that he ate distractedly while he worked, the useless reports picked up at the faculty, a sprig of parsley and one of basil, some silver paper, bits of cotton, nail clippings, the darkened peel of a pear, the milk carton, the empty medicine bottle, the paper bags made of strong, coarse paper favoured by second-hand booksellers. It all gets packed down, concentrated, covered over and fused together and thus traces the perceptible outline – material and solid – of this sketch of the days of the life of a man. Closing and tying up the bag and putting it outside, the simple act of throwing out scraps and peelings, the act of dispensing with, selecting, discerning what is useless means condensing and bringing to a close the day of which those acts may well have been the only distinguishing features. The result of that discernment is a task that dictates its own end: only when the bin is overflowing is it finished and then, and only then, are its contents rubbish.

I began taking a day-to-day interest in the rubbish bin and its progressive metamorphosis about a year after the night I've just described, at a time when, for a variety of reasons that I will discuss later, I was seeing Clare Bayes less than I wanted to (and had not yet found a replacement) and, were such a thing possible, my workload in the city of Oxford had dwindled still further (or perhaps it was just that I performed my tasks ever more mechanically). I was more alone and at more of a loose end and the excitement of the discovery phase had long since faded. But even before that, right from the start and especially at weekends, I'd always taken a lot of notice of the rubbish bin, for Sundays in England aren't just ordinary, dull Sundays, the same the world over, which demand simply that one tiptoe through them without disturbing them or paying them the least attention, in England they are, as I believe Baudelaire described them, Sundays in exile from the infinite. During the rest of the week, even though my teaching duties remained minimal, there were more distractions, and one distraction in particular, which was never lacking in Oxford (it may turn into the only distraction if you become an addict), was the search for the kind of old, rare, out-of-print books that give pleasure to the morbid or eccentric collector. For those with a taste for them, England's second-hand bookshops are a dusty, sequestered paradise, frequented, moreover, by the most distinguished gentlemen of the realm. The variety and abundance of these shops, the limitless wealth of their stocks, the rapidity with which those stocks are replenished, the impossibility of ever exploring every corner of them, the circumscribed but vigorous and vital market they represent, make them an endlessly surprising and rewarding territory to explore. During my two years of scouting out and hunting down such books with my gloved hands, I obtained many apparently unobtainable marvels at quite ridiculous prices, such as the seventeen volumes of the first and only complete edition of the translation of *The Thousand Nights and a Night* by Sir Richard Francis Burton (better known to booksellers as Captain Burton), which began to appear more than a century ago in a limited edition of a thousand numbered copies of each volume, available only to subscribers of the Burton Club on the understanding (which they honoured) that it would never be

73

enlarged or reprinted: in fact that exuberant Victorian text has never again been reprinted in its entirety, but only in selections or in bowdlerised editions, which, whilst apparently complete, were in fact expurgated of everything considered at the time (or by Lady Burton) to be obscene. The hunter of books is condemned to specialise in subjects related to his main prey, which he tracks down with the greatest eagerness, and at the same time, as he becomes infected with the unstoppable collecting bug, he grows irremediably and increasingly more generous and accommodating in his enthusiasms. That's certainly what happened to me and, seeing my interests grow ever wider and more disparate, I decided to restrict the prime objective of my systematic searches to just five or six authors, and my choice of those authors was based as much on the difficulty of finding them as on any actual desire to read or possess their books. They were minor authors, who were all in some way odd, ill-fated, forgotten or unappreciated, known only to the few and not even commonly reprinted in their country of origin; the most famous (but much more famous in my country than in his own) and the least minor of them was the Welshman Arthur Machen, that fine stylist and strange narrator of subtle horrors, who, in a survey carried out during the Spanish Civil War amongst fifty British men of letters, was the only one publicly to declare his preference for Franco's side, perhaps merely as an affirmation of his affinity with purest terror. Despite his reputation, his books are not easy to find in English, particularly in the old editions greatly prized by collectors, and when I saw the difficulty I was having finding many of the titles I lacked, I contacted several booksellers and asked them to put by any that came their way and even to seek them out for me.

In England second-hand booksellers still travel round the country visiting ancient bookshops in obscure towns and remote villages, turning up at country houses owned by the illiterate descendants of some late but lettered man, snapping up bargains at shabby local auctions, never missing even a makeshift or spur-of-the-moment provincial book sale (often held in such places as the local fire station, the foyer of a hotel with no guests, or a church cloister). Since their lives are an endless round of travelling, researching and hunting things down it makes sense to tell them what you're looking for, because the chances are they can find it for you. Amongst the booksellers whose acquaintance I cultivated was a married couple by the name of Alabaster, who made a major contribution to my stock of eccentric acquisitions. Their shop was small, dark and comfortable, simple and insalubrious, a cross between a cosy nook and a haunted house, with beautiful fine wood shelves all of them warped and barely visible beneath the weight and inconceivable disorder of the thousands of books that did not so much fill the shelves as crush and bury them. The Alabasters must have made a reasonable living for inside that dark, stuffy, dusty place, lit even at the brightest hours of the day by a couple of lamps with glass shades, was the additional glow of a television screen which, in the closest of closed circuits, allowed them to see what was going on beneath the one flickering bulb of the shop's basement without their having to keep going up and down the stairs every time a prospective buyer ventured down there to explore its depths. As if wishing to participate in a modernity with which their merchandise was so at odds, the couple seemed to spend their days watching on television (in black and white) what could be seen only a few yards away, right under their noses (in colour). Mrs Alabaster was a smiling, authoritarian woman, with one of those very English smiles that you see adorning the faces of famous stranglers in films as they're about to choose their next victim. She was middle-aged with greying hair, fierce eyes and capped teeth and, wrapped in a pink woollen shawl, she would sit at her desk, writing incessantly in an enormous accounts book. To judge by her constant activity, which she interrupted only (but frequently) to gaze with intent interest via her screen upon the lower levels of the bookshop (almost always empty, always uneventful) the amounts of money handled by the Alabasters must have been vast and the accounts accordingly complex. Mr Alabaster, the husband and original bearer of the name, was equally smiling but his smile was more like that of the strangler's anonymous victim just before he realises his fate. He was a good-looking, well-groomed but casually dressed man still blessed with a thatch of immaculate grey hair and with the slight air of an ageing, theoretical Don Juan (of the type prevented by social class or by an early, rock-solid marriage from ever savouring the charms of the role), who still retains a suggestion of the coquetry and cologne of his less hypothetical years. But, despite the fact that he too was almost always in the shop, I can't recall him ever once answering my questions or queries. He would smile and greet customers in the manner of an energetic, lively man (his whole bearing was intrepid) but he delegated anything requiring a reply, however insignificant, to the greater knowledge and authority of his wife. He would turn to her and repeat with great vivacity and exactitude the question he'd just been asked – appropriating it as his own, as if he were the one interested in knowing the answer: "Have we had anything in by Vernon Lee, darling?" – adding only that one word, "darling". While she enjoyed the benefits of the desk and a comfortable armchair, he had to content himself with sitting on one of the stepladders from which I myself, not without a twinge of guilt, would often dislodge him in order to browse along the more neglected and less accessible upper shelves. He would remain standing until I'd finished up above and then, after wiping down with a cloth the one step that was his seat, he would sit down again without even a hint of impatience. Every time I went into the shop, I found them there, in the same immutable places and positions, she scribbling numbers in a huge ledger or scanning the television screen with her fierce eyes, he leaning back a little on the ladder, his arms crossed (I never saw him reading a book or leafing through a newspaper, still less talking to Mrs Alabaster) in an attitude of expectation, his most strenuous activity (which he shared with his wife) being that of (indirectly) surveying the basement. The cheerfulness and urbanity with which Mr Alabaster greeted any customer entering the shop indicated that, in his role as passive subaltern, the mere appearance of someone through the shop door was the highlight of his day, and his effusive greeting of that customer its most glorious and sociable moment. For, as I have said, the fact is that subsequently he was incapable of answering the simplest question or even of indicating the shelf the buyer was looking for ("Have we got a travel section, darling?") Their absorption in the televisual observation of their basement made me wonder if the Alabasters were not perhaps empowered to see something invisible to other mortals. Often, when inspecting the basement, I would spend less time examining the books than peering into corners and at the floor in the hope of discovering some tiny animal they kept there or of hearing the tenuous breathing of a ghost. But I never saw or heard anything and when I descended to that cobwebbed basement to rummage around in the half-shadows, I imagined that the appearance on their boring screen of my figure – seen in the flesh upstairs only seconds before – would have the Alabasters catching their breath with excitement and more than once I was tempted to perform some prank or steal a book just to provide them with a little entertainment or to arouse alarm. In fact I did neither but I would try to loiter there as long as possible and move about the basement swiftly, randomly, unexpectedly, or repeatedly take my gloves off and put them on again, button and unbutton my coat, smooth my hair, make a lot of noise blowing the dust off books then leaf through them ostentatiously or with exaggerated slowness, take notes in my diary, tap my foot in feigned impatience or doubt, cough, sigh, mutter and exclaim in Spanish and generally lend as much variety as possible to the meagre spectacle I doubtless presented for those four eyes (two childlike and two perverse) observing me in my hunt for books.

Shortly after informing them of my interest in any book by Machen they might come across (although the truth is they never seemed to stray even a mile outside Oxford) and over a period of several days of forays into bookshops, I observed a man who seemed to be following almost in my footsteps. I saw him nosing around in Waterfield's vast antiquarian bookshop, in the mysterious upper floor of Sanders the engravings shop, in Swift's and in Titles, both in Turl Street, in the second-hand section of Blackwell's monumental and comprehensive emporium, on every one of Thornton's three floors, in out-of-the-way Artemis and even in the tiny Classic Bookshop that specialised in Greek and Latin texts. I consider myself to be a fairly observant person but it took no special talent to notice that particular man: he himself was fairly remarkable, but what most drew the eye was the dog he always had with him and that waited for him outside. It was a nice little mahogany-coloured terrier with an intelligent face but with one leg missing – its left back leg had been neatly amputated. That's why it always lay down while it waited, though it stood up as soon as it heard anyone leaving the shop at whose door it was tied, in the hope, I imagine, that it would be his bibliomaniac master. Since I usually arrived at the bookshops before the latter, I also left before him and each time the terrier would hop to its feet and reveal its small polished stump like an atrophied wing. I'd stroke its head and the dog would sit down again. I never heard the dog bark or growl even when it was raining or blustery outside; it never seemed disgruntled. Its owner, who was more or less my age, was still in possession of both his legs, but he complied with the old saying that owners always look like their dogs in that he was rather lame in one of them, his left. Although during those two or three days I never actually saw them together (the man inside the shop, the dog outside), the association was easy enough to make, their two recurring presences rendering it unequivocal. The man dressed in good albeit rather threadbare clothes, wore a hat as to the manner born and, judging by his complexion and hair colour, was Irish. Inevitably, though I'd paid him little attention, I had noticed him inside the bookshops, for even in the most extensive and labyrinthine of establishments I had at some point found myself perusing the same bookshelf as him, but we'd only exchanged the most fleeting of neutral, that is veiled, glances. At no point did it occur to me that he could have any connection with the path traced by my own random footsteps, still less that he might be following in them, although it did seem odd that I'd never before noticed such an immediately identifiable couple, not even whilst walking round the town, and yet now I met him often enough to find their maimed figures, his and the dog's, slightly and momentarily troubling, however little notice I took of them. Perhaps they were strangers passing through, a bookseller and his dog up from London on a recce to Oxford.

On the morning of one of those Sundays exiled from the infinite, I was working in my distinctly uncosy pyramid of a house and, as was my custom on that particular day of the week, kept looking up from time to time to gaze out of the window at the pleasant young gypsy flowerseller in her high boots, jeans and leather jacket, who on Sundays and bank holidays – come rain or snow – used to set up her stall on the pavement opposite. Sometimes, in the midst of my exile, I would go out and buy a bunch of flowers from her simply to exchange a few words with another living soul. Looking up for the nth time in only a brief period, I saw the man and the dog coming down St Giles', the former clearly exhibiting his handicap and the latter his conspicuous lack. They were walking along the opposite pavement and I watched for some time as they hobbled up to the

79

flower stall. I thought: "So the man goes out on Sundays too, even when all the bookshops are closed." I saw him take off his hat to buy something or just to chat to the girl and went back to my boring university tasks. Some seconds later the doorbell rang and I thought it was probably the flowerseller come to ask me for a glass of water, as she did sometimes, receiving instead a Coca-cola or a beer, but when I looked up before going downstairs, I saw that she was still there on the other side of the road. I went down and opened the door and the man who owned the dog with the missing leg stood smiling timidly up at me from the bottom of the front steps, holding his brown hat pressed against his chest.

"Good morning," he said. "My name's Alan Marriott. I should have phoned first. But I haven't got your number. Just your address. And anyway I'm not on the phone. I'd like to talk to you for a moment. If you're not too busy. I waited until Sunday, that's when people tend to be freer. Generally speaking, that is. May we come in?" He spoke as if punctuating each phrase, rarely using conjunctions, as if his speech too were lame. Although he wasn't wearing a tie he looked as if he was, perhaps the effect of the hat, perhaps because he wore his dark blue shirt buttoned to the neck. He could never have been mistaken for a university man, but neither did he look like someone indigent or unemployed. He wore two rings – he lacked taste – on the hand clasping his hat. There was something mean and unfinished about him, though that may just have been the impression left by his lameness.

"Would you mind telling me what this is about? If it's anything to do with religion, I've no time."

"Oh, no. It's nothing to do with religion at all. Unless you consider literature to be a religion. I don't. It's about a literary matter."

"What happened to your dog?"

"He was in a fight."

"OK. Come upstairs and tell me about it."

I ushered them in and led them towards the spiral staircase, but before going up, as if he knew or could imagine the house, the lame man took a step towards the kitchen and asked politely: "Shall I leave the dog in the kitchen?"

I looked down at the poor three-legged beast, so obedient and peaceable. "No, bring him up, he deserves our respect, and he'll be better off upstairs with us."

On the next floor up, the second floor, in the room that served me as both living room and study, the man could not resist an immediate glance at the few books I kept in Oxford (every so often I despatched bulky packages to Madrid containing the books I'd already collected) and which barely occupied two shelves. With the Latin hospitality I never managed to rid myself of, I asked if he wanted anything to drink, to which he said no, more because he was taken aback by the offer than because of any genuine disinclination to have a drink. He obviously felt he was intruding. I sat down on the chair I normally worked in and left the sofa to him. He didn't take off his raincoat when he sat down, it was already extremely creased. The dog lay down at his feet.

"What happened to him?"

"Some hooligans at Didcot station. They started having a go at me. The dog came to my defence. He bit one of them. He hurt the fellow. Badly. Between them, they caught him and put him on the railway line of the train we were waiting for. Somewhere beyond the platforms. They held me down too. They covered my mouth. It was late at night. They intended the train to cut him in half. Lengthways. But when the train came they weren't brave enough to hold him there right till the end, with their hands so near the line. The train didn't look as if it was going to slow down. In fact it didn't stop. It wasn't our train. He managed to roll over and so only lost his leg. You can't imagine the amount of blood he lost. The hooligans took

leg man

fright and ran off across the fields. I got off lightly with just a few blows with a stick. My own lameness is due to polio. I contracted it as a child."

"I had no idea Didcot station was so dangerous."

"Only on match days. Well, it was when Oxford United got into the First Division. Not something that's likely to happen very often."

I couldn't resist giving the dog a few pats on the back. It received them with total indifference.

"Was he a hunter?"

"Yes, but not any more."

"A hunter of books, perhaps," I said, uncertain as to whether or not I should mention it.

The man smiled slightly. He had a friendly face and very large, pale blue eyes with a slight squint. When you looked at them it was difficult to determine exactly the direction of their gaze.

"Yes. I'm sorry about that. Mrs Alabaster told me about you. She gave me your address."

"Mrs Alabaster? Ah, yes, I gave it to her so that she could let me know if she managed to find some books I'm interested in. I'm not sure she should have given it to you."

"Yes, I know. Don't be cross with her. You must forgive her. She knows me well. She told me about you and I wanted to meet you. I did rather insist. I've spent the last few days following you around the bookshops. I didn't want to approach you in the street. You probably realised."

"Following me? But why?"

"To see what you bought and how you went about it. How much time you spent perusing the shelves and how much you spent. What you spent it on. You're Spanish, aren't you?"

"Yes, from Madrid."

"Do people there know Arthur Machen?"

"A few things by him have been translated. Borges wrote about him and spoke very highly of him."

82

"I don't know who Borges is. You must give me the reference. It's Machen I've come to see you about actually. Mrs Alabaster told me you were looking for some books by him."

"That's right. Can you get hold of any for me? I haven't found many up till now. You're a bookseller, are you?"

"No. I was for a few years. It's not easy finding anything by Machen these days. I've got nearly everything by him. Well, not everything. But if you find some title you're not interested in or that you've already got, buy it for me anyway. If it isn't too expensive. I'll always find a buyer for it. I've never found *Bridles and Spurs*. That's a book of essays. It was published in America." Alan Marriott fell silent and, when I said nothing, he seemed suddenly embarrassed. He began turning his hat round and round in his hands. He looked down at the floor, then over at the window. I wondered if he could see the flowerseller from where he was sitting. He couldn't. He loosened his raincoat. The dog yawned. At last Marriott said:

"Have you heard of the Machen Company?"

"No, what is it?"

"I can't tell you yet. I just wanted to know if you'd heard of it. Before I tell you about it, I would have to know if you'd be interested in joining. We haven't got anyone in Spain. Or Latin America. You'll be going back to Spain, I take it."

"Yes, in a year or so, not at the end of this year, but the next."

"There's no hurry."

"I go back every now and then, in the holidays. I teach at the university here. But, listen, it's a bit difficult to know if I want to join something without knowing what it's about."

"Yes, I understand that. But that's the way it is. What matters is the name. How you react to the name. People always react to names. They tell you a lot."

"Can you at least tell me what I would have to do?"

"Oh, to start with, you'd just have to pay a modest subscription, ten pounds a quarter. Then you'd be on the list. There are nearly five hundred of us in England. More in Wales. We have some very eminent people as members."

"Five hundred Machenians? And what do they get out of it?"

"That depends. It varies each year. For the moment you'd receive bulletins. Publications too. Not regularly. Some you pay for separately. But they don't cost much, there's a discount and you can elect to receive them or not. I've been a member for twelve years now."

"Congratulations. And nothing's happened since then, apart from what happened to your dog in Didcot. Just a bit of a beating, eh?"

"What do you mean?"

"I mean, nothing else bad has happened to you."

"Oh, no, nothing. You wouldn't be running any risks, if that's what you mean. It won't affect your life in any way. There are eminent people involved."

"What, no horror, no terror? It is, after all, the Machen Company."

Marriott burst out laughing.

"Do you know, I wouldn't mind a beer now, if it's not too much trouble."

His teeth were set very wide apart; they cried out, retrospectively, for braces. He pulled out a Kleenex from his jacket pocket and dried the tears which, strangely, that one burst of laughter had brought to his pale eyes. I brought him up a glass of foaming beer, which he downed almost in one. Then he spoke more fluently: "Machen's horrors are very subtle. They depend in large part on the association of ideas. On the conjunction of ideas. On a capacity for bringing them together. You might never see the horror implicit in associating two ideas, the horror implicit in each of those ideas, and thus never in your whole life recognise the horror they contain. But you could live immersed in that horror if you were unfortunate enough always to make the right associations. For example, that girl opposite your house who sells flowers. There's nothing terrifying about her, in herself she doesn't inspire horror. On the contrary. She's very attractive. She's nice and friendly. She stroked the dog. I bought these carnations from her." And saying that he produced two bent, rather crushed carnations from his raincoat pocket, as if he'd only bought them as a pretext to speak to the flowerseller. "But she could inspire horror. The idea of that girl in association with another idea could. Don't you think so? We don't yet know the nature of that missing idea, of the idea required to inspire us with horror. We don't yet know her horrifying other half. But it must exist. It does. It's simply a question of it appearing. It may also never appear. Who knows, it could turn out to be my dog. The girl and my dog. The girl with her long, chestnut hair, her high boots and her long, firm legs and my dog with his one leg missing." Marriott looked down at the dog, which was dozing; he looked at the dog's stump of a leg. He touched it lightly. "The fact that my dog goes everywhere with me is normal. It's necessary. It's odd if you like. I mean the two of us going around together. But there's nothing horrific about it. But if she went around with my dog. That might be horrific. The dog is missing a leg. If it had been hers, it would certainly never have lost its leg in a stupid argument after a football match. That's an accident. An occupational hazard for a dog with a lame master. But if it had been her dog, perhaps it would have lost its leg some other way. The dog is still missing a leg. There must be some other reason, then. Something far worse. Not just an accident. You could hardly imagine that girl getting involved in a fight. Perhaps the dog would have lost its leg *because* of her. Perhaps the only explanation of why this dog should have lost its leg if it were her dog would be that she had cut it off. How else could a dog that was so well looked after, cared for and loved by that nice, attractive girl who sells flowers have lost its leg? It's a horrible idea, that girl cutting off my dog's leg; seeing it with her own eyes; being a witness to it."

Alan Marriott's final words sounded slightly indignant, as if he were indignant with the flowerseller. He broke off. He seemed to have frightened himself. "Let's drop the subject."

"No, go on, you were on the point of inventing a story."

"No, forget it. It's a poor example."

"As you wish."

Marriott put his hands in his raincoat pockets, as if announcing with that gesture that he was about to get up.

"Well?"

"Well what?"

"Would you be interested in joining?"

I stroked a finger up and down between my nose and my upper lip, as I do when I'm unsure about something. I said: "I might be. Look, here's what we'll do, if it's all right with you that is. I'll give you the ten pounds for the first quarter and that way I'll be on the list along with the eminent people. Later on, I'll tell you if I'm interested in continuing."

"But when? And the members aren't *all* eminent people, you know."

"Soon. Let's say after the three months covered by my first subscription."

Marriott looked hard at the two five-pound notes I'd taken out of a drawer and placed on the low table as I said this. At least I think he did, his transparent eyes were very deceptive.

"It's not our usual way of doing things. But since you're a foreigner. And we haven't got anyone in Spain. Or in Latin America. I'm going to give you my address. Just in case you find anything by Machen that you've already got. Or *Bridles and Spurs*. Or his introduction to John Gawsworth's *Above the River*. It's very difficult to find his complete works. I'll write it all down. I'll pay you for them. If they're not too expensive. Up to twenty-five pounds. First editions. I don't live far away." He scribbled rapidly on a piece of crumpled paper, gave it to me, picked up the two five-pound notes and put them in his raincoat pocket. He took the opportunity of returning his hands to his pockets in order to lean into them and get to his feet. "Would you like a receipt for the membership subscription?"

"No, I don't think that's necessary. I'm on the list now, am I?"

"Yes, you're on the list. Thank you. I hope you stay on it. I won't hold you up any longer. And I'm sorry I didn't phone first. I haven't got your number. Nor a phone at home. I think I might well get one. Right. Come on, let's go," he said to the dog, who got up again on his three legs and shook himself out of sleep. Marriott picked up his hat.

I didn't give him my number. They went downstairs and I accompanied them to the door. I, who had never been a member of anything in Madrid, had in a few months become a member of the Oxonian congregation by virtue of my job, a member of St Antony's College, to which, as a foreigner, I'd been assigned from the Taylorian Institute, a member of Wadham College, to which I'd been assigned according to the caprice of my head of department, Aidan Kavanagh, and now I was a member of the Machen Company, to which I'd assigned myself without knowing why and without knowing a thing about it. I watched them walking away down the pavement, back down St Giles', stumbling like two drunks along that broad, monumental street also in exile from the infinite. It was nearly lunchtime. Before closing the door I waved to the gypsy flowerseller who was already busily devouring a sandwich. She wasn't as attractive as Marriott had said. She had big teeth and a huge smile; even at that distance I could see the bits of lettuce stuck to her teeth. I *could* imagine her involved in some quarrel at Didcot station or somewhere else, with her black leather jacket and her tangled mane of hair, kicking out with her high boots, biting – like the dog – with her big teeth. Her name was Jane, she was a bit dense but very sweet and I knew that she'd got married, at all of nineteen, to the man – invisible to me, since he never got out of his car to help her – who every Sunday and bank holiday dropped her off and picked her up opposite my house, together with her merchandise, in a clean, modern van. It could have been her husband who cut off the dog's leg.

Back upstairs, I collected Marriott's empty beer can, the tearstained Kleenex and the two crushed carnations still in their silver foil that he'd taken out only to leave behind on the sofa where he'd been sitting. I noticed these three things as they dropped into the rubbish bin on that Sunday in the March of my first year in Oxford.

I DON'T TAKE so much notice of the rubbish now, whole weeks and even months pass without my paying it any attention, it may be that I don't notice it at all or only very occasionally, just for a second, as you might recall something so long disowned or extinct that you banish it at once from your thoughts to preclude all possibility of its ever existing again or to make it seem like something that in fact never did exist, something that never took place. In the short time that has passed since I left the city of Oxford too many things have changed or begun or ceased to be.

I no longer live alone or abroad, I'm married now and living in Madrid again. I have a son. That son is still very young, as yet he can neither talk nor walk nor, of course, does he have a memory. I don't understand it yet, how he came to be, I mean, he seems foreign to me, strange and alien, although he lives with us day and night and hasn't left us for a minute since he was born and despite the fact that for him there's no expiry date, as there may be for his mother or for me, as there was for Clare Bayes or (perhaps) for me two and a half years ago, at the end of my residence in Oxford. For him, on the contrary, there's no time limit. Only a short while ago he did not even exist. Now he's an eternal child. Sometimes I look at this child of only a few months and I remember Alan Marriott's words. I wonder what would be required in order for this child to inspire horror, or to whom the child has been attached in order that that other person will inspire it. I'm troubled by the fantasy that I – his own father – might be the missing factor, the one necessary for the two of us to provoke terror, that he might be the one idea necessary for me to do so. I watch him sleeping. So far he's a completely normal child. Alone, he can't inspire horror, on the contrary, both his mother and myself, in common with all the people who surround us and visit us here in Madrid, feel the protective urge that very young children usually provoke. They seem so fragile. One wouldn't protect something that inspired horror, although I also wonder if perhaps that horror enjoys the protection of what Alan Marriott called its horrifying other half, of that or of whatever reveals or causes the horror by association, by conjunction. Just as the dog would have protected the flowerseller and the flowerseller the dog, in the example proposed by Marriott. This son is, I think, much loved by his mother and by me (for his mother he is doubtless a transient deity condemned to lose his godliness), but there's something compulsive about him, as I suppose there is about all children during their first months of life, and there are moments when I would not want him to disappear exactly – that isn't it at all, that would be the last thing I'd want, it would drive us into madness – but rather I would like to return to the situation of having no children, of being a man with no prolongation of himself, of being able to embody for ever and in unadulterated form both son and brother, the true figures, the only ones to which we are accustomed, the only ones in which from the start we are and can feel at ease. The exercise of the paternal or maternal function is something that comes with time, is doubtless a duty imposed by time. It requires adaptation, concentration, it's something that happens. I still cannot comprehend that this child is here and is here for ever, the harbinger of an extraordinary longevity that will survive us both, nor can I grasp that I am his father. Today I had some meetings to go to and some business to deal with (business that involves a lot of money: that too has changed, I now earn and handle large amounts of money, although not as much as a college bursar), and in the middle of one of those conversations I completely forgot the existence of my son. I mean that I forgot he had been born, forgot his name, his face, his brief past which it was my responsibility to witness. I don't mean that I just stopped thinking about him for a moment, which is not only normal but beneficial to both, I mean that the child simply did not count. I did not, on the other hand, forget my wife, for whom there never was nor foreseeably will be an expiry date as there was for Clare Bayes from the moment I set eyes (full of the sexual admiration I also feel for Luisa) on her lovely, hard, sculpted, square-jawed face and her tasteful evening décolletage. (Despite the fact that I haven't known my wife that long and I could quite feasibly have forgotten her, I did not do so.) So this morning, while I talked to a financier called Estévez, fiftyish and very extrovert (three or four times he proudly referred to himself as a "go-getter"), my son became not something that has ceased to exist but something that had never existed. For no less than forty-five minutes, while the go-getting Estévez regaled me with splendid business propositions, I forgot I had a son and in my head I made plans for myself and my wife (especially travel plans) as if this son who still cannot walk or talk did not exist at all. For no less than forty-five minutes his life was literally wiped from my mind. He disappeared, he was cancelled out. Then, although nothing in particular, nothing concrete reminded me, I suddenly remembered him. "The child," I thought. I didn't mind remembering him – I felt glad to do so – nor did I mind immediately jettisoning the plans I'd been rapidly sketching out as I chatted to that most encouraging and enthusiastic of fellows, Estévez the go-getter. It didn't bother me in the least. What did bother me and make me feel guilty was my having forgotten him, and that made me wonder again today, as I have on other occasions when I've watched him sleeping, if I will not prove to be his horrifying other half, if, seeing that only a few months after his birth I'm capable of completely forgetting his existence, I'm not therefore destined to play that role. There's no reason why this should be so, it could happen to anyone, but forgetting gives rise to rancour and rancour to fear. He will forget me, because he will not have known me as a child or as a young man. A little while ago I asked my wife who, despite motherhood, remains very calm and serene, if she thought this child would always live with us, as long as he was a child or at least while he was still very young. She was getting undressed for bed and her upper body, her breasts still swollen, was uncovered.

"Of course he will, don't be so silly," she replied, "who else would he live with?" And she added while she removed her dark tights. "As long as nothing happens to us, that is."

"What do you mean?"

She was almost naked. In one hand she held her tights, in the other her nightdress. She was almost naked.

"Nothing bad, I mean."

Clare Bayes' son didn't live with her and her husband. Or rather, he was generally with them in Oxford only during the holidays, when he came back from his prep school in Bristol. He went there firstly because it had been decided that when he was thirteen, he would go to the well-known and extremely expensive Clifton School, on the banks of the Avon, just outside Bristol – it was his father's old school – and secondly to ensure that from as early an age as possible he should become accustomed both to the place and to being far from home. His holidays were much shorter than mine and those of his parents (in Oxford, classes are taught for three terms of exactly eight weeks each – Michaelmas, Hilary and Trinity – and the rest is idleness for those who, as was my own case, have no administrative duties, not even the invigilation of exams) and besides I was always away then, visiting Madrid or travelling in France, Wales, Scotland, Ireland or England itself. I never stayed in Oxford unless I had to, except once, right at the end. I was never, therefore, in Oxford at the same time as Clare's son, and that was the most convenient state of affairs for me, and the best suited, I suppose, to our adulterous affair. One shouldn't involve children. They're both too inquisitive and too squeamish. They're overdramatic and full of apprehensions. They cannot bear anything shadowy or ambiguous. They see danger everywhere, even where there is none, and can always spot a potentially dangerous situation, even if it is not dangerous exactly but merely confused or unusual. For more than a century now children have ceased to be brought up to become adults. Quite the contrary, and the result is that the adults of our era are brought up – we are brought up – to continue to be children. To get worked up over some sports event and grow jealous at the slightest thing. To live in a state of constant alarm and insatiable desire. To be fearful and angry. To be cowardly. To observe ourselves. Within Europe, England has shown the least interest in following that path and until only very recently she still enthusiastically and rigorously beat her most tender shoots with a consequent and much commented upon burgeoning of deviations (of the sexual variety) amongst its more impressionable citizens. However, according to what Clare told me, caning was no longer permitted at the school in Bristol and so I imagined that, as well as escaping the sufferings endured at school by his real and fictional predecessors, once home her son Eric would bask in the special privileges reserved for children who are boarded out for most of the year. Despite her innate lack of consideration and her natural expansiveness, Clare was considerate enough not to talk that much about him, at least with me, for I, even without knowing him, could not but see in him the vestiges or the living evidence of her past love. However dead a past love may be, new lovers are much more upset by them than they are by real and current disaffections even if the latter

93

create all kinds of practical difficulties. However, with me, Clare only spoke about her son Eric if I asked after him.

During my second and last year at Oxford, at the beginning of the term known as Trinity, whose eight weeks are spread over April, May and June, Clare Bayes' son fell ill whilst at school and Clare and Edward had to drive down to Bristol and bring him home. He remained in Oxford for four weeks to recuperate and during that period of convalescence and recovery I practically stopped seeing Clare altogether. As I mentioned earlier, although we didn't see each other very regularly or on all that continuous a basis, it's also true to say that from the time we met – with the exception of the vacations – we never went more than a week without meeting at least once, even if it was only for a swift, turbulent half hour between classes. Those four weeks were the worst weeks of my two years in Oxford (though perhaps the weeks that followed were no better). Not only was I more alone and at even more of a loose end (during their final term students either skip classes or the classes end up being cancelled to allow the undergraduates to devote themselves to preparing for the exams and the dons to preparing ever more fiendish questions) but I also discovered with great displeasure that the tenuous and sporadic feelings of jealousy I had very occasionally felt about Edward Bayes (or about their past love, unrepeated with or for me) became focused on her son Eric and the care his mother lavished on him to my immediate detriment. It was she who decided not to see me while the child Eric was at home and although his affliction was not a serious one, merely slow in passing (after the second week he was allowed out, as long as he took it easy), Clare Bayes decided to make it up to him for all the months of the year he spent away from her. Taking advantage of his illness, she wanted to nurture him, to make him more of a child, to feed her retina with images. Or so I surmised.

I called her at her office every two or three days (which was all she allowed me to do) on the pretext of finding out how the boy was coming along and with the intention of persuading her to agree, at her convenience, to just one more swift, turbulent encounter. I was never more available, more accommodating, more full of suggestions, all of which were – one after the other, day after day – declined. I was also at my most ardent (verbally). But Clare wanted no adult distractions or interruptions while the child Eric was at home. She was prepared to receive my calls, even to call me to give me a progress report, believing or pretending to believe that I was really concerned about the infection or the broken bone (I can't even remember what it was that brought the boy home, so little attention did I pay to her explanations), which, in the body of someone who was no more to me than an intrusive stranger, was presumably being fought off or was healing. She wouldn't agree to see me and when we met in the street or in the echoing corridors of the Taylorian, she greeted me with even more restraint and indifference than she normally showed me in public – as a precautionary, though instinctive measure. And then she'd continue on her way. In an all too southern European gesture, I would turn to watch the strong, slightly muscular legs poised on their high heels as she walked away. Now that I never saw her barefoot, they never seemed slender or boyish in their movements. I couldn't force her to stop by grabbing her arm and remonstrating with her as I've seen desperate lovers do in films, for in the streets of Oxford (and even more so in the echoing corridors of the Taylorian) there are, at any given moment, large numbers of dons or colleagues (they've taken the town over) who, on the pretext of walking from one college to another or from a meeting in one building to another meeting in another building, mill around in front of the shop windows or the billboards outside the (scarce but adequate) theatres or cinemas or contrive over-long exchanges of greetings and impressions (on university life). (Maybe they're spying.) And the Taylorian is constantly filled with an impassioned, almost furious thread of a voice, a distant metallic murmuring, which is Professor Jolyon delivering his magisterial lectures, banished (mercifully) to the top floor. Anyway, I couldn't really be said to be desperate. Clare Bayes had banished me from her Catte Street rooms for the duration and, of course, forbidden me to phone her at home, even at times when Edward's absence could be guaranteed. Now it didn't matter if her husband was there or not, because the child Eric was always certain to be there. Though I had never met him, I felt an intense antipathy for that child who had snatched from me the only affection – unsteady, precarious and with no future, but still the only one in evidence – that I'd enjoyed in that static city preserved in syrup. But I never (quite) reached the point of desperation.

During those four interminable spring weeks I intensified my wanderings round the city in search of rare books, and one consequence of that unwanted, artificial and ultimately unwholesome intensification was that my feeling of unease and my uncertain sense of identity reached crisis point.

The city of Oxford, especially during Trinity with the arrival of what passes in that part of the world for "the good weather", is peopled by or, rather, is packed to the gills with beggars. For the whole of spring and part of summer the city, which in other seasons also entertains a fair number of them, undergoes a wild and disproportionate increase in its mendicant population. One gets the impression that there are nearly as many beggars as there are students. The latter are the main reason for the proliferation of the former, who represent a genuine (undisciplined) army of occupation. If, with the arrival of spring (indeed it's the waves of beggars that announce the coming of spring), all the English, Welsh, Scots and Irish beggars abandon their respective winter refuges or quarters and as one man begin their pilgrimage to or march on the city of Oxford, it's because Oxford is a wealthy city (very wealthy) and because there are a couple of poorhouses or shelters where they're afforded one meal a day and occasionally (for those less given to night wanderings) a bed, but the main reason is that the vast majority of Oxford's inhabitants have young, innocent hearts. These British beggars, who invade the more prosperous towns of the south when the climate there begins to make paving stones or asphalt (or more likely benches) seem suitable places to bed down, have nothing in common with our traditional southern European beggars, who always retain a remnant of awareness that, however much they may feel it to be their due, they are in fact *asking* for money. These English and Irish beggars are sullen, fierce and extremely drunk. I never saw them ask for anything, which is not to say that they demand it either. They simply say nothing, they do not speak, they do not behave in the time-honoured manner of beggars, they make no mention of their trade or its meaning, rather they take it for granted that their attitude and their appearance (which is of course impoverished) somehow in themselves make any holding out of hands, any timeworn postulant phrases redundant. They will never tell you their life story or attempt any kind of sales pitch; they haven't got the gift of the gab. They're practically dumb. They're monosyllabic. There is, I think, an element of laziness and pride, a measure of boredom and fatalism in them. They don't beg because – unless the petition is false and merely the first, furtive step in an actual mugging – one who begs cannot at the same time maintain the boastful, bored, loutish, gruff mien so peculiar to them. They're not humble, they lack slyness. They're simply not interested. They make not the least attempt or pretence at cleanliness, their eyes are barely visible for the dark circles round them, they all boast long beards and prehistoric tangles of hair, their clothes are in holes or frayed or torn (but whilst all of them have a jacket or coat, almost none has an anorak or a tracksuit or any other item of sports clothing), they are of all ages and all are tireless. Not one of them is sedentary. They walk along brandishing bottles of beer, gin or whisky in hands innocent of water, they only stay in one spot long enough to sit down and drain the contents of a bottle or when they fall down exhausted by their endless perambulations. The Oxford beggars seem possessed by a fury or fever for walking that leads them to cover the whole city several times a day, striding along, remonstrating as they do, making swaggering or obscene gestures at the passers-by, muttering oaths, blasphemies and curses that remain indecipherable. The Oxford beggars are wanderers. They are the only members of the population who do not know where they are going and thus keep walking round and round the red-grey streets in the rain or beneath lowering skies. Every now and then one of them will pause to lean over a bridge and vomit into the River Isis, or prowl around for a while outside the door of a pub in case some customer (of those who choose to drink outside) should depart in a hurry and leave within reach of the beggar's grimy hand a generous amount of alcohol in their abandoned glass. But for the rest they are ceaseless rovers. There are a few who work, if you can call it that, at something other than cultivating their needy appearance, and they tend to remain in one place, or at least on their wanderings carry with them the tools of their trade. They are the ones who play an instrument, own a performing animal, do clumsy juggling acts, croon ballads or tell fortunes (the latter are very rare, given that there's no market for it in Oxford, no curiosity about the future). These active beggars are the richest and therefore the most hated by their less gifted colleagues. Late one afternoon I saw two of the fiercest and most inveterate of the wandering variety (always heavily bearded) attacking a little man getting on in years to whom I regularly used to give a few pence because he looked so tidy and peaceable and because he played old Madrid dance tunes on a barrel organ salvaged, he claimed, from a dockside bonfire in Liverpool. To walk down Cornmarket and hear in the distance the vibrant sound of a barrel organ grinding out

such tunes caused a hilarity in me comparable only to that provoked by the lively groups of Spanish tourists I occasionally
came across on Saturdays who, as is their custom when abroad,
would invariably be walking along clapping (flamenco style).
So the least I could do whenever I heard him was to go over to
the organ grinder's pitch, even though it was somewhat out of
my way, and give him whatever loose change I had on me. On
that occasion, as I said, I saw two bearded beasts laying into the
old man and his barrel organ. I ran up to them full of indignation and panic, hurling awful insults at them in Spanish and
it was doubtless the sonorous quality of a foreign language so
well adapted to insults (I think they were particularly impressed
by "culo", the Spanish word for arse) that put them to flight
before I had a chance to get near enough for them to lay into
me (equally pitilessly), which would, in the ordinary run of
events, have been my fate: I'm neither very strong nor very
brave. Luckily, neither the barrel organ nor the old man suffered
any irreparable damage and some minutes later I saw both man
and barrel organ disappearing with slightly stumbling steps
along St Aldate's into the advancing dusk. The sky was red and
I was breathing hard.

But what I did perhaps have the courage and strength to do
was to recognise and realise that I was becoming like them, like
the beggars, even though the Oxford beggar's worst enemy is
the Oxford professor or don who, unlike the undergraduate,
has an old and wily heart and sees off beggars with a few sharp
remarks and a well-aimed flick of his gown. Since at the time I
was an Oxford don and no doubt looked the part, I was consequently regarded by the beggars with a hostile eye. But I was
only a temporary don and as yet had scant feeling for the
role, and the habits peculiar to it, amongst them a talent for
intimidating vagabonds and a repertoire of loud cries cultivated
for the purpose, were not yet that deeply rooted in me. As
regards my upbringing and degree of learning, that in no way

belied the perceived similarity, for there are some very cultivated beggars in England. The condition of beggar does not necessarily have its origin in a background of great poverty or the collapse of a business or in paralysing ignorance, but rather in a liking for drink, the loss of one's job, disillusion, a passion for gambling or a mental breakdown – usually of a minor nature – which the state chooses to ignore. John Mollineux, the solo violinist, who at one time often played with a leading chamber orchestra, is now another anonymous wino sleeping by the Thames after having enjoyed a brilliant career as a musician for more than five years and having travelled (feted and honoured wherever he went) all over the world. Now he just drinks, he never plays, indeed he can't bear the sight of a music stave. Professor Mew, a Catholic, a hopeless case suffering from some kind of mental disorder, spent years wandering the streets of Oxford, brandishing a bottle, swearing, talking nonsense, raving and pestering his former colleagues and subordinates when he bumped into them (the latter at a loss as to whether to send him packing or to continue treating him as if he still had his Chair), and yet he left behind him theological writings of great note, and reached the heights of his profession as an academic and even, for several years formed part of the Papal Council for Culture over which the Pope himself presides. Both men (the first violin and the theologian, not the Pope) were drunks who had subsequently become mentally unhinged and at a certain point in their careers were expelled from their respective jobs. For a good part of the day during those first weeks of the Trinity term of my second year, I too wandered from one place to another or rather from one of the city's bookshops to another, and in my wanderings I came across the same unsociable faces again and again, dressed in the same ragged, stinking clothes, with the same alcoholic fumes and resounding belches issuing from mouths that could barely articulate a word. The beggars who wandered the city as I did were the most violent, desperate, inactive and drunken of the lot and some were perhaps wasted talents from the arts and sciences like the violinist and the theologian. The city of Oxford, or at least its centre, is not that big, so it's perfectly possible to come across the same person two or three times in one day. You can imagine how easy it is then if both oneself and the other person spend the whole day in the street, wandering, roaming around, aimlessly drifting, probably not even aware of what they're doing. Particular faces and outfits began to grow painfully familiar to me. "Ah, the ginger-bearded bloke with the blackened teeth and the broken nose," I'd think as I passed him yet again. "There's the one with the moss green mittens." "There's that woman with the toothless grin who long ago lost her looks but who still walks as if she hadn't, like a sixties woman confident of her own prettiness." "There goes that Scotsman who's bald as a coot under his jockey cap and who rolls his r's so tremendously when he rails against Great God and his Virgin Mother." "And that's the young black chap with all the tattoos and the right leg of his trousers slit almost to the groin." "There's that frenzied, dishevelled old man who looks just like Fragonard's painting of the philosopher." I feared that they would begin to recognise me too and assimilate me into their ranks, that they would begin to realise that, although I was not a beggar and did not speak or dress like them, but rather had the unmistakable look of a man in a gown even when I wasn't wearing one, I too, over a period of one week, two weeks, three weeks and eventually four weeks, cropped up several times a day during their mechanical, directionless wanderings, like a stray domestic animal banished to the streets because the child Eric was ill.

IN A WAY I DID BEGIN to feel that I was one of them and to fear that one day, in Spain or England, or wherever in the world fortune or interest led me, I might end up like them. But lest this seem the product of a mere delirium, however fleeting, I should say that my sense of unease was not in itself powerful enough to feed that fear, illusion, fantasy or identification, fomented or sustained by nothing more substantial than a mutual wandering of Oxford's streets, a mutual inactivity. There was something else feeding that baneful fear, that sombre illusion, that gloomy fantasy, that nebulous identification, even if it too were tenuous.

Following Alan Marriott's first visit, a year or more before, I had added to the list of rare authors whose books I sought a writer unknown to me until then, John Gawsworth, whose name Marriott had mentioned and jotted down before saying goodbye and for whom Machen had written a foreword. As Marriott himself had said, Gawsworth's works were very difficult to find. Of his scant œuvre nothing remains in print in England but, little by little, with patience, luck and the progressive sharpening of my hunter's eye, I began to find the odd short work by him in my second-hand bookshops in Oxford and London, until after some months I came across a copy of his book *Backwaters*, published in 1932, signed moreover by the author himself. Inscribed in ink on the flyleaf was: "John Gawsworth, written aged 19½". There was also a correction in his own hand on the first page of text (after the name "Frankenstein" he had added the word "monster", in order to make it clear that he was referring to the creature and not its creator). It was precisely that feeling of temporal vertigo or of time annihilated that is provoked by holding in one's hands objects that still speak in muffled tones of their past that first aroused my curiosity, and from that moment I initiated a research project that for many months proved distinctly unfruitful, so elusive and unfamiliar was, then as now, the figure of Terence Ian Fytton Armstrong, the real name of the man who usually signed himself Gawsworth.

Nevertheless, despite the fact that his writings were at most either passable or bizarre and made both his fall into oblivion and the lack of reprints of his book quite understandable (there was no book, nor it seemed a single article on Gawsworth and he scarcely rated a mention in even the most voluminous and exhaustive dictionaries and encyclopaedias of literature), as I tried to find out more, my interest in him grew not so much because of his rather indifferent literary output but because of the strange man behind it. The first thing I discovered were the dates of his birth and death, 1912 and 1970 and then, on a page of otherwise mute bibliography, the fact that several of his works had been published (at times under different pseudonyms, each one more absurd than the last) in such exotic and improbable places for a London-born writer as Tunis, Cairo, Sétif (Algeria), Calcutta and Vasto (Italy). His poetic works, collected between 1943 and 1945 in six volumes – mostly printed in India – enjoy the peculiarity of having a missing fourth volume, or so it would seem, for it was never published despite having a title (*Farewell to Youth*). It simply does not exist. His prose work – mainly short literary essays and horror stories – can be found scattered throughout obscure anthologies of the 1930s or saw the light of day – if I may use that expression – in private or limited editions.

And yet in his day Gawsworth had been a personality, a literary golden boy. An indefatigable promoter of neo-Elizabethan poetic movements in reaction against Eliot and Auden and other innovators, when he was still little more than an adolescent, he knew and was friendly with many of the most important writers of the time; he took an interest in the work of the famous avant-garde writer and painter Wyndham Lewis and of that of the even more famous T. E. Lawrence, he of Arabia; he received literary honours and in his day was the youngest elected member to the Royal Society of Literature; he knew Yeats as an old man as well as the then dying Hardy; he was the protégé and later the protector of Machen, of the famous sexologist Havelock Ellis, of the three Powys brothers, of the formerly (and once more to some extent) well-known novelist and short-story writer M. P. Shiel. I could discover little more until, at last, in a dictionary specialising in the literature of horror and the fantastic, I found out something else. In 1947, on the death of his mentor, Shiel, Gawsworth was named not only literary executor but also heir to the kingdom of Redonda, a tiny island in the Antilles of which, in 1880, in a colourful naval ceremony, Shiel himself (a native of the neighbouring and much larger island of Montserrat) had been crowned king at the age of fifteen at the express wish of the previous monarch, his father a local Methodist preacher and shipowner, who had bought the island years before, although no one knows exactly from whom since the only inhabitants at the time were the boobies who populated it and a handful of men who spent their lives collecting the birds' excrement in order to make guano. Gawsworth was never able to take possession of his kingdom, for the British government – with whose Colonial Office both the two Shiels and he remained in tireless dispute – were attracted by the aluminium phosphate the island produced and decided to annex his territory in order to prevent the United States from making it theirs. Despite that, Gawsworth signed some of his writings as Juan I, King of Redonda (king in exile, one supposes) and bestowed dukedoms on or named as admirals several admired writers or friends, amongst them Machen (whose title he confirmed), Dylan Thomas, Henry Miller and Lawrence Durrell. The entry in that dictionary, after failing to explain all this (I only learned the details some time later), ended thus: "Despite his large circle of friends, Gawsworth became something of an anachronism. He lived his last years in Italy, returning to London to live on charity, sleeping on park benches and dying forgotten and penniless in a hospital."

That this man, garlanded with honours, who could have been king, and who, one day in 1932, in an access of undoubted enthusiasm and youthful pride, signed the copy of *Backwaters* I have in my possession should end his life like that could not but shock me – even more than the stories of the violinist and the theologian – even though many other writers and better men than he have suffered a similar fate. I could not help but wonder what had happened in between, betwixt his precocious, frenetic literary and social beginnings and that anachronistic, tattered end; what could have happened during (perhaps) those visits and journeys of his to half the world, always publishing, always writing, wherever he was? Why Tunis, Cairo, Algeria, Calcutta, Italy? Just because of the war? Just because of some obscure and never recorded diplomatic activity? And why did he publish nothing after 1954 – sixteen years before his pathetic end – a man who had done so in places and at times when finding a publisher must have verged on the heroic or the suicidal? What became of the – at least – two women whom he married? Why, at the age of fifty-eight, that denouement more fitting in a burnt-out old man, why that Oxford beggar's death?

The Alabasters, with their vast but prudent fund of learning, had been unable to find anything by him and knew nothing about him, although they did know of the existence of a man in Nashville (Tennessee) who, all those thousands of miles away, had almost all the information available on Gawsworth. Troubled by some baseless fear, I delayed putting pen to paper but, when I finally did so, this individual referred me to a short text by Lawrence Durrell on the man who had been both his first literary mentor and his great boyhood friend, providing me also with some supplementary facts: Gawsworth had had three wives, of whom two were known to be dead; his downfall had been alcohol; his hobby – I read with apprehension and a touch of horror – was the morbid searching out and collecting of books. "Morbid", that was the term the man from Nashville unhesitatingly plumped for.

Durrell's text presents Gawsworth or Armstrong as an expert and highly gifted hunter of unobtainable literary gems, with an extraordinarily fine eye as a bibliophile and an even finer bibliographical memory, who, when he was just beginning, used to start the day buying for three pence some rare and expensive edition his eye picked out and recognised amongst all the dross in the bargain boxes set out in Charing Cross Road, only to resell it straight away for several pounds a few yards from where he'd found it, to Rota in Covent Garden or to some classy dealer in Cecil Court. As well as his collection of exquisite books (many of which he kept and treasured), he owned manuscripts and autograph letters from admired or renowned authors and all kinds of objects that had once belonged to illustrious person- ages, bought at the auctions he frequented with money acquired who knows how: a hat worn by Dickens, a pen of Thackeray's, a ring that had belonged to Lady Hamilton, Shiel's ashes. A large part of his energies went into pestering the Royal Society of Literature and other institutions, whose most elderly mem- bers he plagued with persistent and vexatious literary and mon- etary comparisons, trying to wheedle out of them pensions and other financial aid for old, once-successful writers with money problems or quite simply living in penury: Machen and Shiel were two such beneficiaries. But Durrell also recounts that some six years before (since the text dates from 1962, when Gawsworth was still alive and a man of fifty, he must have seen him when he was forty-four yet, curiously, Durrell, who was the same age, talks of him as one would of those who have already departed this life or who are, at any rate, on their way out) he saw him for the last time in Shaftesbury Avenue, pushing a pram. A Victorian pram of vast proportions, notes Durrell. On seeing the eccentric Bohemian, the "Real Writer", who had astonished the young Durrell (fresh up from Bournemouth) with how much he knew, and had introduced him to the literary world and to London's night haunts, Durrell thought that life must finally have closed in on Gawsworth (that, as Durrell says, life had caught up with him at last) and he now had children, three sets of twins to judge by the vast perambulator. But when he approached to view the infant Gawsworth or Armstrong or Prince of Redonda he was expecting to find beneath the hood, he discovered to his relief that it contained only a pile of empty beer bottles that Gawsworth was on his way to return, get his money back and replace with full bottles. The Duque de Cervantes Pequeña (that was Durrell's title) accompanied his exiled king, who never once visited his kingdom, watched him refill the pram with new bottles and, after drinking one with him to the memory of Browne or Marlowe or some other classical author whose birthday it was that day, saw him disappear, calmly pushing his alcoholic pram, into the dark, perhaps just as I sometimes do as evening falls on the Retiro Park in Madrid, except that my pram contains my son – this new son – whom I still barely know and who is sure to survive his parents.

Later, I saw a photo of Gawsworth which, as far as one can tell, more or less coincides with the physical description Durrell gives of him: ". . . of medium height and somewhat pale and lean; he had a broken nose which gave his face a touch of Villonesque foxiness. His eyes were brown and bright, his sense of humour unimpaired by his literary privations."[1] In that one

[1] Lawrence Durrell: *Spirit of Place* (Faber & Faber).

photo I've seen he's wearing his RAF uniform and has an unlit cigarette in his mouth. The collar of his shirt is a bit loose and the knot of his tie seems rather too tight, although that was the fashion at the time. He's wearing some kind of insignia. His forehead is marked by clear, horizontal lines and beneath his eyes he has, not bags, but small folds of skin, and his eyes look out with a mixture of mischief or fun, dreaminess or nostalgia. It's a generous face. His gaze is clear. His ear striking. He looks as if he might be listening to someone or something. He's probably in Cairo, doubtless in the Middle East, or perhaps not, perhaps he's in North Africa, in French Barbary and it's 1941 or 42 or 43, possibly not long before being transferred from the Spitfire Squadron to the Desert Air Force of the Eighth Army. That cigarette would not last long. He must be about thirty, although he looks older, a bit older. Because I know he's dead, I see in the photo the face of a dead man. He reminds me a little of Cromer-Blake, although the latter's hair was prematurely grey and the moustache he allowed to grow for a few weeks before shaving it off again and remaining moustacheless for a further few weeks was also grey or at least threaded with silver, while Gawsworth's (his moustache and hair) are dark. The ironic look in the eyes is very similar, but Gawsworth's eyes are more affable, there's no trace in them of sarcasm or anger, nor even a glimmer or a hint. His uniform needs pressing.

I've also seen a photo of his death mask. When they made it, he had just renounced both age and the passage of time but only the moment before he had been a man of fifty-eight. The mask was made by Hugh Olaff de Wet on 23 September 1970, the same day or the day after Gawsworth died in London, in the Borough of Kensington where he was born. His old friend from Cairo, Sir John Waller, donated it to the Poetry Society, but such courtesies came posthumously or simply too late. The man who was John Gawsworth and Terence Ian Fytton Armstrong and Orpheus Scrannel and Juan I, King of Redonda and

also at times plain Fytton Armstrong or J.G. or even just G, has his eyes closed now, with no expression visible in them. The folds of skin beneath them are now unmistakably bags, the lines across his forehead are muddled (his cranium grown convex) and he looks as though he had thicker eyelashes now, perhaps just the effect of those sealed shut eyelids. His hair appears white – but that might just be because the mask is of white plaster – and his hairline has receded a little since the 1940s, the boundary of his youth, since the war against the Afrika Korps. The

moustache looks thicker but more flaccid, it's simultaneously bristling and limp, that of a retired soldier grown weary now of grooming it. His nose has grown larger and broader, his cheeks flabby, the whole face is puffy, with a false plumpness, with despair. He has a double chin. There's not the slightest doubt that he is dead.

But it was with this final face that he must have wandered the streets of London, wearing one of those coats or jackets that beggars always manage to obtain. He would have brandished bottles and, to the incredulity of his peers, pointed out in the bargain boxes of Charing Cross Road books he had written but that he could not now afford to buy. He would tell them about Tunis and Algeria, about Italy and Egypt and about India. Much to their amusement, he would declare himself to be the King of Redonda. It was with that face that he slept on benches in parks or went into hospital, as that dictionary specialising in the literature of horror and the fantastic said, and with that face he would perhaps have been incapable of holding out the hand that had wielded a pen and piloted aircraft. Perhaps, as British beggars tend to be, he was proud and fierce, brutal and shy, menacing and arrogant, and would not have known how to beg for himself. He was doubtless a drunk and at the end of his life he did not spend years in Italy but only a few weeks in the Abruzzi, in Vasto, for one final drunken binge of which I know nothing. "One final drunken binge", that's what it said in the letter from the man in Nashville with whom I've had no further contact. There was no Gawsworth to save Gawsworth, no promising, enthusiastic young writer to try to bring him to his senses and make him write again (perhaps because there's nothing very admirable about his work and no one wanted him to continue), to go and beg and wheedle a pension out of the Royal Society of Literature, of which he was once an elected member, the youngest ever. There was no woman, of the many he had known, to curb his wanderings or accompany him on them. That's what I believe, anyway. Where do those British-born or colonial women live? Where did they find their last resting place? Where are the books he collected, the books he could identify at a glance in the midst of the labyrinths of chaotic, dusty shelves, as I could on the shelves in the Alabasters' shop and in all those other booksellers in Oxford and London? (With my gloved hands and agile fingers that barely brushed the spines they ran over more quickly than my own eyes, like a pianist playing a *glissando*, I too always found what I was looking for, to the point where I often had the feeling that it was the books themselves that looked for and found me.) They had probably returned to that world where all or at least the vast majority of books return, to the patient, silent world of second-hand books, which they leave only temporarily. Perhaps one of the books I own, besides *Backwaters*, also passed through Gawsworth's hands, was bought and immediately sold again to buy breakfast or a drink or – as one of the elect few – remained for years perhaps in his library or accompanied him to Algeria and Egypt, to Tunis and Italy and even India, and was even a witness to battles. Perhaps one of the sinister beggars whom I passed and repassed daily in Oxford, those I could identify and those I feared and those in whom my insubstantial, temporary wandering state made me see myself as if in some (possibly not so distant) future reflection, had once owned books. Perhaps one of them had actually written books or taught at Oxford or had a mistress-mother who was at first clinging and then (when she was more mother than mistress) evasive and unscrupulous, or perhaps he came from a country in the south – with a barrel organ that decided his fate when he lost it, perhaps on disembarking in the port of Liverpool – a country to which he had not yet forgotten that one cannot always go back.

I REPEATEDLY ASKED and ask myself these questions not out of compassion for Gawsworth, who was after all nothing but a man with a false name whom I never met and whose writings – which are all the visible remains I have of him, that and the photographs of him alive and dead – mean little to me, but out of a curiosity tinged with superstition, convinced as I came to be on certain endless evenings in that spring or Trinity term, that ultimately I would meet the same fate.

The English spring is a peculiarly distressing season to those already in distress for, as everyone knows, it is then that the days grow inordinately long but not in the way they can and do in Madrid or Barcelona at the approach and arrival of summer. Here in Madrid, as the days grow endless, the light undergoes continuous subtle changes and thus communicates the fact that time is moving on, whilst in England – and further north – for hours on end absolutely nothing changes. In Oxford the light remains the same from half past five, when the shops close and teachers and students return home and when the cessation of all visible activity first obliges you to notice it, until gone nine o'clock when the sun sets – as suddenly, apart from a lingering distant, ghostly glow, as if turned off by a switch – the signal for those who have determined on going out that night to rush impatiently into the streets. That same unchanging light, that accentuation of the static quality or stability of the place, makes you feel as if you yourself were at a standstill and even less a part of the world and the passing of time than, as I have explained before, one normally feels there. If, as was of course my own case, dining in daylight hours was out of the question, then there is simply nothing to do during those motionless hours. And so you wait. And wait. Shut up in your house, watching television or listening to the radio, deprived even of the possibility of visiting bookshops where you could feel active, useful and safe, you wait for the longed-for night to fall, for that warm, suspended light to fade, for the weak wheel of the world to start rolling again and for the stillness to end. While the sun hangs paralysed in the sky, the dons are resting in their rooms at college or dining at high table and the students have closeted themselves at home in order to prepare for exams or to go out on the town as soon as they're sure night has come. During the long, fixed hours of those spring evenings in Oxford, the city belongs more than ever to the Gawsworths of the day. The city is theirs for the duration of that long, false, endless twilight, intruded upon only by the town's innumerable bells (the city's religious past) loudly calling the faithful to Evensong. The beggars have no homes to go to, no colleges to return to, nor are they ever guests at high table. I doubt if they rush to the churches either, when these latter call them. They continue to roam the streets, though finding them empty of passers-by in broad daylight so bewilders them that they slacken their pace and even stop for a moment to kick a can, stamp on a newspaper caught up by the breeze and thereby kill a little more of the time they've been killing ever since they woke.

I used to hide at home to wait for night to come, on Wednesdays trying to find a Spanish radio station that might be re-broadcasting an international match involving Real Madrid, constantly tempted to pick up the phone and call Clare Bayes at home, where she would be seated at the foot of the child Eric's bed to give him his supper, watching children's television with him or distracting him with some new game. I was sorely tempted every evening but in order not to succumb and in order to withstand the hours of sameness and inertia – the flat hours and flat days – I would sometimes shave for a second time and get ready to go out into the streets, just like the livelier and more dissolute undergraduates and lecturers, to mingle with other people as night fell. Sometimes I dined at that pleasant restaurant Brown's, close by my pyramid house, with its attractive mini-skirted waitresses, and at others, just to recapture the feeling of being back on the Continent and not marooned on the islands, at one of the French restaurants in which the town abounds, or I would even force myself to make frequent appearances at the ghastly high tables I had not attended since the first months of my stay in Oxford, a year and a half ago now. I tried those of various colleges, some already known to me, others as yet unvisited, in the faint hope, too, of once more finding Clare Bayes amongst the hosts (at All Souls or Exeter, her husband's college) or amongst the guests (at Keble, Oriel, Balliol, Pembroke, Christ Church, each more tedious than the last: the high table at Christ Church being at once the most sumptuous and the most boring). But it was too much of an effort and did not suffice to banish the sense of numbness, or to escape my obsession with Gawsworth and his fate.

During those evenings, after about half past eight or nine o'clock, I started going to a discotheque near the Apollo Theatre, which, on the whole, was more popular amongst the people who worked in Oxford's factories and offices (for Oxford, unlike Cambridge, does have industries and workers and people who don't belong to the university) than amongst its gowned inhabitants of whom I was one. I say "on the whole" because I did get a few surprises there. Each night I found myself confronted by a scene straight out of the seventies, a very English seventies that had not impinged in the least on the outside world. It was all very provincial and domestic from the strident music (well, it was a discotheque) to the decor with its vaguely Moorish motifs, from the (green and pink) lights that played over the dance floor to the clothes of the dancers, which could be dated with extraordinary accuracy. Nevertheless, to judge by the crowds that filled it every night, from who knows what bright evening hour onwards, the discotheque enjoyed enormous success. I remember there being an unusually high number of fat girls in miniskirts and permed hair: there were whole tables occupied solely by large groups of large girls (the term "fat tart" springs to mind) who sat in groups of six or seven, constantly elbowing one another and chewing gum, sunk into the sofas beneath their own weight and torpor, unashamedly displaying a row of vast thighs (in a state of constant friction) and even glimpses of their knickers. And then there were the young Oxfordshire dandies (from the local towns of Banbury and Charlbury, Witney and Eynsham) who gloried in the sort of cheap, loud taste in clothes one only finds in the south of England. It was clear that those rustic, effeminate young men hated the fat tarts and that the fat tarts hated the affected yokels. They never mixed but when they did meet in the queues for the toilets or found themselves dancing in the same spot in the crowd or on the dance floor, they'd exchange looks which were either scornful (on the part of the young men) or mocking (on the part of the young women) and shoot knowing glances at their sympathisers seated at the tables or standing at the bar, openly pointing out their risible adversary with an ostentatious wave of a thumb, thin or plump as the case might be. Although those two species were generally speaking the predominant clientele in the Moorish-style discotheque, it was not unusual to see students there (especially the more refined ones who are likelier to have a weakness and a taste for the plebeian) and even certain dons – the bachelors amongst them – disguised as youths. Most I knew only by sight, distantly enough to avoid the need to greet each other in such circumstances, but on my fourth night there I spotted my own boss Aidan Kavanagh, the author of the horror blockbusters, performing a wild, loose-jointed dance out of time with the music. I couldn't see very well – amongst all those bodies lit by that feverish light – and at first I thought with some alarm that his usually sober, anodyne clothes had given way to an eau de nil waistcoat and little else, but I realised immediately afterwards – with only a modicum of relief – that only his arms were in fact bare albeit to the shoulder: that is, he was as usual wearing a shirt and tie (apricot and bottle green respectively) beneath the eau de nil waistcoat, but it was a strange kind of shirt comprising only a shirt front. I wondered if he wore the same model to the faculty and determined to have a good look next time I met him in the Taylorian to ascertain whether or not his shirtsleeves were visible beneath his jacket cuffs. (As well as being a writer of horror novels under a pen name, he was also, after all, an international expert on my country's Golden Age.) Anyway, his disco wear did allow me to discover that he was extremely hirsute on his (upper) extremities, which were crowned within by dense jungles of underarm hair upon which I had no option but to gaze, since a combination of his frenzied dancing and the lack of space demanded that he keep his arms raised at all times. He saw me from a distance and, far from blushing and trying to hide, came over to me at the bar, still dancing, and greeted me in the most jovial and hospitable manner. He was dragging by the hand (still raised in the air) a fat girl who tottered and shoved her way towards me, smiling broadly. Kavanagh had to shout to make himself heard so that, like Alan Marriott, he spoke in clipped phrases.

"Fancy meeting you here! I thought you didn't like these places! It's taken you nearly *two* years to discover it!" And he thrust two fingers into my face. "This is the best disco there is! The only really fun place in town!" He glanced back at the dance floor with a look of genuine appreciation and satisfaction: the dance floor resembled nothing so much as an operatic mutiny. "I come almost every night! Well, every night I can! I know everybody here!" And with one strong arm, bare to the shoulder, he made a sweeping gesture taking in the whole club. He took a long swig of his drink. "Would you like to meet someone? I can introduce you to anyone you want! Have a good look around! If you see someone you fancy, tell me and I'll introduce you, no problem! There are dozens of girls," he lowered his voice, "dozens. Ah, let me introduce you to Jessie. Jessie!" He hesitated a moment. "This is my friend Emilio! He's Spanish too!"

"What?"

"Emilio!" Kavanagh jabbed at me with a finger that only just missed poking my eye out. "Another Spanish friend."

"Buona sera!" shouted Jessie above the racket.

"Ciao!" I said so as not to disappoint her. She was wreathed in smiles.

"It's best they don't know our real names," Kavanagh whispered in my ear in Spanish. "It's perfectly safe, they only come to Oxford at night. She thinks I work in the motor industry. I've promised her an Aston Martin."

"Do they still make them?"

"I don't know, but she swallowed it." And he added, in English this time: "Come and join us. We're sharing a table. There are simply dozens of girls," he murmured, "dozens. Del Diestro's here too. He arrived today."

Kavanagh grabbed me by the arm and, with me in tow, gyrated his way over to one of the fat tarts' tables, which was all too familiar to me and which, on the previous three nights, I had rejected with an emphatic scorn worthy almost of one of the effeminate, rustic young men from Oxfordshire (Jessie followed, treading on her own toes and shoving people to one side). Sure enough there was the celebrated Professor del Diestro, in his own opinion the greatest and youngest world expert on Cervantes, and known in Madrid (according to how much one disliked him) either as Dexterous Diestro or Dastardly Diestro who, at the Department's invitation, was due to deliver a magisterial and suitably dexterous lecture the following morning. I recognised him from his photographs. The professor, a distinguished, opinionated man in his forties, wearing his designer shirt and his bald pate with equal panache ("A distinguished Spanish professor," I thought when I saw him, amazed and suddenly understanding the reason for his success), was slobbering over and allowing himself to be slobbered over by one of the fattest of the fat girls. It should be said that the sole aim of all these girls, as well as of the rural dandies, the bachelor dons and the more refined students (and my aim too, although at the time I neither realised it nor, therefore, admitted it to myself) was to make the acquaintance of some complete stranger (which was not that easy given the fixed and repetitious nature of the clientele), one's principal goals then being to ask a few superficial questions, to respond untruthfully to the other person's equally superficial questions, to offer them some chewing gum (dancing wasn't obligatory), to kiss them after a decent interval had elapsed and perhaps – depending on the progress and quality of the kisses and on whether one of you had a condom handy – to have a quick fuck in the toilets or in the darker recesses of the discotheque itself or a slower fuck at home later.

Professor del Diestro was already well enough advanced in acquainting himself with his chosen stranger to permit himself a momentary interruption in order to exchange a few cordial words with me, and Kavanagh, after introducing me to the five or six girls present, forced me down on to the sofa in between two of them. I remained lodged between four of the aforementioned thighs (two per girl) and in the sudden knowledge or acknowledgement of the fact that I would not be leaving the discotheque alone that night, I immediately looked to my left and right in order to weigh them up, with the intention of choosing the more lightweight of the two. I perceived at once that the girl on my right was not really fat, only plump, and in that case – or so I calculated – I would after a while find it possible to feel a certain sexual interest in her. Knowing beforehand the degree of intimacy I would eventually enjoy with them, her features seemed most agreeable and her leonine curls were stupendous, although they had very much the appearance of having only come into existence a few hours before (it was Thursday). I turned my back on the other girl, who was undeniably and undisguisedly fat, and with the one who wasn't quite so fat, Muriel by name, I began an intermittent and rather desultory conversation conducted at shouting pitch of which I recall almost nothing (it was after all just a formality), only that she said she lived in a tiny village – or was it a farm? – near Wychwood Forest, between the Rivers Windrush and Evenlode. But that might well have been false, as false as the names Emilio and Muriel. Like her companions she chewed gum incessantly and, although she wasn't as full of smiles as young Jessie, who had returned to the floor to dance with Kavanagh and thus secure her Aston Martin, she seemed quite jolly and pleased to meet me and didn't move away when my legs, covered by their lightweight trousers, rubbed against hers, so preeminently abundant but covered only by finemesh tights; more than that, she tended to transform that contact (unavoidable given the cramped conditions) into a deliberate pressure. I did nothing to avoid it either and at one point she put her hand on my knee in familiar fashion and yelled dutifully into my ear:

"D'you want some gum?"

"No, thanks," I said, and only after I'd said it, did I realise that it might not be the most appropriate of answers in a place so steeped in the seventies.

For a while she said nothing more. She remained rather pensive, her chewing gum stationary somewhere on her palate or gums. Then she said, as if it were the most natural thing in the world:

"I'm only chewing it in case we kiss. But if you like I'll take it out now."

(I still had time to notice the strong taste of mint in that round, absorbent mouth.) (Mine no doubt tasted of tobacco.)

When I left the disco with her an hour later I met with two gazes, one multiple and the other singular, although I can't be sure of the latter. Several dandies whom I was already beginning to know by sight were regarding me critically, or rather classifying me as deserving of great scorn for my choice of companion; and a few yards ahead, at the very door of the discotheque, I think I passed (she was just going in and if it was her I think I received from her no more than a lightning glance) the girl from Didcot station who was later also, though more briefly, the girl from Broad Street – near Trinity and Blackwell's – who was walking along one windy afternoon with a friend who would not let her stop. As on that second occasion (if it *was* her on this third occasion: it was over a year since I'd seen her, and I'd seen so little of her before) I only realised it was her – or thought I did – once we'd turned our backs on each other. I turned round, as I had the time before, but she did not, not on this occasion when I cannot be sure it was her. I just saw her back disappearing into the discotheque along with the man accompanying her, whose presence I had not even noticed when face to face, or at most for a second, with the two of us men walking along and trying perhaps to avoid bumping into each other. From behind he looked like Edward Bayes. But that was impossible: Edward Bayes would be seated at the foot of the child Eric's bed, reading him a story that Clare Bayes would have stayed behind to hear. It was too late now to confirm anything or to go back; as on that other occasion in Broad Street someone was tugging at a sleeve, only this time it was mine. It wasn't windy outside this time, but Muriel, who was already out in the street, was growing impatient.

Back at my house, on the second floor, she went back to

chewing gum for a while, combining it with the gin (a generous Spanish measure) that I served her in a glass with ice and tonic. I wasn't in the least drunk but she was somewhat drunk, or at least gave that impression (I don't know how much she'd had to drink before we were introduced). But it was only later, upstairs, on the third floor, when we were undressed and in my bed, that I really began to think about Clare and to miss her again or, rather (because it wasn't exactly that I missed her), to realise with surprise and some perplexity that this girl verging on plumpness, with her pleasant face and curly hair was not Clare. Fidelity (the name given to the constancy and exclusivity with which one particular sex organ penetrates or is penetrated by another particular sex organ, or abstains from being penetrated by or from penetrating others) is mainly the product of habit, as is its so-called opposite, infidelity (the name given to inconstancy and change, and the enjoyment of more than one sex organ: the literal promiscuity in which, as far as I knew, Cromer-Blake engaged, as too did Muriel and possibly Kavanagh and Professor del Diestro). When, over a period of time, one has become used to one mouth, other mouths seem incongruous, and present one with all kinds of difficulties: the teeth are either too big or too small, the lips too thin or too fleshy, the tongue moves at the wrong time or just lies there, rigid, as if it were flesh and bone not muscle; the smell of the more odorous regions (the groins, the sex, the armpits) is disconcerting as is the disparate intensity of the embrace, the anaesthetic contact of skin on skin, the sour sweat on thighs (due perhaps to remorse), the ill-fitting shapes, the unfamiliar colours that disturb the light in the room, the size and moistness of the orifice. One's hands cannot take in the different size of breasts that perhaps overflow or seem to withdraw from them or, when they grow hard, have a rather rough nipple that almost rasps when one licks it. The new body is not manageable (no new body is) and there is always a certain feeling of reserve or uncertainty about the order in which one should kiss different parts of the body or the force with which one should kiss or squeeze or bite and explore with one's fingers or about the effect it will have on the other if one stops and looks at those parts, withdraws all contact and simply devotes oneself to looking. "I have my cock in her mouth," I thought at a certain point, and I thought it in exactly those words which are the only appropriate ones when you are expressing in words or thoughts what you're doing with the thing they designate (when the designated object is active), even more so when one scarcely knows the other body and especially if the words refer to parts of one's own body and not to those of the other person, about which one is always more respectful and for which one would seek and use euphemisms, metaphors or more neutral terms. "I have my cock in her mouth or rather she has her mouth round my cock, since it was her mouth that sought it out. I have my cock in her mouth," I thought, "and it isn't like other times, all those other times in recent months. As I noticed the first time I kissed her, Muriel's mouth is absorbent but not as spacious and liquid as Clare's mouth. It lacks saliva and space. She has nice lips but they're a bit thin and immobile or, rather, not immobile exactly (for they're not, I'm very aware of them moving) but lacking in flexibility, rigid. (They're like taut ribbons.) While I have my cock in her mouth I can see her breasts, they are large and white with very dark nipples, unlike Clare's, whose breasts combine their two colours very subtly, like the transition from apricot to hazel. On my thighs (that gently squeeze her breasts, though not enough to hurt them) I notice the texture of those white breasts, and although this girl is very young, her breasts are soft, like new Plasticine that has been neither kneaded into shape nor hardened by use and by the prints left on it by the child who plays with it. I used to play with Plasticine a lot, but I don't know if the child Eric does. It's incomprehensible to me that I should have my cock in her mouth (who would have thought it only three hours ago, when I was killing time before leaving here, shaving and keeping one eye on the evening light and she, perhaps, was standing in front of the bathroom mirror in her house or farm in Wychwood Forest, putting on her lipstick and thinking about a stranger, applying it to those lips now so bare of colour). It's far less comprehensible than the fact of placing my cock, as I very soon will, inside her vagina, for – or so one hopes – there will have been nothing else in her vagina in the last few hours whilst in her mouth there's been chewing gum and gin and tonic and ice and cigarette smoke and peanuts and my tongue and laughter and also words that I did not listen to. (The mouth is always full, abundance itself.) Now she doesn't drink or smoke or chew or laugh or speak, because my cock is in her mouth and that keeps it occupied, there's no room for anything else. I don't speak either, but I'm not occupied in doing anything, I'm thinking."

And then, a little later, still upstairs on the third floor of my pyramid house, still naked on my bed, I started thinking again and I thought: "With her I don't miss what I always miss when I go to bed with Clare, that is, that my cock has no eye, no vision, no gaze, that can see as it approaches or enters her vagina. I want neither to see it nor her. But I do see her. Although I like Muriel and she's helping me pass the night in the best possible way, I don't know her. I know she's not Clare but one of the plump girls from the discotheque near the Apollo Theatre. I have various ways of knowing this: her size and height (she's slightly shorter); her thighs, which do not separate quite enough (perhaps because of all that flesh; will the thighs of the even fatter girl Professor del Diestro was kissing be capable of separating at all? Perhaps the Professor is grappling with the problem even at this very moment); also her bones, which are scarcely detectable beneath their generous padding (I can feel her pubis but not her hipbones); and her sighs, which are timid and shamefaced (I'm a stranger and, when she half-opens her eyes, she looks not at me but at the blank wall above the pillow on which I lean). But more than anything else I know it because of the different smell. It's not the smell of Clare Bayes nor even that of Oxford or London or Didcot station, but perhaps it's the smell of Wychwood Forest, of the Rivers Windrush and Evenlode, between which Muriel lives and grew up, as Clare Bayes lived and grew up by the River Yamuna or Jumna with its trifling songs, its rudimentary barges and its iron bridge from which unhappy lovers threw themselves. She's panting now but she's thinking too. She's thinking perhaps about how I smell, and thinking it's a foreign smell, the smell of a Continental, a passionate (reputedly), hot-blooded southerner. My blood can be hot or lukewarm or cold. How must I smell to her? The English don't use much cologne and I do, Trussardi, and that might be the biggest difference, a complete novelty; maybe the Italian cologne I always bring back with me from Madrid is the only thing she can sense as regards smells. She may not like it, she may love it, the only way I can find out is by asking, later, because now she's absorbed in herself (she's thinking only of herself). Perhaps she hasn't even noticed it, perhaps she can't smell a thing, she doesn't seem to have a cold, though there are a lot of colds about in this English spring, this furtive winter, not to mention allergies to pollen, hay fever they call it, young people are the main sufferers, although Clare – who is not so young any more – also gets it. Last spring she sneezed several times whilst lying in the very place now occupied by this girl from Wychwood Forest, a forest that no longer exists, apart from a few remnants, it was cut down and flattened last century, but it's difficult to give up a name, names tell you a lot. Muriel doesn't look as if she's about to sneeze, if she did, given our relative positions, I'd get the full blast of it and it would really shake me, I would notice a violent thrust that is absent now. Perhaps she's getting tired, she did have quite a lot to drink. The room was cold when I left the house but now it's hot because Muriel's body is hot, whilst Clare's body is only luke-warm and that of the girl on the train from London might well have been cold, to judge by her appearance. I think I saw her but it doesn't matter to me now, I haven't thought of her for over a year and for over a year now I've thought about Clare nearly all the time, although we've never seen each other with the urgency of people with plans for a future together. But if I'd waited tonight – if I hadn't met the smiling Jessie and Professor del Diestro – perhaps I would have ended up leaving the discotheque with that girl from the London train and – though not yet, because it would only have happened later, but soon enough – she would be here (if it was her, even if it wasn't her), in place of Clare and in place of this plump girl Muriel – who is neither fat nor a tart – who says she lives between the Rivers Windrush and Evenlode in what was Wychwood Forest. She's the one here, on my bed, on top of me – hiding or containing my cock – because Clare won't see me in these weeks she's reserved for the child Eric who's come home ill, and because it was her and no one else – it was her and not the girl from Didcot station – who was chewing gum in case we kissed. And she was right to do so because we're kissing now."

"Tell me you want me," said Muriel, for a moment separating her round, absorbent mouth from mine.

I heard the bells of the neighbouring church of St Aloysius (or those of St Giles'?) still awake or perhaps they never sleep. There was no need to look at the clock on the bedside table, no need to hurry or start to worry about where I'd hidden her high heels and where her scattered clothes had been left around the room. It was darkest night. "I want you," I said. "I want you," I thought, and stopped thinking once I had thought it.

DURING MY TWO YEARS in Oxford, I think the only real friend I made was Cromer-Blake. I found many of the dons insufferable (the economist Halliwell was but a pale example, and I remember with particular pain Dr Leigh-Justice, our department's expert on the Indies, a punctilious, monkish type with an abdomen broader than his chest and a habit of wearing trousers that were too tight and too short, so that every time he sat down, he revealed a vast expanse of calf, and with whom I had to give the most horribly prim, methodical classes) and, as I mentioned before, I often put myself in Edward Bayes' place and came to appreciate the good humour and nonchalance of the reviled and determinedly frivolous Kavanagh (reviled because he was easy-going and Irish and wrote novels), and to respond – in equal measure, although he would never have known it, since I was even more reserved than he was and never revealed my feelings – to the affection shown me, perhaps despite himself and without realising it, by Alec Dewar, the Inquisitor, a.k.a. the Butcher or the Ripper. And above all I came to admire the literary scholar, Professor Emeritus (he was almost emeritus in my first year and definitively so in my second) Toby Rylands, whose friendship Cromer-Blake had rather rashly recommended to me. For one couldn't exactly have a friendship with Toby Rylands, not because he wasn't welcoming and kind or pleased to receive anyone who came to see him, but because he was too wise and truthful a man (I mean that what he said always had the ring of truth), and it wasn't easy to feel anything for him other than open admiration mingled perhaps with a little fear (what the English call "awe").

I used to visit him at his home in a leafy suburb east of the city, outside of the university area proper, a luxurious house (he was a man of private means, not dependent on any academic usufruct) with an extensive garden that sloped down to one of the wildest and most magical parts of the River Cherwell as it flows through Oxford and its outskirts. I used to go there on Sundays, the day of the week that – especially in my second year there when he was retired – must have cost him, like me, the greatest effort and most taxed his enthusiasm if he was to get through it all and thus move on into the next day (like the beggars he was killing time). He was a very big man, really massively built, who still had a full head of hair: his statuesque head was crowned with wavy, white locks like whipped cream. He dressed well though, with more affectation than elegance (bow ties and yellow sweaters, rather in the American style, or the way undergraduates used to dress) and he was regarded as a future – indeed almost extant – never to be forgotten glory of the university, for in Oxford, as in all places where people perpetuate themselves by some form of endogeny, individuals only achieve glory when they begin to relinquish their posts and become passive beings about to be shuffled off to make room for their legatees. He and Ellmann, Wind and Gombrich, Berlin and Haskell, are or were all destined to end up as members of the same race: the retrospectively desired. Toby Rylands had received every conceivable honour and now lived a solitary life. Other honours, ever less sincere, arrived by every post; he tended his garden; he fed the swans that spent certain seasons on his stretch of the river; and he wrote another essay on *A Sentimental Journey*. He didn't much like talking about his past life, about his little-known origins (it was said that he hadn't always been English but South African, but if that were true he retained not a trace of an accent), nor about his youth, and still

128

less about the dim distant past of his supposed activities – as was whispered in Oxford – with MI5, a department of Britain's famous Secret Service. Though probably true, the link between that particular government department, so familiar from novels and films, and the two principal English universities is too much of a cliché to be very interesting. The juiciest stories told by his acolytes, disciples and ex-subordinates were, in fact, those to do with his war activities: it seems he was never at the front (at any front), but was engaged instead on strange, confused missions (always involving huge sums of money), vaguely related to espionage or the pursuit of politically neutral figures in places as far from the heart of the conflict as Martinique, Haiti, Brazil and the islands of Tristan da Cunha. I never learned much about his past; very few people did, I imagine. His most impressive feature were his slightly slanting eyes, each a different colour: his right eye the colour of olive oil and his left that of pale ashes, so that if you looked at him from the right you saw a keen expression with a hint of cruelty – the eye of an eagle or perhaps a cat – while if you looked at him from the left the expression was grave, meditative and honest, as only that of northern races can be – the eye of a dog or perhaps a horse, which of all animals seem the most honest; and if you looked at him from the front, then you encountered two gazes, or rather two colours with but a single gaze which was simultaneously cruel and honest, meditative and keen. From a distance the olive-oil colour predominated (and assimilated the other colour) and when on certain Sunday mornings the sun shone directly into his eyes, illuminating them, the density of the iris dissolved and the tone lightened to become the colour of the sherry in the glass he sometimes had in his hand. As for his laugh, that was certainly Toby Rylands' most diabolical feature: his lips barely moved, or rather only enough – though exclusively on the horizontal plane – so that beneath his fleshy, purple upper lip some small, slightly pointed but very even teeth appeared, possibly some private dentist's excellent copy of those lost with the advancing years. But it was the audible rather than the visual aspect of that short, dry laugh that lent it its demoniacal quality because it resembled none of the more usual written onomatopoeic forms of laughter, all of which depend on the aspiration of the consonant (for example, "ha, ha, ha" or "heh, heh, heh" or "hee, hee, hee" or even, in other languages, "ah, ah, ah"). When he laughed, the consonant was indubitably plosive, the clearest of alveolar English "t"s. "Ta, ta, ta", that was what Professor Toby Rylands' spine-chilling laugh sounded like. "Ta, ta, ta. Ta, ta, ta."

On the day I remember best and the day on which he seemed most prodigal with truths, he laughed only at the start of our conversation, while we were talking about my colleagues, who were no longer quite *his* colleagues, and he was recounting to me through hints and insinuations some humorous diplomatic or university anecdote, never touching on the war or on espionage. By then (Hilary term of my second year, so it was between January and March, in fact it was the end of March, just before Clare decided to turn her back on me for four weeks) we all knew that Cromer-Blake was ill and, we supposed, seriously so. He'd still said nothing to us about it (he'd been vague, not to say evasive), not to me, to Clare, to Ted, to his brother Roger who lived in London, not even to his revered Rylands, though perhaps to Bruce, the person closest to him for some years, with whom he maintained what used to be called (especially in French) a loving friendship, in which there was neither progress nor withdrawal, neither exclusivity nor constancy. (Bruce was a mechanic from Vauxhall and had no dealings with us: Bruce was his other world.) But Cromer-Blake's visits to the hospital in London – his admissions to hospital were sporadic, each stay there shorter than the last – and the worrying mutability of his appearance – you were as likely to find him back to his normal weight, his skin glowing, as emaciated and ashen – made us worry with that unspoken concern, very common in England or at least more common there than elsewhere, which has at its root a degree of stoicism and also – in contrast – the optimistic belief that things only exist if you talk about them or, which comes to the same thing, that they don't prosper and will ultimately dissolve into nothing if you deny them verbal existence. None of the people close to Cromer-Blake talked about him (about his now visible illness) behind his back, and in his presence we limited ourselves, if he looked well, to forgetting immediately how he'd looked before – as something we gaily condemned to the realm of what has been – and, when he looked bad, to recalling how he looked before that – silently and intensely longing for the return of what once was.

Cromer-Blake was one of Toby Rylands' dearest and most enduring friends – the loyal scion, the pupil who had not withdrawn once he reached maturity – and for that very reason Rylands was the last person I would have expected to mention the nameless disease, whatever it was. That's why that Sunday, when the two of us were standing in his garden at the river's edge, watching the waters flowing easily by without the illusory resistance put up by the vegetation that in other seasons seemed to push against it as it passed and contributed greatly to the sylvan look of that part of the river, I was surprised when he mentioned Cromer-Blake and his health or lack of it. He was throwing pieces of stale bread into the water to see if the swans who occasionally lived around there would appear.

"They're not coming out today," he said. "They may well have moved on; they spend the whole year going up and down the river. Sometimes when they disappear for weeks on end, they've actually only been a few yards away downstream. It's odd, though, because I saw them yesterday. This is one of their favourite haunts because of the royal treatment they get here. But then there's always got to be a first day for their disappearances. Otherwise, they wouldn't be disappearances, would they?" And he continued throwing crumbs, smaller now, into the cinnamon-coloured water. "But it doesn't matter, some ducks have arrived instead, look, there's one of them looking for food. And another, and another. They're so greedy, they don't turn their noses up at anything." And then almost without a pause, he added: "Have you seen Cromer-Blake lately?"

"Yes," I said, "two or three days ago. I had coffee with him in his rooms."

The literary scholar was standing on my left, so I caught the keen gaze of his olive-oil eye, which, seen from the side, looked larger than the grey eye. It was some moments before he spoke again.

"How did he look?"

"Very well. He looks much better since he got back from Italy. I suppose you know he took a week's leave. I covered some of his classes for him. He needed a rest, to get away from here. It seems to have done him good."

"So, it did him good, eh?" And the eye shifted fleetingly to the right (towards me) then immediately back again to the ducks. "I knew he'd taken some leave and that he was in Tuscany, but I only found out from others. He hasn't come to see me once since he came back, what, two or three weeks ago now. He hasn't called either." He fell silent, then turned to look me full in the face, as if that were necessary in order to speak of deeply held feelings or to confess to weaknesses. "I find that strange and, I don't see why I shouldn't admit it, it hurts me too. I thought it might be because he looks ill. But you say he looks well. That's what you said, isn't it?"

"Yes, he was very bad in February and now, by comparison, I think he looks much better."

With some difficulty, owing to his immense weight which was due entirely to his size and build, not to fat, Toby Rylands bent down to pick up more bread from the wicker basket he'd placed on the ground. Four more ducks had appeared.

"I wonder when he'll stop coming here altogether. Which day will be the last time I'll see him, unless of course that day has already been and gone without my realising it, in February. That was the last time I saw him, in mid-February. Perhaps he doesn't intend coming here again. Just look at those ducks."

I looked at the ducks. Then I said: "I don't know why you say that, Toby. You know perfectly well that no one enjoys your company more than Cromer-Blake does. I don't believe he'll ever stop coming to see you, not of his own free will anyway."

Professor Rylands abruptly emptied the rest of the bread from the basket into the water, without bothering to break it up, crumbs and whole slices of bread floating together for a moment on the muddy waters of the Cherwell, then he threw the basket down – it remained upside down on the grass, like a peasant woman's hat, with the handle as the bow – and went back to the small table on which Mrs Berry, his housekeeper, had placed sherry and olives. Although it was only the end of March, it wasn't cold outside if you kept out of the wind. It was a Sunday of sunny spells interrupted by sparse cloud and the sun wasn't to be wasted, because it helped you to get through this day and move on into the next. Rylands was wearing one of his bow ties and a thick yellow sweater with a wool-lined windcheater on top; the sweater was longer than the windcheater and formed a band of yellow below the brown leather. He sat down on an upholstered chair and drank a glass of sherry. He downed it slowly in one, then refilled it.

"Of his own free will," he said, "of his own free will. To whom does the will of a sick man belong? To the man or to the illness? When one is ill, just as when one is old or troubled, things are done half with one's own will and half with someone else's in exactly equal measure. What isn't always clear is who the part of the will that isn't ours belongs to. To the illness, to the doctors, to the medicine, to the sense of unease, to the passing years, to times long dead? To the person we no longer are and who carried off our will when he left? Cromer-Blake is no longer the person we think he is, or the person he used to be, he's not the same. And unless I'm very much mistaken, he will become less and less himself until he simply ceases to be altogether. Until he's neither one nor the other, not even some third or fourth party, but no one, no one."

"I don't understand you, Toby," I said, hoping that the phrase in itself would dissuade him from continuing and that he would stop. Hoping that he would say something like "Let's drop the subject," or "Forget it," or "Pay no attention to me" or "It doesn't matter." But he said none of those things.

"Don't you?" And Toby Rylands stroked his thick, white, well-combed hair, the way Cromer-Blake did (perhaps he'd copied the gesture from Toby Rylands), except that Rylands' hair was much whiter. "He must have been very blond once," I thought, just before he said what I (as a superstitious *madrileño* or an anglicised stoic) would have preferred him not to say: "Listen," he said, "listen to me. Cromer-Blake is going to die. I don't know what's wrong with him and he's not going to tell us, assuming that is that he knows for certain or hasn't managed to put it out of his mind, at least for short periods, through sheer irresponsibility and will power. I don't know what's wrong with him but I'm sure it's something very serious and I doubt that he'll last much longer. He was in a dreadful state when he came here last in February, he looked as good as dead to me. He looked like a dead man. You say he's better now, and you can't imagine how pleased I am to hear that; I only hope it lasts. But he's been better before only to get worse again shortly afterwards, and that last time I saw him he had the look of a condemned man. It broke my heart to see him like that and, when he dies, it will break even more, but it's best to get oneself used to the idea. Yet it hurts me that he doesn't come and see me because of that, while he still can. The reason he doesn't e has nothing to do with his appearance, I mean, whether

134

he looks all right or at death's door; it isn't because he doesn't want to distress me, or because he doesn't want me to see him when he's really bad. I know the real reason he doesn't come and see me. Before, I was an old man (though I've looked like an old man for a long time now; you've only known me a year, but I've always looked older than my age), I was inoffensive, even useful, my digressions were instructive and my malicious comments and jokes amusing, and I still had things to teach him, even though I don't know much about your particular field, Spanish literature – I still don't understand why he didn't study English literature, so much more varied. But that isn't how he sees me any more, now I'm the mirror in which he's afraid he'll see himself reflected. His end is near and so is mine. I remind him of death because, of all his friends, I'm the one nearest to it. I'm the illness he's suffering from, I'm old age, I'm decay, my will has gone wandering off somewhere on its own, like his, only I've had time to get used to that, and getting used to losing one's will means learning to hold on to it as long as possible, to delay its departure, to do as little harm as possible. He hasn't had that chance, and he can't be blamed for it. I shouldn't blame him for avoiding me, poor boy. Although you'd never know it, he must be utterly bewildered. He must be terrified. And unable to believe what's happening to him."

Toby Rylands drank a little more sherry and half-closed his eyes whose opposing colours, now that the sun shone full in his face, blended into one. He picked up an olive.

"I don't know," I said. "I'm not sure you're right, Toby. It would never occur to me to think of you as being near death, as you put it, nor in anyway reminiscent of or like some kind of harbinger of death. You're not even that old, and you're in excellent health. You look wonderful. Last year your classes were packed out and if you hadn't been due for retirement this year they would have gone on being packed out. No burned-out old has-been could fill a lecture hall in Oxford. Maybe Cromer-Blake simply hasn't had time to come and see you."

"Ta, ta, ta," Toby Rylands exploded into bitter laughter. Then he said: "I know what you're thinking, you think I'm just saying all this because of that, because I had to retire. You think that's why I suddenly see myself as being near death and other such nonsense just because I'm not doing anything and spend too much time thinking, alone in this garden by the river, that eternal image of the passing of time. Or at home . . . with the silent Mrs Berry. That's pure platitude and anyway I'm not inactive. I'm writing the best book ever on Laurence Sterne and his *Sentimental Journey*. You may say that doesn't matter much or matters only to a select few, and isn't much of a reason to feel that people still . . . expect something from me, but it matters to me. I love that book and it matters to me that it should be properly understood and that I should understand it as I study it one more time and explain it to you all: I expect something from myself, you see. No, it's got nothing to do with retirement, nothing at all. For years now I've watched the days pass with that slow downhill feeling we all experience sooner or later. It doesn't depend on age really, some people experience it even when they're children; some children already have a sense of it. I felt it early on, some forty years ago, and I've spent all these years letting death approach and it still frightens me. The worst thing about the approach of death isn't death itself and what it may or may not bring, it's the fact that one can no longer fantasise about things still to come. I've had what is commonly referred to as a full life, or at least that's how I regard it. I haven't had a wife or children, but I've had a life spent in the acquisition of knowledge and that was what mattered to me. I've always gone on finding out more than I knew before and it doesn't matter where you put that 'before', even if it's only today or tomorrow. But I've had a full life, too, in the sense that my life's been crammed with action and the unexpected. As

136

you'll no doubt have heard, I was a spy, like so many of us here, because that, too, can form part of our duties; but I was never just a penpusher like that fellow Dewar in your department, indeed like most of them. I worked out in the field. I've been in India and in the Caribbean and in Russia and I've done things I could never tell anyone about now, because they would seem so ridiculous no one would believe me. I know only too well that what one can and cannot tell depends very much on the timing, because I've dedicated my life to identifying just that in literature and I've learned to identify it in life too. I shouldn't be telling you any of this now, but the fact is that in my life I've run mortal risks and betrayed men I had nothing against personally. I've saved a few people's lives too, but sent others to the firing squad or the gallows. I've lived in Africa, in the most unlikely places, in other eras, and I watched the suicide of the person I loved." Toby Rylands stopped short, as if he'd been led to make that last remark by his memory, not by his will (the will he held on to so hard but which was now no longer his alone); he recovered at once, doubtless because to continue was the best way of undoing it. "Oh, and battles, I've been a witness to those too. My head is full of bright, shining memories, frightening and thrilling, and anyone seeing all of them together, as I can, would think they were more than enough, that the simple remembering of so many fascinating facts and people would fill one's old age more intensely than most people's present. But it isn't like that, and even now, when it seems that nothing unexpected is ever going to happen to me again, I mean, *nothing*; when the life I lead here in my garden and my house with the all too predictable Mrs Berry seems designed to guarantee that nothing happens; when anything surprising or stimulating seems over and done with, out of the question, I can assure you that I do still want more: *I want everything*; and what gets me out of bed in the mornings continues to be the expectation of what might happen, all unannounced. I'm always expecting the unexpected, and I still fantasise about what might still be, as I did when I was sixteen and left Africa for the first time and absolutely anything was possible because when you know nothing there's room for all kinds of knowledge. I've been slowly wearing away at my ignorance and, as I said, I've always kept on learning. But that ignorance is still so vast that even today, at seventy, leading this quiet life, I still cherish the hope of being able to embrace everything and experience everything, the unknown and the known, yes, even things I've known before. There's as intense a longing for the known as there is for the unknown because one just can't accept that certain things won't repeat themselves. That's why I sometimes envy Will, the old porter at the Taylorian, who must be twenty years older than me and yet, now that he's let go of his will for good, he lives in a constant state of joy and anxiety travelling back and forth in time throughout his life, both enjoying great new surprises and repeating things he knew before. That's a way of not renouncing anything, even though he's unaware of it and even though his life spent in his porter's lodge has been anything but full from my point of view. But my point of view is irrelevant here, as is anyone else's. Knowing that some time one will have to give up everything, whatever that everything is, that's what's unbearable, for everyone, it's all we've ever known, all we've ever been used to. I can understand someone who regrets dying simply because they won't be able to read their favourite author's next book, or see a new film starring an actress they admire, or drink another glass of beer, or do today's crossword, or continue to follow a particular television series, or because they won't know who won this year's FA Cup. I can understand that perfectly well. It isn't only that anything still might happen, some unimaginable piece of news, a sudden turn-around in events, the most extraordinary experiences, discoveries, the world turned upside down . . . The other side of time, its dark back. It's also because so many things hold us here. There must be dozens of things holding Cromer-Blake here. As many as there must be for you or for me or for Mrs Berry." And Toby Rylands pointed towards the house. "Imagine it, poor chap. But it seems that when it comes to his final hour, I won't be one of those things."

Professor Rylands fell silent. He zipped up his windcheater still further, concealing the upper part of his yellow sweater completely – though not the part below the jacket, where a band of yellow was still visible – and put two olives into his mouth at once.

"You wouldn't like me to have a word with him, would you?"

"Absolutely not." And his eyes, one the colour of olive oil and the other of pale ashes, the eye of the eagle and the eye of the horse, flashed me an imperious look. The literary scholar finished his second glass of sherry and, patting his enormous, convex chest, got up and took a few steps towards the river. He picked up the wicker basket he'd thrown on to the grass and, carrying it on his arm, like a wandering seller of yore who's sold all his merchandise, turned towards the house and shouted: "Mrs Berry! Mrs Berry!" And when Mrs Berry appeared at the window of the kitchen, where she would already be preparing a light lunch for which I would not stay, he said to her, raising his voice as I would later at the discotheque in order to speak to Muriel from Wychwood Forest: "Mrs Berry, would you be so kind as to bring me some biscuits, some stale ones!" Then he turned and looked at me (no longer imperious) and shook the basket in the air, laughing: "Ta, ta, ta. Let's see if that will tempt those lazy swans out of hiding."

EVERYTHING THAT HAPPENS to us, everything that we say or hear, everything we see with our own eyes or we articulate with our tongue, everything that enters through our ears, everything we are witness to (and for which we are therefore partly responsible) must find a recipient outside ourselves and we choose that recipient according to what happens or what we are told or even according to what we ourselves say. Each thing must be told to someone – though not necessarily always to the same person – and each thing will undergo a selection process, the way someone out shopping one afternoon might scrutinise, set aside and assess presents for the season to come. Everything must be told at least once although, as Rylands had determined, with all the weight of literary authority behind him, it must be told when the time is right or, which comes to the same thing, at the right moment, and sometimes, if you fail to recognise that right moment or deliberately let it pass, there will never again be another. That moment presents itself sometimes (usually) in an immediate unequivocal and urgent manner, but equally often, as is the case with the greatest secrets, it presents itself only dimly and only after decades have passed. But no secret can or should be kept from everybody for ever; once in its life, once in the lifetime of that secret, it is obliged to find at least one recipient.

That's why some people reappear in our lives.

That's why we always condemn ourselves by what we say. Not by what we do.

I knew that if the little time left to Cromer-Blake allowed, I would end up telling him what Toby Rylands' imperious look had forbidden me to, although it could not, strictly speaking, be considered a secret. But since at that point it was clear that I should keep silent (at least for the time being) and that those particular words would take some while to reach the ears of their chosen and most vital recipient, I immediately, albeit temporarily, forgot everything that Rylands had said about Cromer-Blake and his prolonged absence from the house by the Cherwell (by that I mean that I didn't agonise about it or keep turning it over in my mind). On the other hand, I couldn't forget those hints – not to say statements: the most explicit I'd heard him make – about his own past. But as regards those, the most I could do was communicate them to Cromer-Blake, to Clare, to the two principal figures in my life in the city of Oxford (paternal and maternal, fraternal and desired, respectively) apart from Rylands himself (who was the third figure, that of teacher, and the one most resigned to his role). I say "the most I could do" because whilst they could share and be the external recipient of those revelations, neither they nor anyone else (think of all the dead that must haunt Toby Rylands' clear shining recollections) could clarify them or fill in the details of that story of betrayal and espionage, of obscure origins and of battles, of men whom Rylands had either condemned or saved, still less the story of the person he had loved and who, even *while* being loved, had committed suicide before his eyes – although immediately I began to doubt what he had said, to doubt my own ability to understand English, to think that I must have misheard and misunderstood.

The first chance I had, I talked to Cromer-Blake about it but, since he paid the story scant attention, he seemed to be in agreement with Rylands as regards consigning it all to the past and to oblivion. He just didn't seem interested. (Perhaps he really was no longer the person we thought he was or the person he used to be, because, as I've said before and as he himself said,

Cromer-Blake reacted to everything with either irony or fury, but never with a total lack of curiosity, never with indifference.)

He merely asked distractedly and sceptically (and there is no greater proof of indifference than scepticism): "Are you sure that's what he said?" "I think so," I said, "although now I'm not so sure. But I couldn't have invented it, it just wouldn't even occur to me to invent a story like that." And he said: "Who knows, maybe it happened during the war, maybe a friend of his, a soldier, got so frightened before a battle that he preferred to put an end to the uncertainty once and for all by shooting himself. It happened a lot, even more so in the trenches in the First World War, which were full of adolescents, hardly more than children some of them." "Is Rylands homosexual, then?" I asked. "Oh, I couldn't really say, he's been on his own for as long as I've known him and, anyway, he'd never talk about such ungentlemanly things. He seems more asexual than anything else." But that seemed to me to contradict something he'd said one night after high table when the port was flowing. "Anyway, you should know by now that, unless I'm told otherwise, when people talk about those they love or desire, I just automatically assume they mean men. Perhaps he said it to shock you. He talks very little about his past, but he likes it to be known that it was very intense. I wouldn't give any importance to the remark, always assuming that *is* what he said, of course." And he went on to ask me about my relationship with Clare, of which at the time – at the end of Hilary term in my second and last year – there remained, in principle at least, a further term of life and to which he'd become so used that, when he was in the mood, he acted as confidant to us both. At that time – like a gossipy midwife – he showed an all-consuming interest in other people's sexual or romantic relationships (as if he himself had renounced all such things), a passion for the present moment and for the most everyday of problems, as if the future no longer counted (as neither, it seemed, did the past). "Anyway who cares what happened forty years ago?" And spreading his hands eloquently, he crossed his long legs and adopted the pose (his gown like a fall of black water) that was the mainstay of the aesthetic disguise of his appearance. That was all he had to say about the revelation for which I had chosen him as recipient.

As for Clare, I told her (in full) about my talk with Rylands. But she seemed interested mainly, or rather exclusively, in the latter's sadness at Cromer-Blake's prolonged absence, and it was only by pleading with her that I managed to dissuade her from intervening in the matter, as she intended, and to convince her not to tell the truant pupil of his master's complaints. At that time her son Eric was safe and well in Bristol and, true to her expansive self, she was still interested in everything, still lingering in the present moment. However, when I brought the conversation round to Rylands' past and to that highly melo-dramatic episode involving one particular death with but a single witness, her whole expression changed (in fact, she grim-aced) and she grew impatient, as if she were no longer prepared to talk or even hear me talk about it. Perhaps the most surprising thing, though, was that she didn't seem particularly shocked or surprised by the revelation Rylands had made to me only half voluntarily. She seemed rather annoyed.

"Who knows," she said, just as Cromer-Blake had said that same morning, "maybe it's true." We were at my house, upstairs, that is, in my bed, when it was still exclusively my place and hers. As so often happened there, due to the poor heating and our haste, we were both still fully clothed, talking hurriedly before she left to walk back to her house – beneath the fickle, mellow moon, her face to the wind – her cheeks still rather too flushed for our safety and my liking. We talked hurriedly because it gave us the illusion of time slowing down, of having fitted more into the brief time available to us and not just passionate outpourings, which no longer (nor had they for a long time) sufficed, for they were no longer the only thing we found interesting about each other. So she said: "Who knows, maybe it's true," and tried to change the subject. But I persisted: "Who would know about it? I'd like to find out more about that story of Toby's but I daren't ask him." "What difference does it make to you?" she said. "Perhaps he was in love with some woman who was very ill and in so much pain that she took her own life. That sort of thing doesn't just happen in films, you know." "So Toby Rylands is heterosexual?" I asked. "Oh, I don't know, I suppose so," she said, "I just assume that all men are unless, like Cromer-Blake, they tell me otherwise. Why shouldn't he be? Just because he's never married? I've never heard anyone say he wasn't." "Well, no, neither have I," I replied, adding: "But if the story's true and whatever the facts of the matter are, doesn't it strike you as terrible and worth finding out about?" It was then that she grew impatient and pulled a face and looked annoyed. She lit a cigarette so carelessly and irritably that a spark fell on to one leg (as usual when she didn't take her skirt off, she was sitting with it pulled up to reveal her tights, her strong, slim legs and her shoeless feet); she swore and got up from the bed, rubbing her leg. She took three steps across the room to the window, looked out mechanically – gazing out perhaps at the church of St Aloysius and the wind in the streets – then walked another five steps to the opposite wall, leaned one hand on it, jangling her many bracelets, tapped her cigarette from which no ash fell – it had already fallen on to the carpet – and said: "Yes, of course it strikes me as terrible, and that's exactly why I don't want to find out any more about it, or talk about it, far less try to imagine what horrors might have happened to Toby in some foreign land thirty years back. Who cares what happened so far away, all that time ago?" "Forty years," I said, "I got the impression that he was talking about something that happened forty years ago. And he didn't say anything about it being in a foreign country, although it might well have been." "A lot of things happened thirty years ago, too, you know," said Clare Bayes, inhaling and exhaling her first puff of smoke, for until that moment she'd simply held the lit cigarette in her hand, gesturing with it but not actually smoking it, "and twenty years ago, and ten years ago, and even yesterday, here and in other countries, horrible things have always happened, I don't see why we have to talk about them now, nor why we should try to find out about those we had the good fortune not to know about, about those things we didn't witness and that we had nothing to do with. What we've seen with our own eyes is quite enough, don't you think?" And she began to gather up her files and bags and to put on her jacket to go, even though the bells of Oxford had last intervened only a short time before to tell us that we still had another quarter of an hour and even though the alarm clock on the bedside table had not yet gone off. There were no long drawn-out farewells on this occasion (no grief for the ending of time) despite the fact that the Easter holidays were about to begin and we wouldn't see each other now until term started again. That was the day she left behind the pair of earrings I still have in my possession.

During my conversation with the literary scholar, a third figure had emerged – again only in passing – who had also attracted my attention and intrigued me and about whom it *would* be possible to find out more, although it could prove difficult to check the facts thoroughly. I saw in that figure the anti-Rylands, and more than that, the anti-Gawsworth, the opposite of what I feared I might become, an opposite that frightened me just as much, because I saw in him the perfect usufructuary, one who would take no personal profit from his life nor leave the slightest trace of having been, one on whom nothing and nobody (nobody's fate) would depend apart from himself (with neither prolongation nor shadow) and his activities, or rather, his routine and his purely imaginary life (like the life of many writers). I saw the dead soul of the city of Oxford, a soul, which, once it had disappeared, not even Will would think to resuscitate, just for a moment, with a cheery wave from his post in the porter's lodge. And although I wouldn't remain in Oxford and would never become one of its true souls, it occurred to me that that anti-Rylands, that anti-Gawsworth, might suffer a worse fate than the real Rylands and Gawsworth, for he would never find a recipient or a repository for his secrets (the only true secret being that of the living dead, not of the dead).

However, I thought about none of that on the Monday or the Tuesday or even the Wednesday following the Sunday of my visit to Rylands (it had been on Tuesday that I had made Cromer-Blake and Clare my chosen recipients, to little effect); but on Thursday, the last teaching day before the Easter vacation, I made a brief visit to Blackwell's in the empty hour between two of my classes and instead of going straight up to the third floor, as I usually did, in order to investigate and poke around in the old and second-hand book department, I stopped at the second floor to have a look round the foreign or Continental department, where translations lived cheek by jowl with the imported texts in their various original languages. And there, from a distance, I spotted Alec Dewar (a.k.a. the Ripper) standing near the Russian section. He was consulting – or rather, given the time he was taking, reading – a thick volume the cover of which bore, as I at once noticed, Kiprenski's widely reproduced portrait of Pushkin. At first I gave the matter no further thought since Dewar was a specialist in the nineteenth-century literature of Spain and Portugal (he was an enthusiastic devotee of Zorrilla and Castelo Branco and was always ardently recommending me to read a long poem by the former entitled either *The Clock* or *The Clocks*, I can't remember which because I never followed his advice) and I assumed him to be motivated by some devious piece of comparative literary manoeuvring. So absorbed was he in his reading of *Onegin* or *The Stone Guest* (probably the latter, I thought, so as to compare it with

Zorrilla's *Don Juan Tenorio*) that he didn't even notice me and I felt disinclined to greet him outside the confines of the Taylorian and during what was for me a break from work. But when I walked by him on my way to the Italian section, some way beyond, and passed unnoticed right behind him, I caught a glimpse of the text he had before him and saw that it was in Cyrillic. I moved a little further off in order to observe him more carefully. He stood for some time reading the Russian tome, turning the pages as he read on, and when, after some minutes had passed, I again approached him stealthily from behind, overwhelmed by curiosity and so close I almost brushed against his back – whilst he, so engrossed was he in his reading, remained immersed in the deep thoughts of one or other of those rakes – I had ample opportunity to look over his shoulder and see that the book was not even an English edition containing footnotes or an introduction in English which might explain the time he was taking to read it, but a genuine Soviet edition of which there were quite a number in that section. It was then that I heard a tenuous whisper, only perceptible from close to and only when the nearby cash register was silent: the Butcher was muttering the words he read under his breath, a faint smile playing about his huge mouth, and he was delicately, rhythmically (he was utterly enraptured) beating time to the perfect cadence of those iambic stanzas. There was no doubt about it, the Inquisitor wasn't merely reading Russian, he was positively revelling in it.

I wouldn't have found it in the least odd to come upon Rook in that ecstatic pose (Rook, the old and much-vaunted friend of Vladimir Vladimirovich, eminent and eternally future translator of *Anna Karenin* just as Vladimir was the eminent and eternally past translator of *Onegin*). But the Ripper was already fluent in the two languages to which he dedicated himself professionally and it seemed excessive that he should also know Russian and with a mastery that allowed him to give fluent voice (in public) to its finest lines. And it was then that I remembered that Rylands, in what he would have later regarded as that Sunday morning's indiscretions, had spoken of Dewar as being a spy. "A penpusher," he'd called him and therefore, in his eyes, despicable; but he had not then shown the slightest hesitation in attributing that role to him and in associating him with that line of work, which, besides, was so very Oxonian. That was something I could ask Rylands himself about, but, as it happened, I didn't do so until after Easter, in Trinity term, when the child Eric was ill and Clare did not care to see me, when I spent more time than usual walking the streets of Oxford in company with the beggars with whom I was becoming increasingly obsessed and when I was about to make my first visit to the discotheque near the Apollo Theatre, only then did I again visit the house by the Cherwell and dare to question him about Dewar. And although he tried at first to avoid the question ("Oh, yes, that Dewar, from your department. Did I really say that?"), thus demonstrating the reaction I could have expected had I thrown discretion and respect to the winds and asked more about his own intense past, when I persisted, he finally agreed to tell me, sprinkling the tale with his customary digressions and malevolent details: "Oh, yes, Dewar," he said, "from Brasenose, isn't he? Or is it Magdalen? Anyway, unless I'm very much mistaken, he'll be retired by now. How old is he, fifty-something? Impossible to tell his age really, he's been middle-aged for as long as I've known him; but the Service tends to retire its men early, even the penpushers, unless they're irreplaceable. I should think if they haven't done so already, they're certainly about to retire him; he's a very nervy chap, a chronic insomniac, and that will have taken its toll on him. Did you know that the only way he can get to sleep is by having white noise playing in the background? White noise, that's what they call it. It's some kind of apparatus, an acoustic device that emits a strange uniform sound which isn't really a sound at all,

148

something almost inaudible but nonetheless there, enough to suppress all other sounds and pave the way to sleep. Never fails apparently. They use it a lot in the Secret Service, which is full of people who can't sleep. Dewar must have got hold of one in exchange for some extra jobs he did. He showed it to me once, at his college . . . I still can't for the life of me remember if it was Magdalen or Brasenose . . . It looked like a small radio, but I couldn't hear a thing. Dewar. Yes. He never really did that much and, as far as I know, he never went on any mission outside England. Mainly deskwork, nothing more, his only merit being his mastery of Russian. He's a man with a real gift for languages, he learned Russian as a student just as he learned Spanish and then Portuguese later on to complete his chosen speciality. I think he speaks several other languages too . . . He could have chosen to study Slavic languages but if he had, the Service would never have used him. Anyone in a Slavic languages department is automatically ruled out for any work to do with the Soviets. They'd be no good at all. Dewar's been called to London sometimes to monitor broadcasts, translate recordings, interpret nuances of intonation or explain the finer details of some particularly complicated or dense texts, but never anything more than that. Oh and, yes, he had another function, but the work involved was only ever sporadic . . . he may still do it . . . When any ballet dancer or athlete or chess player or opera singer (the kind of Soviet citizen most likely to defect) escapes and crosses over to the West when they're on tour or involved in some competition in this country . . . although it happens less all the time now, not just because of the changes taking place over there, but because they all prefer to try America first before making up their minds . . . anyway, before giving any help or offering asylum to the athlete or singer in question (a boring lot, terribly mechanical), they'd call in Dewar to interrogate them in Russian or, rather, to have him translate the questions of the inspector in charge and give his opinion as to the fugitive's sincerity, good intentions and general level of disaffection towards the Soviet Union. Not one of those escapees . . . there were never many, I seem to recall that the last one who passed through his hands, it must be a couple of years ago now, was a dancer who later, as they all do, carved out a brilliant career for himself in America . . . Not one of those escapees could walk our streets freely without Dewar's say so. That doesn't mean his agreement was definitive or absolute, he's never been that important; it was more that he gave his personal opinion based on tone, voice inflections and the manner in which the interrogated party replied in his own language, something there was no way the inspector conducting the interrogation could possibly gauge. People used to say that Dewar enjoyed (or enjoys) himself so much in his role as vicarious interrogator that he was suspected of taking certain liberties, I mean, it was noticed that he seemed to take an unnecessarily long time over his translations of the questions into Russian and people got the impression he was departing from the questions he was given and adding others off his own bat, though he didn't of course translate into English the answers given to the latter. Naturally the inspectors could never prove the existence of these private and parallel dialogues held between Dewar and the defectors and (assuming they did exist) still less what the devil Dewar was talking about with those would-be ex-Soviet subjects. For that they would have needed a second interpreter to supervise Dewar's translations both ways, checking and retranslating everything the latter heard and said in Russian. Too complicated and with the added risk of setting off an endless chain of interpreters, ta, ta, ta . . . One thing is certain, Dewar took his work very seriously and his participation in an interrogation always meant the defectors would be kept sitting in their chair for hours on end, being badgered by questions that were possibly personal or even intimate, maybe even rude. I imagine he milked to maximum effect the few occasions he got to exercise this second role. Given the life he leads, he must have considered it all a great adventure."

I think my affection for the Butcher was born at that moment. It isn't that his work as a spy was so very brilliant or even admirable, but every time I recalled Rylands revealing to me Dewar's polyglot, inquisitorial skills (now I understood the origin of one of his nicknames), I couldn't help imagining him in a poky room in some London police station, shut up for hours with a frightened, newly escaped ballet dancer, who, during those hours – Dewar's fierce, unctuous face being his first and rather unappealing impression of the so-called free world – must have had serious doubts about whether he'd really cast off the yoke of oppression or whether it was just about to be placed once more upon his shoulders. Perhaps the Inquisitor flexed and bounced his leg up and down as he used to do in class in front of the undergraduates, his huge voracious shoes resting – for lack of a desk – alternately on the arms of the chair occupied by the dancer or perhaps, higher up, on the back of the chair or worse still, on the seat itself, the toe of his shoe (so broad and square) placed like a wedge between the defector's thighs, a threat to the dancer's skintight trousers or tights (I couldn't help thinking that the dancers would have fled immediately after their London performance, after all the ovations and bouquets and would, therefore, still have been wearing their ballet costumes – with that look of Robin Hood they all have – and perhaps a purple, *fin de siècle* cloak wrapped about them against the cold). "So you've decided to defect, have you?" the Ripper would perhaps start off by saying, treating them initially with some scorn and incredulity, addressing them with the informal "you" just to bring them down a peg or two; and with a rapid movement he would make as if to strike him, although he would never actually touch him (except for the lightest of taps with the toe of his lace-up shoes). "And how do we know you're not just pretending and that you're not planning an attempt against the Crown?" (the Butcher is pompous). "And don't give me the usual sob story," he would add off his own bat, "I know it by heart: there's no future for you there, you're bored, you feel like prisoners in shackles" (he would throw in that word to impress them with the breadth of his vocabulary), "you can't grow as a dancer; all you artists really want is more glitter, more show, more adulation and more money, isn't that right?" "It's not just that," the dancer might venture to reply, not yet quite having lost the impulse or élan of the dance. But the Inquisitor would be in no mood to be bamboozled by someone in a Peter Pan outfit (the security of the state, or at least one of its many fronts, lies in his hands, for several hours he is in charge and everything depends on his sagacity and cunning if a potential dancer-cum-spy is to be unmasked). Dewar lifts one ostentatiously shod foot, with a gesture that could as easily presage a doubt as a kick, but on that first occasion he lets it fall to the floor again, loud enough for the thud to resonate in martial tones around the room. Someone is dependent on him, although only for that one day. "Well, well, well," he says with the self-important smile I know so well from our shared classes, having seen him bestow it on the students he most hates. The Ripper flexes one leg and his foot wanders over the interviewee's chair (once even carelessly pinching his flesh) while he translates the inspector's questions and slips in his own: "What made you decide to ask for asylum in the United Kingdom? (And tell me, comrade, this love of dancing, has it been with you since childhood?)" Or perhaps: "Did you plan your escape on your own or was some other member of your ballet company involved? (And tell me, comrade, in the Soviet Union is it difficult to find work in an established company? Do you have to perform any sexual favours in order to get in?)" Or perhaps: "Do you know person-ally any of the leaders of the Communist Party or any member of the government in your country? (And tell me, comrade, what do you think of English audiences? Real connoisseurs, eh? Well, there's a long tradition of ballet here. How did the performance go today? And how many hours a day do you rehearse? Do you have to follow any kind of diet? Which is more strenuous, classical or modern ballet? Nijinsky or Nureyev? That's a lovely purple cloak. And how do you get on with your partner? Any jealousies?)" The Inquisitor never lacks for questions. After his dull life in the city of Oxford everything interests him, and he'll be able to dine out on what he gleans from the lips of this Russian at various future high tables, astounding his fellow guests with his insider knowledge of the life and habits of Russian dancers. And so the Butcher always ends up giving the defector the all-clear, although that may only be because after all those questions and answers he almost regards him as a friend, or at least as an acquaintance, whom he probably knows as well as all those stern, haughty dons in the city where he teaches and whom he's observed over the course of decades, without ever finding out a thing about them. And the Ripper, after the long hours of questioning, turns to the inspector and gives him an affirmative nod. "Bring me some vodka," he orders the police constable, who has accompanied them in the shadows, keeping close to the wall and remaining utterly silent throughout the interrogation. "Perhaps the gentleman would care to drink a toast to his new life. *Za zdorovie!*"

It's possible that, as Rylands suggested, poor Dewar felt bold and important on those occasions; it's also possible, to judge by his Pushkinian trance, that he missed having the opportunity to exercise his extraordinary knowledge of Russian; and, lastly, it's possible that he took advantage of the circumstances in order to spend some pleasant hours in conversation with someone who couldn't flee from him, who had no option but to answer his questions, someone whom he could ask openly about the customs and landscapes of his native land, about family and friends, about his childhood, about his political opinions and religious beliefs, about his loves and his sexual preferences, about his career and the obligations this imposed on him, or about the Moscow metro and Russian cuisine and the prices in the market and the current state of Russian literature (much to his irritation and offence this last remained unanswered – none of the chessplayers, dancers or gymnasts kept abreast of contemporary literature: "You must answer all my questions! Do you understand? Every one of them must be answered!").

That dark, bony, formal man, with the enormous mouth, pointed skull and high cheekbones of an Otto Dix portrait (and possessed of a child-like ferocity, by which I mean one that could only frighten those barely out of childhood, namely his students, who faithfully, year after year, passed on to the new crop of undergraduates his three bloodcurdling nicknames), no doubt took as much pleasure in the Russian language as he did in Spanish words of four or more syllables ("En-a-je-na-miento, tra-ga-sa-bles, sin-gla-du-ra, va-sa-lla-je"). He knew no other life than the university. He was just one more bachelor in the city of Oxford, another upholder of the old clerical tradition of that immutable, inhospitable place, preserved in syrup, in the words, already quoted, of one of my predecessors. (Another troubled spirit, like myself.) Dewar was a dead soul. He had, however, this other small, unusual life, and the day – one of the few days – he was called to London with great urgency because a swimmer, a pole vaulter, a cellist or a dancer (you can be sure those were his favourites) had asked for political asylum, forsaking for ever his or her troupe or orchestra or team, then he would abandon with glee the white noise of his rooms at Brasenose (his dead soul leaping into life again), and take the train through Didcot and Reading and Slough and Southall and arrive at Paddington where he would change on to a packed underground train that would take him to the heart of London. He must have felt he was the most important, most inscrutable, wisest man in the whole university: more important than both Vice Rector and Rector, more important than the Vice Chancellor and more inscrutable and wiser even than the Chancellor himself. That's why whenever I came across him with his thick glasses on, reading a newspaper in the Senior Common Room or in the library at the Taylorian or in the lounge at the Randolph Hotel immediately opposite, I imagined him, his pulse racing, engaged in avid scrutiny of the arts and sports pages to see if a Soviet ballet company or state orchestra or some team of Soviet athletes or chessplayers were coming to perform or compete in some corner of Great Britain, and when he saw them advertised or read reviews of their performances, he must have prayed to Hermes, the god of travellers and commerce, or thieves and orators, of disquiet and dreams, to arm with valour one of their number during the night and persuade him to dodge the security guards and make a bid for freedom.

Dewar will find himself less and less in demand now, his days will pass routinely with no surprises, no phonecalls from London. And that's why – ever less attentive to the phone – he will not hesitate to use his white noise to banish and neutralise for ever all other sounds. I am no longer a solitary like him, nor one of the living dead, but for a time I thought I was.

I SAW THE CHILD ERIC, Clare's son, only once and that was when the days of his unexpected stay in Oxford were coming to an end and my emotional instability was at its height (for if you have already been deprived of something for some time or – its real duration being of little importance – have experienced it as having gone on for a long time, as being perhaps endless, the fact that an end to it is now in sight pales into insignificance beside the continuing fact of your deprivation; I mean that the mere juxtaposition of these two things is not in itself enough for you to perceive as being at an end something which, though about to end, is still not yet over, and what prevails is the fear that by some ill luck – by some misfortune, the very opposite of what you have foreseen – that long-accumulated, patient present might yet go on for ever: you experience not relief but anxiety and feel only distrust for the future). And the time I saw the child Eric I also saw – again only once – his grandfather, that is, Clare's father, the old diplomat now retired and living in London, who thirty years before used to stand at the other end of the garden and watch his daughter, the young Clare, while she waited and in turn watched the trains crossing the iron bridge over the River Jumna. (In those days her silent father smelled of tobacco, alcohol and mint.)

It happened in the museum, that is, in the town's main museum, the Ashmolean Museum of Art and Archaeology, a building that at the end of the seventeenth century housed the kingdom's first public exhibition of natural and historical curiosities (or rather the museum did, not the actual building, which did not become a home to them until two centuries later). I didn't visit the museum often, for the curiosities are of the kind that need to be seen only once, but that day in the fifth week of my second, solitary Trinity term, I had walked the twenty or so paces from the Taylorian (the institute and the museum are adjacent, forming a right angle, so that they seem almost to be the wing and main body of the same building) in order to have a look in the Ashmolean library at the drawings of Spanish cities, not on public display, made in the mid-sixteenth century by the Flemish artist Anton van den Wyngaerde or Antonio de las Viñas, topographer and court painter to Philip II, commissioned to this end by one of my brothers, a historian of architecture in Madrid (that is I walked those twenty or so paces in order to go and see them on my brother's behalf, it was not he who commissioned Van den Wyngaerde to make the drawings, they were commissioned by the person probably known in Oxford at the time as the Demon of the South). A friendly librarian with reddish hair had allowed me to study and measure them and to note down details of the views (executed in pen and ink, sepia and watercolour) and I was leaving the museum with the odd sensation of having seen with extraordinary clarity the Golden Age skylines – or vistas seen obliquely from above – of Sanlúcar de Barrameda, Málaga, Tarragona, Gibraltar, Segovia, the Albufera Lake and the port of Valencia, that is, the lost face of our southern cities, of my cities, almost forgotten, to which I would soon be able to return if I so wished: as soon as the Trinity term drew to a close and with it the academic year, just over three more weeks to go. As I say, on leaving the museum I was preoccupied by that odd sensation and by a sudden awareness of how short a time remained – objectively speaking – before I left Oxford and returned to Madrid (even though I was not going back to Madrid to stay), when at the entrance (or in the revolving door) I passed three people who were just coming in: the father, the daughter and the latter's son, that is, my lover with her son and her father. As had already happened twice with another woman in Oxford – and the second, if questionable, occasion was still very recent – I didn't realise it was Clare until I was outside the museum and they were inside, separated from me by a door. But it was so instantaneous (the realisation I mean: perhaps her companions prevented me noticing it was Clare since I always thought of her as being either alone or with her husband, or perhaps it was the revolving door, or the vivid memory of Sanlúcar as seen by ˙Van den Wyngaerde) that I had time to go back in and see them in the foyer, where they were engaged in looking at the postcards and slides sold there.

I had no way of knowing that the old gentleman holding her arm was her father, the diplomat Mr Newton (Clare Newton – Clare Newton! – that was Clare's name before she married), since I had never seen him, not even in a photograph. But I knew who he was at once. I knew because of their astonishing (perhaps even horrifying) likeness. That man, completely bald and slightly stooped, with his wrinkled skin and pouched eyes, and resting the remnants of his distinguished air on a walking stick, had the same face – exactly – that I knew so well. That old man of cadaverous aspect *was* Clare Bayes, as she might have been in a bad dream in which, whilst still retaining her own identity, she appeared in the guise of a decrepit old man. Half-hidden behind a column, I observed them from a distance – both adults were facing me, but the child still had his back to me – and, while it was likely that she had also failed to notice me when we passed on the way in, now she did see me – my head and torso emerging from behind the column which I was using less as a hiding place than as some form of protection – and, when her companions weren't looking at her or in my direction (they were looking at the slides), she made a gesture with her right hand for me to go away, to leave, to disappear. But it was then that the child, her son Eric, as if he had eyes in the back of his head or somehow knew that was the precise moment he should look – or perhaps he heard the clink of her numerous bracelets as her hand made that brief, clandestine, proscriptive gesture – half turned round for a moment and saw me and looked at me, and doubtless associated me with his mother. And when the boy turned round and stopped looking at the slides and the postcards and stopped listening to what his grandfather was saying to him (it was only a matter of seconds), when he intercepted our looks and I saw his face at last, what I saw was the same, identical face for the third time, Clare's face that I knew so intimately and that I had kissed and whose lips had kissed me so many times. That face, I thought, was the same face that long before had been the face of her diplomat father and then, as yet only briefly, that of the child Eric, Eric Bayes. They were one and the same face, the face whose lips had kissed me in one of its incarnations, representations, figurations or manifestations, for I've never seen such a perfect, precise, exclusive likeness. Those three people had transmitted their features, rejecting all others (those of a mother and a father, those of the first Clare Newton and those of Edward Bayes), and had surrendered them up entirely, unstintingly and freely, I mean without keeping back one single detail for themselves; and unlike most such capricious, unexpected likenesses, in which one or several or many but never all the features are reproduced, or the inherited characteristics are changed (changed by the passing of unpredictable time and by intransigent age), in this instance, in each of the three cases, the transmission had been complete and unaltered: the same deep blue eyes, the same thick, curled eyelashes, the same short, straight nose, the same strong, cleft chin, the pale cheeks, hard forehead, heavy eyelids, faded lips. But for the moment I could see no more, for the child Eric had turned round again and had his back to me, and after Mr Newton had bought a folio-size reproduction – a reduction or an enlargement: a likeness – of some picture or object I couldn't make out, the three moved off towards the rooms inside, this time without Clare looking round at me, on the contrary, she seemed bent on pretending that she hadn't seen me and on trying to ignore me (she'd realised I had no intention of obeying or paying any heed to her furtive hands shooing me away). I let a few seconds pass, then set off after them, determined to visit all the rooms they visited. "So they've brought young Eric to see the museum," I was thinking without wanting to (I wanted to think about the likeness, or perhaps it was the other way round, perhaps I thought this because I preferred *not* to think about the likeness). "Clare's often told me how old he is, what was it now? Eight, nine years old? Judging by his height he looks like a boy of about nine, but he might be tall for his age, both his parents and his grandfather are tall, he might be only eight or seven, possibly even less. It's no age to be going round museums, I wouldn't bring my seven-year-old son to the Ashmolean, even if he was fed up and bored with being at home ill." That's what I was thinking and then I thought: "He looks fine now. He'll leave Oxford soon. But so will I, I'll be leaving very soon, and now I'm not so sure I want to."

The three figures stopped every now and then, before a Greek statue, a Reynolds portrait, a piece of Chinese porcelain or some Roman coins. They looked at everything. I drew nearer then moved away, always keeping a few respectful yards between me and them, according to the length of the rooms and according to my capacity for feigned concentration on each of the objects I stopped to contemplate; and that's why – though also because they were speaking very quietly, as people do in British, though not in Spanish, museums – I could hear nothing of what they said. As I was always following, following scrupulously in their footsteps, each time they moved on after they had stopped to look at something, I saw them only from behind or in semi-profile, or rather quarter face. I never got a good view of them, and I think I preferred it like that, preferred not to be confronted once more by those three identical faces. Clare held the child Eric's hand, while her father, leaning on his walking stick, was always trailing slightly behind as if she were not prepared to wait for him or to adjust her and her son's pace to the slower and more awkward step of the ex-diplomat Mr Newton (as if the visit to the museum were a treat intended for her and the boy, not for the grandfather, who had perhaps insisted on accompanying them without having been invited and was just an appendage, perhaps even an intruder: he brought up the rear, the way nannies did when the mothers were present and took charge of the children, in the days when there were nannies). It wasn't the grandfather either who did the talking, Clare talked most, though always to the boy, and now and again I heard snippets of her comments.

In front of the Alfred Jewel (a ninth-century cloisonné enamel, the pride of the Ashmolean) I heard her read out loud (like any father or mother) the Anglo-Saxon inscription cut into the band of gold filigree that encircles the supposed portrait of Alfred the Great: "Look, Eric, here it says *Aelfred mec heht gewyrcan* which means 'Alfred ordered me to be made'. See? It's the jewel itself saying that, it's the jewel speaking and telling us how it came to be made. It's said the same thing now for eleven centuries, and will go on saying the same thing for ever." The child Eric said nothing.

Later, on the upper floor, before a rapid or unfinished sketch by Rembrandt depicting the painter's wife, Saskia, asleep in bed (only she isn't really in bed, but rather dressed or in a dressing gown and covered with a blanket, as if she were a convalescent), I heard Clare say to her son: "She looks like you in bed all these weeks, don't you think? Except you had the television to watch," and she stroked the back of his neck, setting her bracelets jingling again. Then she added, still looking at Saskia and no doubt ignorant of the fact that Saskia had died when she was younger even than herself and never had the chance to grow old (mistaking Saskia's possible illness for old age): "That's what I'll be like when I'm old." And young Eric said nothing or at least nothing I managed to catch (Eric seemed a polite, timid child, and if he spoke, he did so too quietly to be heard).

Further on, in front of a Cantonese statue of gilded wood (in fact a copy from the last century) representing Marco Polo as a fat Chinaman with pale eyes, wearing an extravagant black hat with a narrow brim and low crown, shod in clogs of the same colour, his face adorned with equally black moustaches twisted back over his cheeks, I heard Clare say: "Oh look, Eric, it's Marco Polo, the Italian explorer. He first reached China in the thirteenth century when it was still very hard to get there and, since getting back was harder still, he stayed on and stayed there so long he ended up looking like a Chinaman, see? But he was really Italian, from Venice. Look, he's got blue eyes. No real Chinaman would have blue eyes." And Eric remained silent, or rather I didn't hear his response, only Clare's; annoyed at my disobedience and my spying, she was doubtless trying to speak as quietly as possible thus urging the boy to do likewise, as if – in keeping with her decision of the last four weeks – she didn't want me to participate even as an eavesdropper in her family world, especially not in the filial and paternal worlds – the world of blood ties – though I knew her husband and occasionally, as I have said, the three of us even lunched or dined together with Cromer-Blake. She just didn't want me to be there, and I began to think that when I did hear what she said, it was because she wanted me to, that it was not by chance that only certain phrases reached my ears, and that when Clare Bayes raised her voice, she did so on purpose in order to communicate something to me. And I thought: "She was referring to me when she said that about Marco Polo, her remarks were aimed at me, you don't talk to a seven- or eight-year-old child like that, at that age you're well on the way to adulthood. Unless, that is, Eric suffers from some form of infantilism and has to be treated as if he were younger than he is – or perhaps she's just made him more of a baby over the weeks he's been at home – or then again, maybe he really is younger than I think, I've come to realise that I'm as useless at judging children's ages as I am at judging how old adults are, and another thing I've realised is that, apart from the women I already know, like Clare herself, the more I desire women the less prepared I am to think about them, I desire them without thinking about them at all, that's how it was with Muriel and how it still is with the attractive waitresses at Brown's, and I don't know if that's indicative of anything – it's certainly a new development – apart from my general state of disequilibrium. I do think about Clare, indeed the less I see of her the more I think about her and try to imagine her, if not I wouldn't be here trailing round the Ashmolean having forgotten all about what brought me here in the first place: Van den Wyngaerde (I've got the notes I made in my pocket); and when she raised her voice to talk about the statue it was so that I should understand that someone who spends too much time in a place other than his homeland ends up belonging to neither place, ends up looking like a Chinaman with blue eyes, like the Marco Polo of this statue. But I haven't spent too much time here, I'm neither an exile nor an emigrant, and anyway I'll be leaving soon. Maybe this summer I'll go to Sanlúcar de Barrameda, I really liked that view of the bay, the castle, the principal church, the Duke's palace, the customs house, that view painted four centuries ago and that no longer exists nor ever existed, since the viewpoint adopted is a purely imaginary one, as perhaps my viewpoint on the city of Oxford is." And in my mind, I added: "She knows that too, that I'll be leaving soon, she's probably worked it out already, just a little over three weeks until the end of term, but despite that she continues to tell me – not with her hand or with a look, nor so casually as in the foyer, but with deliberate, winged words – that I should go away, leave, disappear now, without delay, from Oxford and from her life, where I haven't spent so very long. I could almost leave now, I've scarcely any classes left, perhaps the time has come, a little earlier than anticipated, I must talk to her and not just on the phone or hurriedly as we've always talked, always just about to part right from the very first moment, I must see her, we must make time to see each other unhurriedly, with no bells chiming out the hours, at least once, now that nothing holds me here."

There was scarcely anyone else in the museum, only the odd impatient or lost visitor peering into a room only to leave again without looking at anything and the lethargic keepers on their chairs like Andalusian neighbours sitting deep in thought in their patios after their siesta, just them and the family group spanning three generations and a solitary man, a foreigner, who no longer perhaps seemed so foreign after his not over-long stay in Oxford – or perhaps had the gait of an Englishman but the eyes of a southerner – and who mechanically, always some steps behind, looked at everything they had looked at and, possibly, as quickly forgotten. The foreign chap with the look (albeit imperfect) of an Oxford don followed them out of the museum, and walked behind them through the red-grey streets and went into the same restaurant they did – it was still early but hunger can come on children at any time and they lunch promptly – and sat down alone at a table opposite them, in direct line with that of the father, the daughter and the daughter's son, keeping his fingers crossed that no one would sit at the empty table between him and them and thus block his view of the three identical faces; he was determined now to see them and observe them.

The child Eric sat down opposite his mother, still with his back to me, and the grandfather sat to her left, an arrangement doubtless chosen because Clare intended to continue addressing herself principally to her son (she ignored the ex-diplomat New-ton, showed him no respect, or mistreated him by simply not treating with him at all). I could hear their conversation more clearly now, although in fact, apart from the odd isolated comment, they didn't talk that much while they studied the menu, or even afterwards, while they ate. "I'm going to have sausages." I heard the boy's voice for the first time. "I don't think it's a good idea to have sausages here, Eric," Clare said to him, "they won't be any better than the ones you have at home, but other things might be. Why don't you have asparagus to start with? You liked it that time you had it at your aunt's house. We hardly ever have asparagus at home, and I'm sure you don't often get it at school." "I don't feel like eating asparagus. Unless I can eat it with my fingers, can I?" I saw Clare Bayes give him a look of mock disapproval and heard her say with a pretend drawl of hesitancy: "I suppose so." "Well, I'm going to have asparagus served with scrambled eggs," interposed the ex-diplomat; "wouldn't you prefer to eat it like that, Eric? It has salmon in it too. Do you like salmon?" "I don't know," said Eric, and went back to studying the menu. The retired diplomat ordered white wine and Clare Bayes ordered water. And then, when they were already on their first course and I was still waiting for mine (asparagus with scrambled eggs and salmon) to arrive, Clare asked her son: "What did you like best at the museum, Eric? What would you take home with you if you could?" The coins," said Eric, "and the statues. The Chinese statues, the painted ones. There's a boy at school who collects coins, but you can't collect statues, can you?" "It would be a bit expensive," said the diplomat, with a senile grin revealing teeth just like Clare's (but more translucent and possibly capped like Mrs Alabaster's or false like Toby Rylands'), "and there are far fewer of them." "I'll collect coins then; why don't you each give me one to start my collection now?" said Eric, and Clare and her father each took out a coin, he from his jacket pocket, she after much searching in the handbag she used to leave thrown down anyhow (sometimes even spilling the contents) in my bedroom or in the rooms of hotels in London or Reading, and I remembered the coin I'd thrown to some children who weren't Eric (he wasn't ill then and he was away at school) on Guy Fawkes' Day on the fifth of November last year from the window of her study in All Souls, in Catte Street, across from the Radcliffe Camera, nine months after we'd first met. That was seven months ago, and now all that had changed was that nothing had changed: I'd known Clare for a long time and nothing had ever changed, except that just now I wasn't allowed to see her and would soon have to say goodbye. I wouldn't have minded giving the boy a coin too. "But don't go and spend it," warned his grandfather, "if you show me you're capable of saving them and starting a real collection, I'll bring you some from Italy and Egypt and India that I've got in London." And turning to his daughter, he added: "I think there are still some at home. We travelled such a lot then, didn't we, Clare? But my travelling days are long since over." Clare didn't reply, though, and concentrated on her own plate of asparagus with scrambled eggs and salmon. They were finishing their second course just as I was starting mine when Clare said: "It's back to Bristol on Sunday. Has it been very boring being here with me all this time?" "No," said the boy (who was certainly too young to know anything of coquetry) and, since he said nothing more but just went on eating his sausages, I thought again that Clare's question must be intended for me and I answered in my thoughts: "Yes, it's been very boring here all this time without her."

And during the whole of lunch in that restaurant slowly filling with people, and because Eric was only young and therefore short, his lack of height gave me a view of the whole of his mother's face above the back of his head – Clare was immediately opposite me and facing me, but never once looked at me – and to the left I had a clear view of the grandfather's face; and with them sitting down and me sitting down – and though she never looked at me once – I could see them better than at any point, either standing still or moving around, in the foyer of the museum or in any of its rooms. And by the end of the lunch I was just getting used to the astonishing likeness – to the extraordinary similarity between father and daughter and to the back of the grandson's head concealing his likeness – when, without finishing his dessert and having asked permission to do so (he was a polite boy), Eric got up, turned round and walked by me on his way to the toilets. It took him only a few steps – four or five – to pass me, but during the short time those four or five steps lasted – one, two, three, four, five – I enjoyed a close, clear and simultaneous view of the three identical faces, that of the grandfather and mother sitting down and that of the son as he walked by me. The boy looked straight at me as he passed, as he had done when he turned round in the museum foyer, and doubtless again associated me with the person with whom he should inevitably associate me (but he would say nothing because he was too polite and timid); and as his mother and his grandfather followed with their respective gazes the trajectory of that of their son and grandson, both rested their unveiled eyes on me (she for the first time since we'd entered the restaurant, he for the first time in his life), and for some moments the three of them, all at the same time, regarded me with their unveiled eyes (at least I think they did because I didn't actually see it, my eyes being fixed only on Eric who was taking his four or five steps in my direction). It was only a matter of a few seconds (the time such steps take when made by a child, for children have no concept of walking slowly), but it was long enough for me to see (as I had not had the chance to in the museum foyer) something in the boy which then (but not in the museum foyer) acquired a name: in the child Eric's deep blue eyes I glimpsed the slow downhill feeling that we all experience sooner or later. 'It doesn't depend on age really,' Toby Rylands had said (and he'd said it before the last term had ended, before Easter Week, and before the summer term had begun and Eric had fallen ill and been brought back to Oxford ahead of time. "Some people experience it even when they're children; some children already have a sense of it." That's what he'd said, exactly that, and that was precisely what I saw then, in the time it took for him to walk past me – a child already conscious of that feeling; but I saw it not only in the boy's face but also – by assimilation, by kinship, because of their similarity, their astonishing, indeed alarming, likeness – in the faces of the old man and of the woman I knew so well (and in whom I had never recognised it or seen it before) and whom I had kissed and who had kissed me so very often. In those three people, every feature and characteristic, as I said before, had been passed on without the slightest detail being kept back, including that downhill feeling, "the slow downhill feeling we all experience sooner or later", I thought and remembered and thought again. "Kiss the child and you kiss the old man," I thought. "I've kissed and been kissed by the boy and by the old man, and that's an example of two ideas which, according to Alan Marriott, may or may not ever become associated, but once they do, they instil horror and provoke fear: the idea of the boy and the idea of the kiss, the idea of the kiss and the idea of the old man, the idea of the boy and the idea of the old man. The old man's horrifying other half is the boy, the boy's is the old man, that of the kiss the child, and that of the child the kiss, that of the kiss the old man and that of the old man the kiss, *my* kiss (there are three ideas involved, plus that of Clare, who hovers in the middle), the kiss given by interposing people but not by an interposing face, for the face is the same even though age and sex may vary through the different incarnations, representations, figurations or manifestations. The kiss of all three is the kiss given by someone who has experienced that slow downhill feeling familiar to the demoniacal – the awesome – Rylands and to the ailing Cromer-Blake but not to me (the feeling that Rylands has known for forty years and Cromer-Blake since who knows when, the feeling known too to the beggars and to Saskia beneath her blanket but unknown to me). It is the kiss of one who, in Rylands' words, has spent years letting death approach, or of one who, to use Rylands' words again, knows that a day will dawn when he will no longer be able to fantasise about things still to come. It's only natural that the ex-diplomat Newton should know it, and it's also understandable that Clare Bayes née Newton, should too, but the fact is that the child Eric, Eric Bayes, at the age of only nine or eight or seven, also knows it. In the deep blue eyes they all shared, I saw, the first time I ever saw them, the blue waters of that river gleaming brightly in the blackness, the River Yamuna or Jumna, and the long bridge of criss-crossing iron girders, and the mail train that comes from Moradabad with its rickety many-coloured carriages and the diplomat father, silent (and melancholic and not old then) who watches his daughter watching as he stands, dressed for supper, with a glass in his hand, and a nanny who whispers in the ear of the young Clare (Clare Newton as she was then) or sings some trifling song; and perhaps it's the reflection of those blue or rather black waters (since it was night) that carries with it the slow downhill feeling, the feeling of being burdened down, of vertigo, of falling, gravity and weight, of false plumpness and despair. That feeling was already in the gaze seen and observed for a whole minute across another table, a high table, nine plus seven months ago and yet it was not in mine, also seen and also observed for the same minute those nine plus seven months ago, and which reflected the image of four children walking with an old maidservant along calle de Génova, calle de Covarrubias or calle de Miguel Ángel. I feel deeply troubled, yet my sense of unease has never lacked coherence or logic, it is light, logical, coherent and transient, but now it's greater than ever because I'm thinking all this, thinking about the child and the old man and the kiss and the river, the wide River Yamuna or Jumna that crosses Delhi, and about the River

Cherwell on whose banks Rylands lives and in whose waters he sees an image of the passing of time, and the Rivers Evenlode and Windrush between which lies Wychwood Forest or what *was* a forest, and the River Avon near where Eric goes to school, and the River Guadalquivir that flows out into the sea at Sanlúcar, and the River Isis, the nearest to me, and into which I may well need to vomit. How wearying it is, this permanent state of unease, how wearisome and tedious it is to think these troubled thoughts and because of that to think so much, such ravings always have their origin in thoughts that rhyme and sway and have their own arbitrary punctuation; I must stop thinking and start talking instead, just to have a rest from these thoughts that struggle to make connections and associations and make too many, I must talk to Rylands or Cromer-Blake or Kavanagh or the Ripper or to Muriel (except I didn't get her phone number). I must talk to Clare and put my proposals to her: that we shouldn't say goodbye, shouldn't go our separate ways, that she should let me participate in that downhill feeling they all share and of which I as yet know nothing, or perhaps more simply, to which I have not been a witness."

When Eric returned from the toilet, I heard only his rapid steps and felt the brush of air past me, but by then I wasn't looking at anyone and was hurriedly paying the bill before they'd even removed my plate of half-eaten sausages; I'd declined dessert knowing that if I didn't have time to reach home and the rubbish bin, at least the Isis wasn't too far away.

THE VERY NEXT DAY I decided to ask the advice of Cromer-Blake, my best and only friend, about the proposals I intended putting to Clare Bayes, since we tend to try out our rhetorical skills on friends before submitting those skills to the real test, and make our friends early participants in any plans we don't completely trust (so that those friends may lessen the pain of failure), expecting to wring from them the encouragement and response we hope to win later and which we may well not receive when the plan proper is put into action.

I didn't bother to phone before going to see him, I just dropped by his college after my morning class, as I had so many times before, assuming that he'd be in his rooms. If the worst came to the worst, and he was giving a tutorial, then I'd just wait outside the door for it to finish. On the stairs on my way up to his rooms – on the third floor like mine – I heard his voice and presumed he was indeed lecturing some undergraduate, who would be sitting dozing on the sofa opposite Cromer-Blake, pretending to concur with the latter's disquisitions on *Tirano Banderas* or *Automoribundia*. That's why I did not at first rap on the door with my knuckles, not because I wanted to hear what he was saying or talking about. I listened only in order to confirm that he was busy and to make an on-the-spot calculation as to whether it was convenient or worth my while waiting – outside the door, as I say – until the end of the tutorial or whether I should instead quickly open the door and tell him I needed to talk to him urgently and would return shortly, then take myself off for a stroll. But, when I was already outside his door, the first clear words I heard (the first to rise above a murmur) stopped me in my tracks for long enough, a matter of seconds, so that (once those seconds had passed: one, two, three, four, five) it was already too late to make any further move either into the room or back down the stairs.

There's a verb in English which can only be translated into Spanish by a gloss, that verb is "eavesdrop" which means (and this is the gloss) to listen indiscreetly, secretly, furtively, to listen deliberately, not by chance or unwillingly (for that you'd use the verb "overhear"), and the verb itself contains two separate words, "eaves" which means "the edge of a roof projecting out beyond the wall of a house" and "drop", which can mean several things but basically has to do with liquid dropping (the listener places himself at a certain minimal distance from the house: he stands at the spot where the water would normally run off the eaves after a shower of rain, and from there listens in to what is said inside). Vladimir Vladimirovich, he of the former British colonies, once pondered on the device of "eavesdropping" in the nineteenth-century novel, and more specifically in *A Hero of our Time*, and although Nabokov was at Cambridge, not Oxford, I'm sure that during his time there in the 1920s he would have had ample opportunity to make the same discovery I made in my time at Oxford, which is that eavesdropping was and is not only a practice in active use in both places, but still the best (admittedly primitive) means of obtaining the information one needs in order to avoid becoming the kind of outsider who neither possesses nor transmits any. In Oxford (and in Cambridge too, I imagine), eavesdropping becomes exactly what Nabokov describes in the Lermontov novel mentioned above: "the barely noticeable routine of fate". I had seen circumspect, sententious dons actually down on one knee before a keyhole in a corridor in the Taylorian (getting their trousers dusty in the process), or sprawled on a carpet in one of the colleges (literally prostrating themselves, their gown like a spreading ink stain) with one ear glued to the crack beneath the door, or keeping watch with a spyglass (made in Japan) from some Gothic window; not to mention neglecting their own conversational partners in the lounge at the Randolph in order to catch some sentence unleashed from another corner, or else imprudently craning their neck at high table (or afterwards, more likely, once their napkins were irredeemably soiled). But I had never done this, I had never stood beneath the eaves. I did so then for the first time, and when I did (only momentarily and almost at the end of my stay there) I felt somehow more integrated; although I think the first clear words that reached my ears from Cromer-Blake's apparently bloodless lips were, strictly speaking, merely overheard. What happened afterwards, however, was eavesdropping pure and simple.

"Come on, please, be nice, come to bed with me," those were the first distinct words I overheard Cromer-Blake saying; and in the following seconds, during which I remained stock still, my friend added: "Just this once, just one more time, please, I implore you, it will be the last time." The voice that answered was young, younger, rather unpleasant, rather cracked, as if the young man's voice had not yet completely broken, which was odd because although he was young he was not so young that his voice would not yet have stabilised. And that countertenor voice replied without irritation, patiently, trustingly, like an old friend: "Don't go on about it, I've already said no, and that's that. Anyway, Dayanand says you're ill and you shouldn't overdo things, he says it's dangerous, for me too. That's what he says." His diction was rather crude, not so very different from the way Muriel spoke, or the mechanic Bruce (except that it wasn't Bruce, who had a much deeper voice), the diction of someone who would say things like: "abaht", "fings", "nuffink", "nah" (but then, nowadays, that's not unknown amongst certain television presenters either). And because of that, because of the plebeian accent, I knew at once that it couldn't be an undergraduate (it had crossed my mind that it might be young Bottomley), and anyway Cromer-Blake would never do anything so foolish, even if he were in love and desperate: nothing was taken more seriously in Oxford than an accusation of sexual harassment, or, even worse (and equally possible), of gross moral turpitude, another (anglicised) Latinism, an exquisite euphemism for, in plain language, penetration. "Ah, Dayanand says so does he, our omniscient doctor," remarked Cromer-Blake (almost to himself) recovering the ironic tone that was so much more characteristic of him than pleading; it made me uncomfortable to hear him plead. "Dayanand knows nothing about my health, he's just saying that to take you away from me, to eliminate me, it's ages since he last saw me as a patient; that's about as valid as if I were to tell you now that it's him who's ill. To call someone ill is always a way of discrediting them. It's a way of getting rid of people. I've been a little unwell, but I'm fine now, I'm cured. Do I look like a sick man?" I'd seen Cromer-Blake two or three days before and he looked good, as I imagined he would at that moment, on the other side of the door. I wondered if the young man who was speaking could be the "Jack" whose name Cromer-Blake had let slip months before, just after I saw Clare for the first time (saw her face and her tasteful décolletage); and I waited to hear a name in his – in Cromer-Blake's – mouth that would clarify this for me, but I can categorically state that during my period of eavesdropping no name was uttered.

"No, you look good," said the young man's voice, "but it makes no difference, it's over, it can't go on. Anyway, Dayanand would be furious." "But it doesn't matter if I get furious I suppose." The cracked voice softened for a moment: "Yes, of course it matters to me but it's not such a big deal. Things being how they are." There was a pause of several seconds (perhaps a pause created by a kiss, for kisses do impose silence), and then the voice spoke again, raised in harsh protest now (sounding still younger and even less pleasant): "Let go of me! Stop it! You're hurting me!" "I'm sorry," said Cromer-Blake, and his tone reverted to that of the petitioner: "But please, I'm begging you, please, I swear it won't be dangerous, and there's no reason Dayanand should ever find out. I just want us to lie down for a bit and for me to hold you for a while, it's ages since anyone held me." "Well, get someone else to do it," the voice said acrimoniously (like the voice of a don refusing alms to a beggar and sending him packing). I felt my face flush crimson with a mixture of shame and indignation, it offended me that this young man, whoever he was, should mistreat and reject my friend Cromer-Blake at that moment pleading with him. But I still stayed where I was, by the door. The door had a gold handle, it was closed but certainly not bolted or locked, all it needed was for me to turn the handle and push the door open; Cromer-Blake rarely kept it locked when he was in, no bolts or keys, just the plaque I could see before me which said: "Dr P. E. Cromer-Blake". There was another pause, as if Cromer-Blake had been temporarily rendered speechless, deprived of his usual capacity for irony and anger. I heard the other door leading into the bedroom creak; Cromer-Blake had gone in there, whether alone or accompanied I couldn't tell. But then I heard the door creak again and he returned to the room. He said: "All right. But at least do the photographs for me, there's nothing too dangerous about that is there, no reason for anyone to get angry?" The ironic tone was there again although he was still begging (but not to be held this time). I wondered about his friend Bruce and about the tempting offers and superior methods of seduction he'd mentioned on a previous night. I wondered about the pretty faces and athletic bodies, which, according to him, were sometimes at his disposal in his bedroom. Cromer-Blake was a good-looking man, but, judging by what I could hear from my position beneath the eaves, his good looks were proving of little avail, and this was long before he was to become an old man, long before he was reduced to sifting through the memories he'd manufactured and stored up in the hope of providing a little variety for his old age, at a time when in the normal run of events, the manufacture and storing of memories for the future would still be in full swing. I thought it couldn't be because of his illness, whatever that was and assuming it wasn't yet cured; there are some things before which no danger seems too great. It was Cromer-Blake himself who was asking to be held although perhaps he really shouldn't have been overdoing things. I recalled that Dayanand, whose fiery gaze I had first encountered at that high table, was not a man to be trifled with. Dayanand must have been possessed of a stronger will and a greater ability to get what he wanted, more so at least than Cromer-Blake; his gaze was unveiled, a southern gaze like mine; the Indian doctor carried his demon within him, like Toby Rylands, who some said had originally been South African, or like Clare Bayes, who'd spent her childhood in far-off, southern lands, and possibly also like the dead Gawsworth, who'd been in Tunisia and Algeria, in Italy, Egypt and India (although never on the island of Redonda), and doubtless like myself, who always was, am and will be from Madrid (I know that now). My blood can be hot or lukewarm or cold. But as soon as the occasion arose, as soon as I was given the chance, it would be my turn to play the postulant. I'd already spent weeks playing that part from afar, with Clare, to whom I addressed my pleas.

"All right," replied the young man whose voice was so late in breaking, "but let's be quick about it." "You'll take them?" said Cromer-Blake with sudden undisguised gratitude and relief. "Thank God for that, in the sort of relationships you get into through agencies, they always end up asking you for photographs. It's awfully good of you, without them I'd be really stuck, and if you don't take them, I don't know who else could. I can't ask Bruce." "Come on then, get ready, the sooner we start, the sooner it's over," said the cracked voice helpfully. Cromer-Blake, I deduced, must be having photographs of himself taken in order to send them to some sort of agency, or to someone with whom he'd been put in touch by an agency. During this break in the dialogue, interrupted only by the occasional remark and the unmistakable whirr of a Polaroid camera ("How does it look?" Cromer-Blake was saying. "Make sure you get a good shot of it." "Is this high enough?" "Whirr," said the Polaroid), I began to wonder exactly what they were taking photographs of, what kind of poses these were that they precluded Bruce the mechanic, or, for example, Clare or me from taking them for him. And as I thought that I felt my face grow even redder (as I stood there at the door), but this time it was with pure, unalloyed shame. And although there was no one there to see my blushes (the only thing looking at me was the shining plaque bearing Cromer-Blake's abbreviated name), they were provoked not by my imaginings but by my reaction or by that of my conscience (a remnant of it). For it was then that I felt ashamed of my eavesdropping.

With immense stealth, with a stealth I hadn't required when I came up the stairs because at that point I'd not yet become indiscreet, secretive and furtive, I half-turned and started to tiptoe down the stairs, while one last phrase reached my ears (overheard this time, for I didn't want to hear any more): "It's important to get a view from above," Cromer-Blake was saying. "Whirr," said the Polaroid. All the same, when I'd gone down a few stairs, I couldn't help smiling a little, ironically (as if I were Cromer-Blake), at the imagined scene I hadn't witnessed. However, my smile soon disappeared with the sudden memory of why I'd gone there and the realisation that I would not now have the chance to ask Cromer-Blake's advice or try to lessen the pain of failure beforehand or hear from his lips the encouragement or the response I hoped to hear later, when I put the plan proper into action, because in the cracked voice and on the lips of a stranger, I'd already heard the discouraging tone and the response I didn't want to hear.

ONCE THE CHILD ERIC had departed and Clare had agreed to see me again (alone) to listen to my proposals and to talk to me with time to spare, without undue haste and without alarm clocks going off or bells chiming the hour, the half hour and the quarter hour and inconsiderately pealing out again as evening fell (bells that I will not hear again, but which will continue pealing out until the end of time), she and I went to Brighton. We went down one Saturday (Eric was back in Bristol and Edward Bayes was travelling on the Continent) to spend the night there, the first and last that we were to spend together, for I'd never actually slept the night with her as I had with Muriel. Once there we scarcely left our hotel room, which was different from and less conventional than those in London and Reading and from whose opposing windows we could see, to one side, the minarets and onion domes of the celebrated Royal Pavilion in all its pseudo, grotesque Indian glory, and, to the other side, the beach (it was the only time that being together proved expensive: adultery is usually fairly cheap). It isn't in fact true that we didn't go out, but that's how it felt, as if Clare and I were always shut up in a room somewhere together, in Oxford and in London and in Reading and in Brighton. We went to Brighton not by train but in her car, and that also had something inaugural and new about it (although it was actually bringing something to a close): the two of us sitting in her car heading south, going on a journey, turning our backs on London and Reading for the first time, with me, seated on the left, under the false impression that I was driving and she with the same (correct) impression that it was she who was carrying me along. But it was all false, I think (as regards us, that is, but not as regards others, the person who had died thirty years before in a distant land, for example, and the person who did not die but should have died, there and then). The air was rank with the odour of farewell – always so intense, instantly identifiable – but we pretended that our farewell and separation were not necessarily decided, even though they had been right from the start (I had after all set out to find "someone to love" during my time spent at this stopping-off point, to have "someone" to think about), we pretended, rather, that a final decision might hang entirely on that meeting, on that weekend, that our fate could be determined in a hotel room in Brighton. And I enjoyed the great consolation (or perhaps even the immense pleasure) of proposing the impossible and knowing that it would be rejected: for it is precisely the recognition that it is impossible and the certainty of rejection – a rejection that the person who proposes the impossible and takes the floor first in fact expects – that allows one to hold nothing back, to be vehement and more confident in expressing one's desires than if there were the slightest risk of their being satisfied. And Clare Bayes, I think, pretended to believe me, to take me seriously, and explained things to me as if that were really necessary and as if a simple "no" would not have sufficed, as if she had to be careful not to hurt me and as if it were important that I understood (she behaved with great delicacy). It's a procedure that must be gone through in order to give a false lustre to non-blood relation-ships, which are never fruitful or very interesting, and yet which nonetheless seem essential for the mind, for it to be able to fantasise about things still to come and not simply to languish, or fall into a decline. In order that the mind should not slide into despair.

But we touched on none of that – with me saving up my little speech and she her generous response – until after supper and our walk along the endless beach, until after we'd returned to the hotel room knowing that the most arduous part – the representation and figuration – was still to come. That's why we'd saved our energies (verbal and valedictory) during the car journey and during our visit to the fake palace, the Royal Pavilion, with its crenellations and pinnacles and lattice screens, during our shopping trip in town (there was always a second-hand bookshop waiting for me wherever I went in England, always handbags for Clare and a present for the child Eric) and during supper, looking out over the beach and the incoming tide, and during the walk in bare feet, my feet bare too, my shoes dangling from two fingers, middle and index (with no need for gloves this time). And when we'd gone upstairs after that day of occasional remarks and long silences (not that it was late, for we knew there were still hours to go before we'd call it a day and try to sleep, but perhaps we wanted to avoid making it too tiring or too truthful), she, as was her custom, removed her shoes and I did not, despite the sand in my socks, and she lay down on the bed and her skirt rode up, as it was prescribed that it always would, to reveal her legs, not strong and slightly muscular as they were for others, but slender and almost boyish in their movements. That night we were free to eternalise the contents of our time, or enjoy the illusion that we did so, and that's why there was no hurry, not even to start talking, not even to kiss, not even for my cock to go to her mouth or her mouth to my cock, or for my cock to go anywhere. The spring night had an appropriately spring-like air to it and one of the windows – the one that allowed a glimpse of an occasional incongruous minaret or onion dome floodlit in the background – was open. I leaned my back against the window frame. From there, through the opposite window, I could see the beach and the water.

I lit a cigarette and said: "I don't want to leave, Clare. I can't leave now," and I thought that those two remarkably similar sentences might be enough in themselves to prompt her to take the floor to give some answer (and I was immediately aware too that, although she did begin speaking I was still thinking, not resting). She spoke but didn't answer (not exactly, for she answered with a question).

"You mean leave Oxford?"

I said: "Yes, or rather, no. I suppose I do want to leave Oxford, and anyway I've no option, my contract runs out. But I don't want to leave you. I've missed you so much during these last interminable weeks, and I don't want to be separated from you for purely geographical reasons, that would be ridiculous," and I thought that in saying that I had been even more explicit, as earnest conversations between lovers demand, since they are obliged to flow over flat ground, through all that is diaphanous, all that is yet to be.

"Geography can be a very powerful, not to say, implacable reason for people to part. You don't want to leave and you do want to leave, you don't really know what you want. I know that I can't and don't want to leave. But it doesn't matter whether you know what you want or not, because you have to leave anyway, and you will. There's no point in talking about something that's settled already."

I said: "You could come with me," and thought, to my surprise, that in saying that I had said almost all that seemed necessary to say (given that I had to be explicit) on that Saturday night in June in Brighton (and I also knew that Clare would say it was impossible.)

"Where? To Madrid? Don't be absurd. That's impossible."

I said: "But would you come with me if it were possible?" and thought that I was thereby giving her an opportunity, too, of saying she would do something both of us knew was out of the question. But she let it pass, for that was my role, not hers.

"Just out of curiosity, I'd like to know how you propose that should happen."

I said: "I don't know how, we'd have to find a way; you can

always find a way if you really want to. But first you have to want to find it, I need to know if you want to come with me, or if you're prepared to consider it; and that you won't let there be another four weeks like the last four. And if I see your son I don't want him to look at me oddly, I want him to get to know me and to live with us if we live together, I want him to be my son, or rather my stepson. I can't live without you, even if it is a bit late in the day to realise that, when I'm going to be obliged to live without you. But that's always the way things happen," and I was surprised to find myself daring to say (much too early in the conversation) things I hadn't even foreseen myself saying or was even sure I wanted to say, either at the beginning or perhaps even at the end (the word "together", the word "son", the word "stepson"), but I thought, too, that my last sentences, including the very last, had been acceptable within the narrow range of possible varieties of behaviour in non-blood relationships. Now it was Clare's turn to be surprised, at least a little, although, inevitably, her surprise was only a pretence. But her pretence took the form of not being surprised, which is one way of handing back the surprise (or its pretence) to the other side.

"Whether it's late in the day or not is irrelevant," she said, and lit the first cigarette, the first threat to her tights, that she'd smoked since lying down on the bed: she'd scarcely smoked at all during supper or during the walk, as if she were saving it for the night and for the room. "It isn't a matter of timing, because there never was a set time for that. It was outside of time, there was never any question of it, and there still isn't, now even less so. You'll go back to Madrid soon and in a way it's better that we haven't seen each other over these last few weeks, that way we've got used to it, at least I have, quite a bit. You're all alone here; back in Madrid you won't miss me so much. With each day that passes I'll seem more distant and more diffuse. There's no point talking about it. Let's have as nice a weekend as possible and then say goodbye tomorrow. At least we've had some time alone together. That's enough."

I said: "As easy as that," and thought that at last she'd taken charge of the conversation and that perhaps I would not even need to speak further, just listen and rest.

"No, it isn't easy at all, don't imagine it's easy. I often thought about you while Eric was at home, and I'll often think about you when you've gone."

I said: "But I'll think about you all the time, the way I have these last four weeks. If you don't want to come with me, then I'll have to find a way of staying here, even if it's in another job," and I thought that really I had no desire to stay in Oxford teaching Spanish in some language school, or in London working for the BBC (it was the only thing that occurred to me at that moment, nor to end up looking like a blue-eyed Chinaman, as perhaps she had, having spent her childhood far off, in Delhi and in Cairo.

"You wouldn't last much longer here; you miss your country more than you think. If you were to stay, I wouldn't be with you, or at least it wouldn't be any different from the way it has been up to now. We'd go on seeing each other like this, in hotels, or between classes at your house or mine. We've never talked about this, I suppose out of mutual courtesy and because it was taken as read somehow. There was no need to talk about it, there wasn't time; we didn't want to spoil our little holidays. We've never really talked about anything much. But I'll never leave Ted."

Within the rules governing the steps to be taken in diaphanous conversations about the future (steps that are mere formalities) I had two options then: I could ask (I looked across at the beach) if she would never leave Ted because in spite of everything she loved her husband (but on that Saturday night in June in Brighton I didn't want to run the risk of hearing that or of having to try to deny it by resorting, inevitably, to boasting);

pretending that the former possibility didn't exist, I could reproach her with her lack of daring and her bland acceptance of the status quo (I turned round and looked out at the domes: I threw my cigarette out of the window – like a coin – and kept my back turned to her while I talked), with her acceptance of things that I had never witnessed and for which I felt neither responsibility nor respect. Whether or not I chose the second option became a matter of indifference, however, since Clare answered as if I had decided on the first.

"I'm not going to give you a speech about how I'm still in love with Ted because I don't know if I am or, if I am, in what way I am, and on the other hand I do know that I'm not in love with him the way I was years ago, when we got married, or before or since then. The truth is I don't think about it much, I'm not used to asking myself that question. But even if it were true that I am and I were convinced of it, I wouldn't say so to you. It's absurd for a woman to say that to her lover, or for a man to say it to his, and even less to someone who's not just a casual affair, but someone one has known and cared about for some time. I couldn't say it to you with any conviction, even if I were sure. But it's not necessary. It's enough that I tell you that I like living with him, you know that already. It's not just that it's pleasant, it's that I'm used to it. It's the life I chose, and I continue to choose it out of all the other lives I could choose to have, let alone those I couldn't. Having a lover doesn't contradict any of that, nor would it even if I were to be a little ridiculous and tell you that I loved Ted more than anything else in the world."

I said: "Lovers take time, we're wilful and over-enthusiastic, isn't that it?" and thought that though I had certainly taken up Muriel's time and been wilful with her, I could never have been accused of being over-enthusiastic.

"You're a fool," said Clare as she had that fifth of November in her room in All Souls, in Catte Street, across from the Radcliffe

Camera, and it was therefore the second time she'd called me a fool (without my taking offence on either occasion): she was annoyed by my remark and doubtless annoyed because I'd interrupted her when she was all ready to take the floor and conduct an infantile conversation with me (when she was all ready to put an end to the whole wearisome business), to go through the whole process: the approaches, the consummations, the estrangements; the fulfilment, the battles, the doubts; the certainties, the jealousies, the abandonment and the laughter. "You're a fool," she said. "Yes, lovers do take time, yes, they are wilful and over-enthusiastic, but not for long, and that's just as it should be. That's your function and also your charm. Mine too, don't forget, as your lover, and even though you're not married. Our role in life is not to last too long, not to persist or linger, because if we stay too long, the charm fades, the suffering begins and tragedies happen. Stupid tragedies, avoidable, self-inflicted tragedies."

I said: "I can't say I've noticed many tragedies happening nowadays," and thought that between Clare and me no such tragedies were possible, in Oxford or in London, in Reading or in Brighton. Not even on Didcot station.

"It doesn't matter if they happen now or used to happen in other times, one time is much like another, even though it may not seem like it. And anyway, who can know any time other than their own? Thirty years ago, that is during my own lifetime, I did see a tragedy, doubtless a stupid one, and since then, or perhaps since I realised I saw it, I've spent my whole life trying to make myself invulnerable, to be pessimistic and cold enough to prove invulnerable to just such stupid tragedies; to be immune to them and not to inflict them on myself. You've seen nothing and so there are still many things you can afford to think, but I can't. And I don't want to."

That was when Clare, lying on the bed with, to one side, the beach and the water and, to the other (in the background) the outlandish imitation Indian palace and (in the foreground) the man who'd been her lover for sixteen months and was in the process of becoming her ex-lover, that was when Clare (as if she were a man), decided she was ready to recall out loud things from the distant past. That was when the conversation between lovers stopped flowing over flat ground, through all that is diaphanous and all that is yet to be and to judder instead over rough and rugged terrain, through all that is opaque and all that is already past.

"Listen," she said, lighting a fresh cigarette and leaning her head on one hand, her elbow resting on the bolster on the double bed (that's how she prepared herself to recount to me the melodramatic episode involving a particular death with its several witnesses and about which the only surviving one could remember nothing). "Listen," she said and I turned round again to face her when she said that, turning my back on the inland-facing window again; as I did so, I couldn't help noticing that with that sideways shift towards me her skirt had ridden up even more: it was almost as if she wasn't wearing one. "Listen," she said, "my mother had a lover who stayed too long. His name was Terry Armstrong and I don't know who he was or what he did, it all happened when I was three, and I only found out about him long afterwards. He left no trace. Only when I was old enough to ask more about my mother could I ask others, although since I was only ever given one version or one answer, I've had to assume them to be correct simply because they're the only ones I got. My father's always maintained an aggrieved silence about it, and perhaps not just because he doesn't want to talk about it, but also perhaps, I sometimes think, because he may not know the whole story; he wouldn't be able to tell me the whole story. The only person who wanted to tell me about it, after a while, was Mrs Munshi, Hilla, my nanny, the nanny who looked after me in Delhi. My father, on the other hand, has always refused to answer me when I've asked him about or accused him of something, which means that he's never actually denied anything, he's never denied what I told him the nanny told me. Every time I raised the subject, he'd get up and leave the room, a black look on his face. I'd follow him right to the door of his bedroom, insisting that he tell me, but he'd just shut himself in and not come out until hours later, for supper, as if nothing had happened. But it's been ages now since we engaged in those struggles, now it never even occurs to me to insist on answers or to have it out with him, I never talk about it or even attempt to do so, with him or with anyone else, and Hilla died years ago, here in England where she'd moved to be with her sons and her grandsons. I don't even know if I should talk to you about it, but it doesn't matter, and anyway you'll be leaving soon," and I thought that, although it wasn't strictly necessary, it was nice and something of an honour to be given explanations by Clare as if on that night in Brighton they were necessary; and I thought too: "It's true. Once I've left, what possible importance can what is happening now have? I'll leave no trace. Like Terry Armstrong." And I paused over that name: "Terry Armstrong." But while I was thinking this, Clare had continued talking, her gaze growing ever more abstracted, ever more fixed, the gaze of one reminiscing or telling a story. "According to my nanny, Terry Armstrong, of whom she never knew anything more than his name, was, like all good lovers, over-enthusiastic and wilful. One of those men who write letters and poems with just the right mixture of seriousness and irony, who are full of infectious energy and vitality and engender laughter and hope in the person who feels loved by them. He'd come and go and no one ever quite knew when he'd reappear, he was stationed in Calcutta, possibly in the diplomatic corps or just there on his own account, probably the latter, since his name doesn't appear in the files of the diplomatic corps; I wrote to them for information when my curiosity about the subject was at its height, at its most urgent. Perhaps it wasn't his real name, I don't know; perhaps only my mother knew that, or perhaps not even she did. In any event he must have been in India for some time or had been there before, because he spoke a little Hindi to the nanny, just to flatter her, she said. He flattered the nanny and flattered my mother, that seems to have been his main function. For the nanny he was never more than that, a flattering presence and a name, she never tried to check up on him, that wasn't her place, it was enough for her that he was Mr Terry Armstrong or Armstrong Sahib just as my father was Mr Newton or Newton Sahib and I was Miss Clare, the child of the house, it didn't matter to her what else we were or even if we were anything else. The secret affair between my mother and Terry Armstrong lasted about as long as ours has to date, a year and a half, and although it took my father a while, it seems that nonetheless he did find out about it some time before it ended, and that he tolerated it, put up with it, perhaps in the hope that he'd be transferred somewhere else, or that Armstrong would, assuming he belonged to the diplomatic corps or worked for a company; diplomats don't stay anywhere long, nor do foreigners with no established marital links, just as you won't be staying here much longer. Any burden is easier to bear if it's only intermittently there, and who knows, if Terry Armstrong came and went, if he was hundreds of miles away and only travelled them when he could, then perhaps the situation was not so very unbearable for my father and he was prepared to wait, as perhaps Ted, if he's suspected anything during all this time, is waiting now for you to go. Perhaps I'm waiting too. I don't know. I long ago gave up trying to find out anything through my father, I tormented him quite enough at the time, and he must have felt pretty humiliated if what Hilla said is true. And it must be true." "What else did your nanny tell you?" I asked from my post by the window (the inland-facing window); but more than anything I was turning the name of Terry Armstrong round and round in my mind, although still not daring to think beyond that, beyond the mere name. "Terry Armstrong," I thought again. Names tell you a lot. "My nanny said my mother became pregnant," Clare replied, "and that she thought the new baby would be Armstrong's, although she wasn't sure, or perhaps she was but didn't want to be. Whatever it was, that false or genuine doubt *was* more than my father could bear or tolerate. I do know that my father was aware of her doubts because Hilla heard snatches of what must have been their last conversation. Their last argument." Clare turned round and changed her position: her feet on the pillow now, her chin resting on her hands, both elbows at the foot of the bed. Now what I could see were the backs of her thighs and the curve, covered by her tights, where her buttocks began. And I thought: "You're only that relaxed about revealing so much when you trust the person watching, when it's a brother, or a husband, when it's a family member. I'm not her husband or her brother, but her foreign lover who's about to become her ex-lover. But tonight she's entrusting me with a family secret." "One night, when I was about three years old, when I'd already been asleep for hours and Hilla had only gone to bed some minutes before, she heard me crying. She got up and came to me as she had on other nights, to calm me and console me and sing me a song to lull me back to sleep, and that was when she heard what must have been the real reason for my waking up and for my tears: my parents had just got back and from their bedroom, close to mine, came shouts and now and then the sound of something being hit, of a blow on the floor or on a table. Frightened, my nanny immediately started to sing in order to drown out the shouting and to overcome her own fear, and it was her singing combined with my sobs that prevented her from hearing the conversation, although there were times when the voices grew so loud, that they startled her again, so that she stopped singing and, without wanting to, overheard the odd phrase. Just a few phrases, eight in all, four isolated pairs of phrases, which, on my insistence, she repeated to me so many times that now it's as if I myself remembered them. For I must have heard them too, though I can't possibly recall them. I can barely remember my mother. Nevertheless, I do remember those phrases that at first I wrote down until, effortlessly, they became part of my memory and have stayed with me ever since, and I know that one of the things Hilla told me my mother said that night was: 'But I'm not sure, Tom, it could be yours.' And I know what my father replied: 'The fact that you're not sure means that it can't and won't be mine.' And I know that later my mother said: 'I don't know what I want, I wish I did, I'm worn out with not knowing.' And my father replied: 'And I'm worn out with knowing what I do want and not being able to get it.' My mother's third sentence was this: 'If that's what you want, I'll leave tomorrow, but I'll take the girl with me.' And my father said: 'You're in no position to take any more with you than the clothes you stand up in and what you're carrying inside you, and you'll probably never see Clare again.' And later the nanny heard the last thing my mother said: 'I can't take any more of this, Tom.' And my father replied: 'Neither can I.' Hilla sang me back to sleep, more and more softly as the voices quietened, and when I'd gone back to sleep and the voices had fallen silent, my nanny told me that the door of my room opened and she saw the figure of my father silhouetted there. He didn't come in. 'Has the child gone back to sleep?' he asked. The nanny looked at him and raised a finger to her lips, and my father, lowering his voice, added: 'Mrs Newton is leaving very early tomorrow morning to go on a journey. It's best the child doesn't see her go. Take her to sleep in your room for the night.' The door closed again and then the nanny, very carefully, in the dark, without waking me, obeyed his orders and gathered me up in her arms and carried me to her room to spend the rest of the night with her. She gave up her bed to me and, still watchful, went to sleep in a chair." Clare fell silent, paused. She got up from the double bed that she alone occupied and went to the bathroom, and although we were in an intimate situation we were not so intimate that she left the bathroom door open. Even so I couldn't help hearing the fall of liquid on liquid and while I did so (without wanting to), I thought about that name again: "Terry Armstrong," I thought, letting my thoughts go further this time. "Armstrong's a very common name, so is Terry. For women it's the diminutive form of Theresa and for men of Terence. But Armstrong's very common, there are thousands of them in England and always have been, as many as or more than there are Newtons and almost as many as there are Blakes, although the double-barrelled form, Cromer-Blake is rare. And Terence or Terry are equally common, although not as common as John or Tom or Ted (short for both Edward and Theodore). But Armstrong," I thought. "A strong arm." And when Clare came back, she sat down on the bed, put a folded pillow in the small of her back and leaned against the wall. She lit another cigarette and tucked her legs under her so that her skirt rode up again. She'd splashed her face with water and though her gaze was less fixed, she hadn't lost the thread of her story. "The next morning my mother was no longer in the house, they said she'd gone away for a few days. I still had my nanny Hilla and she stayed at my side from that day on during the several years we remained in Delhi, without a transfer, despite what had happened. She had no way of re-establishing contact with my mother nor of course with Terry Armstrong, whose whereabouts she had no way of knowing. Moreover, during those first few days, my father kept a discreet watch on her, obliging her to remain at home with me all the time, not leaving me for an instant, and that's how it was from then on, she just stayed with me all the time, never leaving my side, until years later, when we at last left Delhi, she chose not to come with us. Hilla never found out what happened to my mother during that time, but one imagines that she went to Armstrong and hid with him in some hotel or in the house of someone he knew in Delhi, some Indian, certainly no one from the British colony, she would have had a difficult time explaining her situation to them. My mother's pregnancy was already becoming noticeable, Hilla said, in a certain blurring of the features, a bulkiness about her figure, perhaps that's why she had to talk to my father, to tell him about it, on that night that ended with her departure. My nanny didn't even know if Armstrong was in the city when my mother left the house, if he was there that night and was waiting for her somewhere the next day or if he came to her later, as soon as he could after she'd called him, which would mean that at first my mother must have been completely alone. My nanny said Armstrong never struck her as a practical or resourceful man, more of a dreamer, that's how she described him, a dreamer, that's the word she used. What she remembered most about him was his unfailing good humour, his continual joking. She told how, often, he'd take a metal flask out of his pocket and, amidst much laughter, hold it to my mother's lips, even to Hilla's, but both always declined, laughing, and then he'd hold the flask high and spout on about something or other, toasting to English names that meant nothing to my nanny and drink long and cheerfully, although she never saw him drunk. My mother was always laughing, she laughed at everything he said or did, the way young people do, the way Armstrong did: he was always joking, Hilla said, that was what she remembered him for, his endless laughter." And while Clare spoke of the man of whom she knew nothing except his name and that one character trait, I changed position at last and left the window to go and sit on the floor at the foot of the bed in order to listen better and think less. But I still listened to my thoughts, which were in fact urgent and succinct, for all I could think of (as I approached the bed and noticed the sand in my socks and at the foot of the bed) was a name: "Terence Ian Fytton Armstrong." "Four days after the argument, we saw him, Terry Armstrong that is. We all saw him, Hilla, me and possibly even my father, although he's never admitted he did and I can't remember it at all, just as I can't remember what it was they said that woke me up and made me cry on that other night. Or perhaps for a long time I forgot what I'd seen and only much later, when I was told about it and was told that I'd seen it, did I regain a kind of memory of what, according to Hilla, I too saw with my own eyes. The likelihood is that if I'm telling it now as if I remembered it, it's only because now I know about it and have spent the years since imagining it. But, you see, I can't avoid knowing what I saw, and although I may not have understood it then nor am I able to remember it with my memory, I *think* I remember it now with my mind." And while Clare Bayes, who was once Clare Newton, talked to me about her knowledge or memory of the first Clare Newton, who must have had another name before, unknown to me (that is, while the child Clare talked to me about her dead mother), I continued to think about the name of Armstrong and this time I thought (at the same time as I heard the story of that melodramatic episode from the lips of one of the witnesses): "It can't be, it wouldn't be, it isn't, Armstrong's such a common name, so's Terry, there must be thousands of Terrys and thousands of Armstrongs and hundreds of Terry Armstrongs, and anyway there's no way of proving it because no one knows anything about the Terry Armstrong who left no trace after returning to Calcutta in the 1950s as he returned to Vasto at the end of his life; perhaps he went back to Calcutta for 'one last drunken binge' that got too complicated for him and that held him there and lasted a year and a half (it was more than a drunken binge) and took him to Delhi; 'a final drunken binge', even though it took place fifteen years before his actual death." "Only four days had passed and I was in the garden with my nanny, watching the river and waiting for the last trains of the late evening to pass; as I've told you before, that was something I did ever since I was a little girl and continued to do until we left Delhi. My father was standing at the other end of the garden, near the house, and that's why while it's possible that he saw everything, it's equally possible that he saw nothing. But I did see what I know I saw but don't remember, what I didn't remember later nor even at the time, not even immediately after it happened, because that night, four nights after my mother's departure, while I was waiting for the mail train that came from Moradabad and always arrived so late, two figures appeared, a woman and a man, walking along the iron bridge that spans the river." "The bridge over the River Yamuna or Jumna that Clare has described to me before," I thought. "The long bridge of crisscrossing iron girders, deserted for the most part, in darkness, idle and shadowy, exactly like one of those faithful but ancillary figures from our childhood who grow dim then blaze into life again later, just for a moment, when they are called, only to be instantly plunged back into the gloom of their obscure, commutable existences, having done their brief duty or revealed the secret suddenly demanded of them. Just like Hilla or the old maidservant who used to accompany me and my three brothers along calle de Génova, calle de Covarrubias, or calle de Miguel Ángel: the Indian nanny Hilla and the old Madrid maidservant, whose lives are commutable and exist only in order that through them, whenever necessary, the child may once more emerge." And while Clare was telling me what she'd seen but remembered now only with her mind, I thought it all myself from my position at the foot of the bed, looking at the front view of her strong, slender legs that offered a glimpse of her knickers: "The English girl is looking at the black iron bridge waiting for the train to cross it, to see the train lit up and reflected in the water, one of the brightly coloured trains full of light and distant noise, that from time to time cross the River Yamuna, the River Jumna that she looks patiently out at from her house high up above when night falls. But the train has not yet appeared and, instead, along the dark bridge two

195

hesitant, fearful figures appear, stumbling perhaps on the rails, skidding on the gravel, two figures who are John Gawsworth and the mother of the watching child, Clare Newton, a woman who is still young, younger than her daughter on this night in Brighton. They're walking hand in hand, with Armstrong leading; they're leaning on the crisscrossing iron girders, clinging on to them as if they feared slipping and falling into the water, although it's possible that that is precisely why they've gone to the bridge, to fall in and drown, or perhaps not, perhaps they're simply crossing the bridge on foot, with obvious difficulty, perhaps they're in flight or stunned or troubled or drunk or ill, perhaps they don't know what they're doing. The child immediately spots the two figures in the darkness because they're both dressed in white and because one of them is her mother (and because the person who will become Clare Bayes only has eyes for the iron bridge and its promise of brightly coloured trains). 'There's Mummy,' says the daughter, pointing at the bridge. The nanny takes no notice of her at first, she doesn't even look up but goes on crooning some trifling song while she sews or does nothing and simply sits with her hands folded in her lap watching over the child left in her charge. The girl sees how the man, who is perhaps Gawsworth, walks to the middle of the bridge, still pulling the mother behind him, and although the daughter does not know it yet – her nanny will whisper this to her during her future childhood, not telling her everything until much later, not telling her until it is demanded of her – they're standing on a bridge from which many a pair of unhappy lovers have thrown themselves. But perhaps they're not going to throw themselves in, although that night they are doubtless unhappy, perhaps they're on the bridge for some other reason, who knows, it might be that Gawsworth himself, who leads the mother, does not himself quite know what that reason is. Armstrong takes out the metal flask from the pocket of his white jacket, but he doesn't toast anyone now or spout on about anything or proffer it to the lips of the first Clare Newton, who laughed so much (to the lips he had so often kissed), but takes a few hurried swigs, almost as if concealing the fact from the woman he loves and who follows behind him. She looks down, while he looks up, possibly she suffers from vertigo and cannot help looking down, down into the broad river of blue or rather black waters (since it is night) and because that is the only way of accustoming herself to them, because perhaps the mother does intend throwing herself in, and perhaps she is the more decided of the two and wonders if Gawsworth, or Terry Armstrong, will jump too, as they've promised and planned to do. It doesn't escape the first Clare Newton's notice that he keeps drinking from his metal flask, perhaps that's his way of accustoming himself to the liquid fate that awaits them; and it doesn't escape the nanny's notice either ('Look, there's your mummy with a man'), although she watches in astonishment and still without understanding what she's seeing. Perhaps the mother and the man made their promises and plans and reached their agreement the night before or during the day in some hotel room, and have agreed (Clare Bayes doesn't know, no one knows) because no other solution other than ending it all occurs to them. Gawsworth is one of life's unfortunates, easily perplexed, never serious, he just makes jokes, plays games (his thinking is erratic, his character weak) and he cannot accept that life has caught up with him, that it has finally closed in on him. The King of Redonda can't have an heir or take care of a child, he can't even take care of the woman he loves and who carries his child, perhaps he couldn't even if she wasn't. And Clare Newton has agreed this with him (Clare Bayes doesn't know, no one does) because she's afraid and desperate, she's been alone and homeless and possibly penniless for three nights and four days spent in cheap hotels or perhaps wandering the inhospitable city while Armstrong still does not come and there's no one to take care of her, three nights and four days of being bewildered, terrified, unable to believe what is happening to her: her will has wandered off somewhere, she doesn't know now how to hold on to it, to delay its going, it's no longer entirely hers, like the will of an invalid or an old man or one troubled in mind. He drinks, she looks at the water. The two stop in the middle of the bridge. They stumble. Gawsworth puts his arm – his strong arm – round her shoulders, as you put your arm around those you wish to protect and love, and with the other hand he grasps hold of an iron girder. In his first hand he still has hold of the flask, which, though he hasn't realised it yet, must be empty by now. It's Armstrong's turn to look down, whilst the mother looks up, trying to make out the garden of her house to which she will never return and her daughter, wondering if she'll still be watching, hoping that she won't be, that the nanny Hilla will have put her to bed and be singing her to sleep because the mail train from Moradabad will have passed already, marking the end of the child's day (Clare Newton doesn't know that as usual the train is running very late). The two lovers, who have only been unhappy lovers for a short time, stand still, they don't continue their walk, they don't cross the whole bridge. And it is then that from around the corner the Moradabad mail train appears, the train for which, as on every night of her present and future foreign childhood in the south, the little English girl is waiting, the train that always arrives incalculably late (no one can ever tell how late it will be, and that night is no exception) and that's why, although it's almost reached its destination, it seems as if it will never slow down. Gawsworth looks towards the oncoming train whose approach the mother hears without having to look up (the metallic noise inaudible to the child), instead she looks down again into the water. The fickle, mellow moon is now just a sliver. And then Armstrong raises the arm encircling the first Clare Newton's shoulders, frees himself and frees her, and now with both hands – with those hands that piloted planes and that will one day beg for alms – he grasps hold of and crushes his body against the crisscrossing iron girders, his drunkenness suddenly evaporated, his flask fallen from his hands, his eyes wide open and fearful like those of Alan Marriott's dog just before the football hooligans at Didcot station severed its back leg. 'There are so many things that hold us here,' Gawsworth is perhaps thinking, 'and anything might still happen.' Or perhaps he doesn't think it, he knows it. The mother must know it too, but nevertheless she holds out until the last moment, with her body so perilously close to the rails – her body that is beginning to swell with what is not yet and will never be Clare Bayes' younger brother or sister – and she does not follow Armstrong's example, the two lovers do not do the same thing, and instead of holding tight to the iron girders, the mother falls or jumps between them, in her white dress (as white as Rylands' hair, as white as the breasts of the not-so-plump girl from Wychwood Forest, Muriel) Clare Newton throws herself into the water. And while Clare Newton jumps and Terry Armstrong does not jump, the train passes, filling the entire length of the iron bridge, lighting up the river with its windows (the men on the barges below look up at the train and grow dizzy) and that is the image that helps the girl to go to sleep and to come to terms with the idea of spending another day in a city to which she does not belong and which she will only perceive as hers once she has left it and when her only chance to recall it out loud will be with her son or with a lover, for lovers serve the same function as children do, to listen to our story. The mother falls, with her slow downhill feeling, with her feeling of being burdened down, of vertigo, of falling, gravity and weight, with her swollen body and her blurred features, with her false plumpness and her despair. And Gawsworth's eyes – that have been closed and void of any gaze for years now – see how the body of the person he loved falls and drowns; and the child Clare observes from high above how the body of the person she loved – the mother she cannot remember on this night in Brighton – disappears into the blue waters of that river gleaming brightly in the blackness; and perhaps the father, from the other end of the garden, near the house, also sees how long it takes for the body of the person he loved to surface and sees that it does not surface. (All three see the person they love kill herself.) And it is the nanny, Hilla, who sees how the men in the barges fail to find the body of the beloved, which is swept away on the current, it's she who will reveal the secret, because neither Armstrong nor the father nor the iron bridge over the River Jumna will. And when the train has passed and Clare Bayes who was then Clare Newton loses sight of the swaying lantern on the last carriage and waves goodbye to it, a goodbye that is never spoken in expectation of any response because there is no one there now to respond, the bridge is once more deserted, in darkness, idle and shadowy. The other white figure remains there for only a few seconds, perhaps he vomits into the River Yamuna like an Oxford beggar into the River Isis, before fleeing, terrified, the last King of Redonda, the writer John Gawsworth, the Real Writer, who will never write again nor leave any trace behind him. Except possibly a metal flask that has perhaps been there ever since that night, crushed and rusty and empty between the rails."

And when Clare finished her story, I got up from the floor and returned to my window and to looking at her, thinking: "But it can't be, it wouldn't be, it isn't."

She got up from the bed and came over to me, and then the two of us looked in silence out of the window that revealed in the distance the fantastic imitation of the palaces of her child-hood; there was a moon and clouds; her breasts brushed against my back. Clare stroked the back of my neck and I turned round and we looked at each other as if we were each the other's vigilant, compassionate eyes, the eyes that look out at us from the past and no longer matter because they've known for a long time now how they're obliged to see us: perhaps we looked at each other as if we were each the other's older brother or sister and were sorry we couldn't love each other more, more at least than an older brother or sister. And it was then that I remembered some lines I'd seen quoted, the lines of another English writer of whose life (unlike Gawsworth's) much is known, but whose obscure death, which was violent and legendary, has had to be imagined, like that of Clare Newton: he was stabbed to death before he was thirty years old one day in Trinity term, on the thirtieth of May four hundred years ago, in Deptford (a name that means deep ford), near the Thames, which is what the Isis is called everywhere and at all times except when it passes through Oxford. The lines were: "Thou hast committed fornication; but that was in another country, and besides, the wench is dead."

The next day Clare dropped me at the door of my house in Oxford (and although it wasn't yet night we no longer made any attempt to hide). I saw that the gypsy flowerseller, who set up her stall opposite my house on Sundays and bank holidays, was just then being picked up by her invisible husband in his clean, modern van. That meant that, despite the warm, suspended, immutable spring light, it was growing late and it would not be long now before the weak wheel of the world would start rolling again and the stillness come to an end. I realised with joy that I'd been spared another Sunday in exile from the infinite.

OF THE THREE, two have died since I left Oxford, but neither of the two was Clare Bayes, they were, as anticipated, Cromer-Blake and Toby Rylands. The man who was both father- and mother-figure to me as well as being my guide in that city died four months after I left and did not see another Michaelmas or another year, and so my second and last year was also Dr Cromer-Blake's last, though he'd spent much longer in that water than I had. And it was Toby Rylands, who would die two years later (just two months ago, in fact), who sent me an express letter and who kept Cromer-Blake's diaries, which later, when he too died, travelled south to my safekeeping as requested in Rylands' last will and testament. His letter was very short and to the point, as if he were loath to say much about the long-expected event, or about the person who, after his death, became the mirror in which he did not wish to see himself: as if now it were Rylands who could not bring himself to visit Cromer-Blake, to visit his tomb or his memory.

Cromer-Blake was buried in London (in north London, where he was born, and although there was no need to make a collection to pay for the burial of the man who was never to be bursar, there were few people at the funeral, mostly colleagues (so supportive, so good-humoured) from the Taylorian. The priest who said the prayer for the dead and delivered the sermon had the ill grace to request the removal of the children of two colleagues, who had accompanied their parents to the Catholic church at Marble Arch to take advantage of the trip to London by spending the rest of the day at London Zoo. Of Cromer-

Blake's family (his parents, an unmarried brother and a married sister) only his brother Roger was there, and it seems that as soon as the service was over he raced off in a sports car (possibly an Aston Martin) without saying a word to anyone. His friend Bruce was absent, as was Dayanand, from whom, according to the diaries, of which I understood only fragments, though I've read them in their entirety, Cromer-Blake had definitely distanced himself in the last months of his life. A few members of his college attended: not the Warden, Lord Rymer, for whom he'd done so many favours – with whom he'd been working hand in glove – but the economist Halliwell, from whom everyone fled after the funeral to avoid being bespattered by his one topic of conversation. Obituaries appeared "in two of the nationals, neither of them very kind", as Rylands enigmatically put it. The Professor Emeritus was succinct in his letter, which had obviously been written in haste, in order to be done with his obligations as soon as possible, but he was also upset. "Cromer-Blake knew what was wrong with him for nearly a year, he knew last December in fact. He was so brave. According to those who continued to see him, he bore his terrible sentence with apparent unconcern. It's odd how the most unlikely people show great courage in the end. How immensely sad. I can't stop thinking about him." The express letter – it concluded by giving me an address in London so that I could, if I wished, send a donation to a charity in memory of Cromer-Blake – said little more.

I sent nothing, although I fully intended to. The truth is that I tried to forget about his death the moment I learned of it and, to some extent, I succeeded because it's not so hard to forget such a thing when the dead person is far away and had already begun to recede into the past even when he was alive. The last time I saw him, his health was average to poor. Kind as ever, he'd offered to give me and my huge suitcases full of books a lift to the station from where I would go to London, then on to Paris by train and hovercraft and by another train south to

Madrid. But the night before my departure he felt worse and called to tell me that he had best spend the next day at home. So I paused in my preparations for leaving and went over to his college to say goodbye. Although it was late June and pleasantly warm, he received me lying on a sofa and covered by a blanket, like Saskia; the check blanket over his legs had replaced the dark cataract of his gown, which hung, black and immensely long, behind his door, as mine does in my house in Madrid. He had lost part of his aesthetic disguise. The television was on, an opera with the sound turned down. He said he felt cold, a bit feverish. I can't remember what we talked about now, I've forgotten as one does forget things to which at the time one gives no importance, the things that don't seem interesting because they're done with no awareness of the fact that what one says or does – or what one sees – has meaning and weight. And at the time that farewell had neither meaning nor weight, or at least not much, perhaps because I wanted to think that Rylands was being excessively gloomy in his predictions (Cromer-Blake did in fact seem quite nonchalant) and my thoughts were more on my leaving, on what awaited me (in the future, in all that is flat and diaphanous) than on what I was leaving behind (in the past, in all that is rough, rugged, and opaque). All I remember is that, while he cast occasional glances at a clamorously silent *Falstaff*, his customary pallor was even deathlier than usual, but that was not remarkable: at exam time dons always looks extra pale. That night he was almost the colour of his prematurely grey hair, which was less and less grey now and more and more white. I didn't stay long, it was late. I had to finish my packing and he perhaps wanted to listen to *Falstaff*.

The last entries in the diaries now in my possession are extremely brief and half-hearted, just two or three lines on the days he managed to write something, which was not, by any means, every day. The third of September, for example, reads:

"Today is my birthday. I've managed to reach thirty-eight. I'm no longer young. Clare gave me a woollen jumper she knitted herself. B nothing, he forgot." And three days later, on the sixth, the entry is even shorter: "B wants to go and live in London. My native city, how absurd. It seems a long way away, although in fact it's only an hour." Then there's nothing until the twelfth, on which he writes: "Today I started re-reading *Don Quixote*, I hope I have time to finish it between this week and the next. Perhaps I should re-read the second part first." And later, on the fourteenth: "Only seven days till the end of summer. I'm tired, tired of not being well and of the summer." And on the twentieth he mentions me: "Today is our dear Spaniard's birthday. He's thirty-four, so he's not so young any more either. I called him in Madrid, but he was out." (And it's true that I wasn't at home that day, nor even in Madrid, but in Sanlúcar de Barrameda with Luisa, who is now my wife, and whom I'd met in Madrid a month before.) The next entry is on the twenty-ninth and seems to have been copied from a diary or calendar because all it says is: "St Michael and All Angels. Seventeenth Sunday after Trinity (eighteenth after Pentecost). First day of term. The sun rises at 07.02 and sets at 18.47. Full moon at 00.08." Then there's nothing more until the seventh of October, when he writes: "Moon's last quarter at 05.04. Toby phoned. I made an excuse to put him off coming to see me. Poor old man, he understands nothing." And on the fourteenth: "New moon at 04.33. Michaelmas begins today as do the classes I won't be able to give. Dewar and Kavanagh have been kind enough to offer to fill in for me until I'm better." The last entry is on the seventeenth and reads: 'St Etheldred, Queen of Northumbria, reluctant to the last, the silly woman. I'm sure that in a few years' time this illness will be curable, nothing much to worry about. God, I'm fed up." He died on the nineteenth, the twentieth Sunday after Trinity (twenty-first after Pentecost) and St Frideswide's day (at least in Oxford). The sun rose at 07.38

and set at 18.01 and there was a crescent moon at 20.13. Cromer-Blake saw the rising and the setting but not the crescent moon.

Of the poor old man's death I know less or almost nothing, because there was no Cromer-Blake to tell me about it, no one even to say: "How immensely sad." It was Kavanagh, more dynamic and more modern than Rylands, who undertook to phone me in Madrid two months ago to tell me about it, no express letters or addresses for donations for him. It was he, too, who sent me the diaries of the first of the men to die. But I know that Rylands, unlike Cromer-Blake, didn't know about his death beforehand, if such a phrase has any meaning. I mean that he hadn't been ill before. He wasn't in hospital, but at home, his heart just suddenly stopped, that's all. I don't know what time or where he was found or what he was doing. Maybe Mrs Berry called him in to have lunch and, when he didn't appear in the kitchen, perhaps she sensed what had happened and cautiously walked down to the banks of the Cherwell where Rylands would be sitting in his upholstered chair so as to make the most of the autumn sun. Or perhaps she didn't even approach him, the all too predictable Mrs Berry, and it was enough for her to see from the window the huge convex torso sprawled in the chair. The sherry glass fallen on the grass. The eyes bereft of all authority and colour. The yellow sweater all twisted. I don't know, it doesn't matter, it isn't immensely sad.

Not much time has passed since I left Oxford, but it all seems very far away now. Too many things have changed or begun or ceased to be since then (now the things I think about and look forward to are my wife Luisa and my new son and the ambitious plans proposed by the go-getting Estévez). Rylands never did publish a book on *A Sentimental Journey* and it seems that no trace was ever found amongst his papers of a manuscript bearing any resemblance to the text he spoke to me about that Sunday at the end of the Hilary term. In fact no writings from his latter years have been found at all, at least nothing unpublished. Either he destroyed them, or else they never existed and he spent the years following his retirement without writing a line, inert, watching the river, that eternal image of the passing of time, and the occasional television programme, calling to his rebellious swans and throwing crumbs to his grateful ducks, with honours (ever less sincere) still arriving by every post. That Sunday, on which he seemed to speak so many truths, he must have lied about his book. Maybe he lied about everything, I don't know, it doesn't matter. My life flows along different channels now. I'm not, I think, the same person who spent those two years in Oxford. I'm not troubled now, and my sense of unease then was never really that serious, it was slight and transient, coherent and logical, as I said, the kind of malaise that does not keep us from our work, or from behaving sensibly, or being polite, or dealing with other people as if in fact nothing were happening to us; the kind of malaise that doubtless passes unnoticed by everyone except the person feeling it, a malaise we all experience from time to time. It all seems very far away, and my strongest link, now that Cromer-Blake and Rylands have both died and there's no way I could keep up a correspondence with Kavanagh and Dewar, is the subscription to the Machen Society that I continue to send from my native city and in exchange for which, plus a supplement, I continue every few months to receive the occasional meticulous, obsessive publication on Machen and his circle, amongst whom Gawsworth is sometimes mentioned though with no further details about his life. Even if more details were given, I wouldn't want to know about them; that's why I've never bought any of the extremely scarce titles written by the king without a kingdom that I've seen offered, at very inflated prices, in the exotic catalogues I still have sent to me from my rare and antiquarian booksellers in Oxford and London (though never *Above the River*, the book he published when he was nineteen, the one that Alan Marriott was interested in). I suppose it's Marriott who puts the pamphlets from the Machen Company into their envelopes and sends them off, but I can't be sure, for there's never any note appended to those remittances franked always in different towns (Chippenham, Lymington, Scarborough; he certainly seems to get around). I saw Marriott again a couple of times during my second year in Oxford, in the distance, dragging his lame dog along with him, but I didn't approach to say hello and neither did he. What's certain is that he never sought me out again after those few days when he followed and found me everywhere and after his one visit. Perhaps all he really wanted was to acquire a new member for the Machen Company, even though I wasn't anyone eminent, and to secure my subscription.

It was purely by chance that I ended up leaving Oxford on my own. I have no complaints: Cromer-Blake couldn't take me in his car and it was too late by then to ask another colleague. I'd said my goodbyes at a small party three days before and, besides, I was leaving very early the next morning. I called a taxi, gave one last look at my final bag of rubbish, my final task completed, then tied it up and put it out; I left my three-storey pyramid and locked it up, dropping the keys through the letterbox (they fell on to the carpet without so much as a clink); I got on the train without waving goodbye to anyone. At Didcot station, where the train stopped for a minute, I looked sleepily out of the window and, on the opposite platform (the one for Oxford-bound passengers), I caught sight of Edward Bayes laughing and embracing a woman who, in the reciprocity of her embrace, had her back turned to me. She was blonde, with short hair and had a cigarette in her hand; her ankles were made fragile (perfect perhaps) by her loving pose. It wasn't Clare, of course, but I wouldn't go so far as to say it was the girl from Didcot station either, even though she was at Didcot station. I don't think I could have said so with certainty even if I'd seen her face – had she turned round – because by then it was as vague and confused with other faces as it is now in my memory. I wasn't surprised, it just seemed like something that no longer concerned me (as if I wasn't really present at it, as if I watched it through a veil), and the only thought that did occur to me was that perhaps in the 1950s Terry Armstrong was married too. I think that's why I didn't worry about Clare, feeling sure as I was and am now that she and her husband would always stay together. And putting myself in his place (in her husband's place), as I had on several other occasions, I simply thought (feeling half-dead from lack of sleep): "I just hope they don't meet Rook when they get on the train. That would give them a fright and put an end to the laughter, because this is no hour to be going back to Oxford." The sun had risen at 04.46 and would not set until 21.26, and I'm not sure if there was a moon or not. At any rate I would not again be witness to that warm suspended light nor hear the bells pealing out inconsiderately as evening fell.

The light changes gradually here in Madrid and now I too sometimes have something to push or drag along: my new son's pram through the advancing dusk in the Retiro Park. That's why now I'm more like Clare Bayes holding her son Eric's hand, and Marriott dragging his dog along, and Jane, the gypsy flowerseller, who dragged her merchandise along the pavement without her husband ever once getting out to help her, and like that old beggar who lugged around with him the barrel organ he'd salvaged from a dockside bonfire in Liverpool and played in the streets of Oxford. And like Gawsworth, who pushed his Victorian pram full of beer bottles along Shaftesbury Avenue, before disappearing into the dusk at a leisurely pace; and yet I'm less like him now, because life has caught up with me, closed in on me and left me with this child about whom I sometimes forget and of whom I as yet know nothing, not even whether he looks more like me or like his mother whom I still kiss so very often. I'm no longer like Dewar or Rylands or Cromer-Blake who never pushed or dragged anything along. Cromer-Blake and Rylands are dead anyway, which makes any resemblance I might have with them even less marked; they no longer fantasise about things still to come, whilst I still do: about the go-getting Estévez, about my wife Luisa and about the new child who in the normal course of events will survive us all, including the child Eric. The others are still alive. Clare, who will have another lover by now and with whom I do not correspond, is alive. Dayanand, the Indian doctor, is alive, although not it seems for much longer. Kavanagh, who occasionally comes to Madrid and reports to me about the static city preserved in syrup and brings me news of the water there, he's still alive. Dewar, who no doubt declaims in three languages in the privacy of his rooms with his white noise playing in the background, continues his living death and will have forgotten all about me by now. Will, the ancient porter with the limpid gaze (the like of which does not exist in Madrid), is still alive, probably still raising his hand when he says good morning, and confusing his time with my time and perhaps now calling someone else by my name (because in his eyes I have not left, because for him all souls are still alive), although, as far as I know, no Mr Branshaw has yet made an appearance in the Taylorian. And Muriel, I suppose, lives on between her two rivers, in what was Wychwood Forest, in what *was* a forest. I have before me a few coins I didn't spend at the time (I hear them clink in the metal box that contains only them and a single pair of earrings). I could have left the coins for the child Eric, who is also alive and growing and must be due to come back from Bristol about now for his holidays. But maybe one day this new child of mine will also want to collect them.

Julio Cortázar

HOPSCOTCH

Translated from the Spanish by Gregory Rabassa

"Anyone who hasn't read Cortázar is doomed . . . something similar to a man who has never tasted peaches. He would quietly become sadder, noticeably paler, and probably little by little, he would lose his hair"   **PABLO NERUDA**

"*Hopscotch*, a superb work, should establish Cortázar as an outstanding writer of our day . . . The dialogue is brilliant, whether the subject is literature, love, Mondrian, jazz or the fallibility of science. Individual scenes are superbly alive . . . the rapid-fire invention of the language makes every page sparkle, thanks to the translation by Gregory Rabassa, which gives a dazzling parallel to Cortázar's stylistic magic"   **DONALD KEENE,** *New York Times*

Giuseppe Tomasi de Lampedusa

THE LEOPARD

Translated from the Italian by Archibald Colquhoun

"The poetry of Lampedusa's novel flows into the Sicilian countryside . . . a work of great artistry"

PETER ACKROYD

"Every once in a while, like certain golden moments of happiness, infinitely memorable, one stumbles on a book or writer, and the impact is like an indelible mark. Lampedusa's *The Leopard*, his only novel, and a masterpiece, is such a work"   **BRUCE ARNOLD,** *Independent*

To join the mailing list and for a full list of titles please write to

THE HARVILL PRESS
2 AZTEC ROW • BERNERS ROAD
LONDON N1 0PW • UK

enclosing a stamped-addressed envelope

www.harvill.com

ALL SOULS

"An intelligent and well executed book with exceptionally funny set pieces"   MARK SANDERSON, *Independent on Sunday*

"In the precision and subtlety of its writing, it is reminiscent of Proust and Henry James. Marías holds the reader enthralled with the elegance and flexibility of his style"

BRUNO DE CESSOLE, *Figaro*

"Marías follows Borges in his practice of creative deception, planting elements of unadorned reality that the reader may or may not be right to take at face value"

HELIE LASSAIGNE, *Libération*

"A brilliant book, charming, amusing, delicate, touching, well structured and limpid in its exposition"

J. A. MASOLIVER MÓDENAS, *Vanguardia*